INTO THE

STORM

Also by Katie Richard

Destiny

My Last Hope

INTO THE

STORM

Katie Richard

Katie Richard LLC

PROLOGUE

He who calls upon the darkness to do his bidding will seek the power he was not given.

With eyes that match the blood he has shed; he shall only have one true adversary.

She is born of sword and sybil of mine own blood thirteen descendants down on the tree of life.

It is she that is destined to be the Immortal Savior.

The maker of rain who calls on dark skies will extinguish the flames he has brought forth to scorch the Earth to ash.

It is she who was gifted by the ancestors to wield water as a weapon more potent than his fire.

The one with hair the color of rich earth and eyes the colors of sun and grass.

Only her light can keep the darkness away, for without it, there is no hope.

ERIC

I step through a portal into the Murud-Janjira Fort in India that Excalibur has taken over. While walking toward my father's office, my scalp tingles at the muffled argument. Wanting to overhear the hushed conversation without interrupting them, I channel my ability to go invisible.

"Where is the girl?" A low growl escapes from Excalibur's rigid body as I step quietly into the open doorway.

His jaw and neck muscles strain beneath his skin as he grinds the distasteful words out. Hunched over Raymond, who's standing stock-still beside his black leather chair, Excalibur curls his tanned, meaty hands into fists on top of Raymond's white oak desk, his taller frame looming over Raymond's husky build.

"We still haven't located her yet, sir, but my boy is on it. We will find her. I promise you that," dear old Dad says in his rushed yes-man voice as he nods like an enthusiastic bobblehead.

"We can't do phase three without Sierra!" Excalibur's bellow booms through the small office with yellow-stained walls.

The shout makes Raymond flinch under Excalibur's piercing glare. "I know that, sir. I have assigned Kairos and Austin to assist Eric." Raymond meets Excalibur's heartless stare levelly as I roll my own eyes and yell fucking Christ inside my head.

Having Kairos and Austin designated to help me is news to me. I hate Kairos, the creepy warlock almost as much as I loathe these two men. Austin's not too bad, other than being tied up in this. I don't need a babysitter. There's a reason I haven't given Raymond Sierra's location. Standing in the doorway to Raymond's hole-in-the-wall room and watching their exchange, I can't help but wonder if maybe my asshole of a father really isn't as bad as I thought. Maybe he's being blackmailed into helping Excalibur just like I am. Raymond is trying to put on a solid front, but the way he's clenching his fists and fiddling with his fingers, it's obvious he fears his boss. I can understand why he's afraid of him.

Excalibur is a huge muscular immortal, possibly the largest man I've ever seen. He could put professional bodybuilders to shame. The boss man's jet-black shoulder-length hair is tied back into a red ponytail, and his irises, the color of freshly spilled blood, have the effect of staring right through you. I know that feeling personally. There's a jagged white scar along his left cheekbone.

Excalibur hijacked a plane out of the sky a few weeks ago and took Sierra's parents hostage. If it wasn't for Sierra's boyfriend Dante, she would've been taken as well. I guess it's not all bad that Dante's in the picture. Excalibur has some kind of hold over the High Council that oversees immortal activities, I just don't know what that is yet, but I plan to find out. That's why he's never gotten into trouble for killing the dozens of civilians onboard the Boeing 737 or for kidnapping several immortals.

My dad and I are both full immortals, but I didn't go through the transition the way they perform it in Graystone like ninety-nine percent of immortals do. Mine was forced on me. I've never even been to Graystone, the immortal country; my dad always forbade it. I was his dirty little secret that he enjoyed abusing and manipulating into doing his dirty work.

It's hard not to feel bad for anybody getting blackmailed. But I don't when it comes to Raymond. He doesn't really care about his kids. Emma and I are just pawns who he uses in his chessboard game of life to get what he wants. He could've found a way out of this before he had kids, but he didn't. Not to mention the total mind fuck he's put me through. I've been forced to do some terrible things, all in the name of protecting my little sister Emma from being involved in this madness. At night when I go to sleep is when my memories are the worst. Sometimes I'm my own worst enemy. Most nights, I can dull the pain with alcohol, but lately, that hasn't been strong enough.

"If you don't get me Sierra before Thursday's full moon, I'll be forced to wait until the next full moon." Excalibur slams his fist down on the worn desk making the wood creak and groan in protest. A cup tips over and sends loose pens skittering across the papers scattered on top.

I hate the way he says her name. It's as if she's nothing more than a tool for him to use and discard as he pleases. Just the sound of her name on another man's lips makes my heart twinge with a jealousy I shouldn't harbor. She has a boyfriend; I had my chance with Sierra, and I blew it. I've tried to keep her at arm's reach because I didn't want her to see how truly messed up I am underneath the frat boy persona I wear all too often. One night when my will wasn't strong enough to keep a healthy distance from her, I kissed her. I was too pushy, and she was so innocent and sweet. My fingers brush over my lips as I remember the taste of her cherry lip balm and the feel of her soft lips molding to mine.

Excalibur takes a step in Raymond's direction, then pauses and sniffs the air around him, like a hound tracking a scent. His head slowly rotates on that thick trunk of a neck he has, putting me in his viewpoint. I hold my breath, and I don't move even a single muscle. I'm using my invisibility gift; he shouldn't be able to see me. I should be blending into the wall behind me. Some immortals are born with extra abilities but not all of us. Sierra's gift is hydrokinesis and Dante's is dreamwalking. All immortals are able to manipulate a human's mind, but Excalibur's also able to control other immortals' minds, which is unheard of, but then again, I don't know many immortals because I wasn't allowed to go to the immortal homeland, Graystone.

Shit, the sweat beading on my forehead trickles down the side of my face. I wonder if my scent has drawn his attention to me. It's hard to imagine anything other than the mildewy stench that seems to be everywhere in this castle. Immortals also have heightened senses, which can be a total pain in the ass at times like this. His eyes lock on mine, while the pounding of my pulse drowns out any other sound. Each thud in my chest feels like the shockwaves that only come after the loudest, most powerful fireworks. Then, like a light switch, he alters his focus back to Raymond. I take in a deep unsteady breath. That was a close one. Too close for my liking.

"If you don't succeed in bringing Sierra to me before the next full moon, Emma will pay the price of your inadequateness. The prophecy must not be fulfilled. At all costs." Excalibur rests his hand on the hilt of his black carbon steel Ka-bar, driving his point home and leaving no question about what he would do to Emma.

Raymond swallows, making his large Adam's apple bobble up and down, and gives his boss a curt nod. "I understand, sir."

Prophecy? Little do they know; my little sister Emma is safe in a place far from this shit hole. They'll never be able to find her. I made damn sure of that. The warlocks on Dante's team were able to mask her location. Even the most powerful witch or warlock won't be able to track her whereabouts. I slowly back away from the door and avoid Excalibur as he makes his exit to the empty, dimly lit hallway. He doesn't pause this time or look in my direction as he passes me, his spicy cologne lingering in my nostrils. Hopefully, that means the big guy doesn't know I was there. Excalibur's mahogany leather Tecovas clunk evenly along the hard pine wood floors, the long planks dull from years of neglect.

Until today, I've never actually met the guy. I've only seen him from a distance. Close up, the man is unnerving. I watch him open the door to another room down the hall and disappear inside. I start walking in the opposite direction until I come around a bend in the corridor, and I stop. I'm a safe distance away from Raymond's office and out of sight of any prying eyes. I lean against the cold stone wall and listen for any signs that anyone could be close by.

Satisfied that I'm alone, I take out my blue benitoite wand-shaped portal stone, point it toward the smooth wall and create a doorway back to my house in Colorado. At first, the stone wall slowly swirls in a circle until the smokiness clears, and I can see my kitchen on the other side. The light wood cabinets never looked so welcoming. I have to get word to Dante and his team. If Excalibur can't do phase three without Sierra, that buys us a little more time before we have to attack this fort and break the prisoners out that Excalibur is holding in the dungeon, including Sierra's parents.

I have to find out what he means by prophecy; that should help us figure out why he needs Sierra. Dante's team plans on attacking and rescuing the prisoners within the fortress in a matter of days. If the team has more time, they can have a better plan and more recruits on their side. The number of minions that Excalibur has is somewhere north of a hundred. Unfortunately, many immortals don't want to risk treason by going against the High Council's orders, which makes it hard for Dante's group to gain additional allies.

Once I step through the portal, I put my hands together to close the doorway to the Fort in India. The reason I went there today to begin with is all but forgotten. I put my stone back into the front pocket of my favorite pair of faded blue jeans.

CHAPTER 1

RUBY

Tony, Ari, and I drew straws to see what location each one of us needs to go to for the ingredients to make more elixirs. Of course, I would draw the short straw and have to travel to the most dangerous location, Germany. But not just any part of Germany; you can only get your hands on pure dragon's blood in its strongest form in the seediest part of the country, where even the tourists aren't stupid enough to be caught in.

For about a year, I was stationed in Germany not too long ago, so I had to learn the language, which makes me a better fit for this mission anyway. There are dragon trees in a few different places in the world, but only the trees containing dark red sap used for our elixirs are found on Socotra Island. Getting the sap directly from the Yemen Island is even more treacherous. The mystical trees are protected by the native tribes living on the Island of Socotra, and they won't hesitate to kill any trespassers. Many who have ventured to the island haven't come back to talk about it.

With so many immortals staying at the compound and training ferociously, we're running low on the one thing that can sustain our bodies for long grueling combat, our elixirs. We need to eat real food too, but we're at our best with our strawberry-banana-flavored drinks. The elixirs are loaded with vitamins and minerals that our hungry bodies devour and use to transform every molecule of an immortal into a more powerful being. I like to think of it as wonder juice. I feel like wonder woman every time I consume the liquid. As if I'm ready to take on the world.

I've only been with Maverick's group for about a week now, but they treat me more like family than any other place I've been. I've known Maverick for years. He used to date my older sister, Summer. After all the chaos with another immortal taking out a passenger plane full of innocents with no justice served, I was done with being the High Council's dangerous little puppet. It was a no-brainer when Mav asked me for my help.

Ari, Tony, and I each travel alone and without any obvious weapons. We're trying to blend in, so the High Council or Excalibur can't find us. Excalibur wants Sierra for some cryptic reason, and the High Council's hunters have been searching for us since they believe we're all traitors. It's considered a crime of treason to not abide by their laws. The council warned us if we didn't check-in within a certain time frame, we would be rogues in their eyes.

After portal hopping from another country, I create a portal to a back alley in Frankfurt. I pull the hood of my black hoodie over my bright red pixie cut hair and start walking toward the main road. The cold metal of my spiked brass knuckles wrapped around my fingers is making me twitchy. I'm used to carrying my twin Smith & Wesson silver-coated steel daggers on my belt where I can grab them if shit goes sideways. I still have them, but they're inside my knee-high black leather boots, not exactly easy to access.

The thud of my combat boots echoes off the run-down buildings. Plywood-covered windows block any prying eyes, and the moon is the only illumination in this part of town. The streetlights all look as if they've been shot out.

Whoa, what is that awful smell? I round the corner to a crap ton of makeshift homeless camps made out of cardboard, tarps, and for the lucky ones, tents. There's a dumpster overflowing with torn open trash bags. The smell of rotting food and cat urine is so overpowering that I have half a thought of just portaling past it, so I don't have to walk that close to it.

If only I didn't have to worry about drawing unwanted attention. This whole being the prey thing is a new experience for me. Usually, I'm the one hunting down suspects for the High Council's off-books team. Every government entity has them, special agents, special forces, black ops, seals, you name it. Ours is called SIA or Special Intelligence Agents; we take care of the things the High Council would like to keep hidden from their civilians. Which is another reason I jumped to help Mav. I hate the secrets and lies that our government has.

I'm known as Nine in our team. Each agent is assigned a number as a code name, and we have to wear a mask that conceals our face when we work as a team. The High Council says it's to protect each of us, but, to be honest, I think it's because they wouldn't want the group of specially trained agents working together against them. They groomed me at a young age. I was the perfect candidate for their program. My only family was my older sister. I was a rough kid and enjoyed violence as a way to get my way.

Footsteps against cement echo over to my right. I turn slightly and glance behind me to see if it's a threat. Nope, just a bum going to bed for the night. Man, why couldn't I have drawn the straw to go get hibiscus petals in Hawaii? Ari deserved to go though; he could use an easy assignment. The young Israeli man got pretty messed up in training today. He didn't pass the evaluation to become an immortal guardian like me. Instead, he ended up working in one of the many offices in Graystone.

Don't get me wrong, every job is important, but this chick can't sit behind a desk. I have to be out in the field where all the action is. Ari can't be much older than nineteen or twenty, but he's a quick learner, and he's passionate about the cause. He believes his dad was also abducted by Excalibur a few years back, and big surprise, the High Council covered that up too.

I never worked on any cases that involved Excalibur that I'm aware of anyway. Ryker was good at omitting certain details. The steely-eyed Master Council who oversaw our team only told us the bare minimum. I kept telling myself I was doing a job that had to be done to protect my people. Over the years, though, I had my doubts that I was doing the right thing. Once I saw for myself the aftermath of the aeronautical disaster, I knew I was out. I was done with those narcissists pulling on my strings. I will not be their instrument any longer.

A whistle lets out as I walk past a dive bar with a couple dozen delinquents lining the worn brick building waiting to get inside. The black stanchion rope barely contains the crowd to the sidewalk. The music pulsing through the open doorway is an odd mix of hip-hop and dance beats. The yellow light billowing out is thick with cigarette smoke. It's a wonder that people can even breathe in there, let alone dance.

"Hey there, pretty lady. Are you lost? I can show you around." A pack-a-day smoker's voice reaches me in German.

"No thanks, I know where I'm going," I reply back in fluent German.

"This isn't a good part of town to be alone in," he warns.

Gee, the barred windows weren't a dead giveaway. Thank you so much, captain obvious. I pull the strap of my backpack a little tighter. It's not far now, only about two blocks away. I would have portaled closer, but I was worried about being seen using my stone. I cover the ground quickly, wanting to get this mission over fast. The hairs on the back of my neck have been standing at attention since I stepped foot in this country.

I round the next corner, and I immediately see the sign that reads Haus der Hexerei, or house of witchcraft in English. I gently push on the cold metal door, and a chime sounds above, alerting the shopkeeper of an incoming customer. I walk through the small storefront skimming over all the dust-covered glass vials and jars for what I'm looking for. I don't see anything. Huh, that's weird. They've always had plenty when I've come here in the past. Maybe we're not the only ones gearing up for a fight.

"Can I help you?" a gray-haired elderly lady with a serious case of crow's feet says as she hobbles over on a wooden cane fraught with knots.

"Yes, I'm looking for dragon's blood?" I answer the woman back in her native language as I fold my hands in front of my stomach.

She eyes me skeptically before retreating behind the counter. She pulls out a large black glass bottle about the size of a half-gallon of milk from the cabinet below. We exchange money for the whole bottle of dragon's blood, and I secure the glass container with bubble wrap and towels I had stashed in my bag. Hard to believe this small amount of tree sap has a going rate of close to two grand. I step outside and head back toward the alley I portaled into. The noises of the club barely reach my ears at this distance.

Bang, bang, bang. The sound of bullets exiting a firearm has me darting in the opposite direction. I run as fast as my legs will go, my daggers in their sheath shuffling inside my boots are rubbing my calves raw. I dart behind a concrete building and wait. Pop, pop, pop. Bullets are still flying, and one takes a chunk of concrete out of the wall inches from my face. They're definitely after me. Again, I take off at a dead run. The attackers are too close for me to be able to stop and take the time to create a portal. This isn't too much of a surprise. There are always thieves watching places like this. Just waiting for somebody else to foot the bill for them.

Another shot rings out from between the tall looming buildings where the alleys cross. Pain explodes inside my stomach, and I fall hard to the pavement, gouging my arms as I try to catch myself. They're getting closer, their footsteps pounding into the asphalt. With what little strength I have left, I get up and lurch to the end of the alley. Ahead is another road with woods on the other side. Each of my strides engages my abdomen muscles and pulls painfully at my wound.

Running across the roadway and through a small patch of grass, I try to take cover in the trees. The assailants are not far behind me. The pounding of their feet against the pavement are not far behind, while bullets ricocheting off of buildings and other objects make me duck at how close they are. The scent of gunpowder is something I'm not used to smelling. We don't use guns in our line of work. I stumble, trying to put pressure on my wound as I run. I'm losing a lot of blood, and I'm getting light-headed. I voice activate the speed dial to Mav's phone linked to the earbud in my ear.

"Ruby, everything okay?" He answers on the first ring.

"No, Mav, I got sh-shot. I'm bl-bleeding a lot," I manage to choke out.

The lids of my eyes grow heavier and heavier by the second. Branches are breaking, and leaves are crinkling under my feet, my stealthiness falling away like the blood trail I'm undoubtedly leaving behind me.

"Where are you? I'm coming." Maverick rushes the words out, his anxiety clear in his voice.

"There's a cabin in the wo-woods. I'm going to tr-ry to hide in there. But they're cl-close Mav, and I can't make a por-portal." I hold pressure on my stomach as I try to swallow the bile that's rising in my throat, burning a path of acid all the way up until the hot saliva starts to pool in my mouth.

I reach the cabin and jiggle the metal handle. Thankfully the place isn't locked. I shut the door and lock it behind me. I don't hear the chasers anymore. I drag myself across the small dirty beige carpet, and I slump down in the kitchen on the cold white tiled floor. I grab the hand towel hanging on the door handle of the oven to my left, pressing the blue cloth hard into my stomach, not caring if it's sterile. If I make it out of here alive, my immortal genes can fight off almost any infection. I had to bite back the scream that tried to escape through my clenched teeth as I put more pressure on the hole that's still hemorrhaging the thick liquid. The pain is so bad it drains the color from my surroundings to black and white.

"I'm on my way. Stay on the phone with me, okay? You're doing good. Just get to a safe spot."

"K, I'm in." I almost forgot I was on the line with Mav.

Everything is fading in and out of focus. I can't hear anything besides my racing pulse. No gunpowder exploding from a barrel, though. Hopefully, they went past here. My eyelids are getting too heavy to keep open. I can't stay awake. I'm vaguely aware of Mav's voice coming through in my ear. I can't make out the words he's saying. It's as if he's speaking gibberish.

Knock, knock. I jolt my eyes back open. Oh no, they found me. I don't know how long I've been sitting here. If I ignore them, maybe they'll go away. I hold my silver dagger in my shaking hand while keeping the other shoved onto my stomach to slow the bleeding. Not like a dagger can fight off a bullet, but I'm not going down without a battle. Now, if I could just bring myself to stand without crying out in agony that would be great.

Getting onto my hands and knees, I push myself off the floor with the hand holding the knife. Pulling my left leg up to plant on the tile, I maneuver so I don't place my foot in my slippery blood that has coated the uneven floor until it looks like a spilled gallon of paint. Even for an immortal that's still far too much blood loss. Still pressing the sopping wet towel into my stomach, I grab the counter with my free hand and pull myself to stand. My legs are as wobbly as a bowl of Jell-O, and the back of my head feels as if a nail gun had target practice on it.

Slumping my shoulders, so they don't pull at the angry wound below, I slowly make my way to the front door. My legs are aching and feel as if they're ready to give out without warning. My sweaty hand grips my knife until my knuckles grow white as I shuffle across the floor. The fierce knock at the front door echoes through the small room, reminding me that I don't know who lurks on the other side of that wood. Please be Mav, please be Mav, please be Mav, the mantra I keep repeating until I finally reach the front of the building.

SIERRA

I've been lying in bed next to Dante watching him sleep for close to an hour, his bare muscular chest slowly rising and falling with every breath. He looks so peaceful and relaxed while he's asleep. There's no hint of the fierce guardian he is during the day. His chocolate-brown hair contrasts with the light gray pillowcase he's on. A small amount of sunlight peeks through the window and highlights his square jaw and the short beard he's allowed to grow in recently. My fingers itch to run them through the coarse dark hair, but I don't want to disturb him. He needs his sleep.

Uncle Joe, Maverick and Dante have been sharing the responsibility of being the leaders, and I know that weighs heavily on him. He's still sweet and thoughtful toward me, but he doesn't often show that side of him to the others. To them, he's an officer in charge, and they all respect him for that, but he's also able to be their friend when they need him.

We've been adding more immortals to our cause. It seems like they aren't happy with how the High Council just dismissed what Excalibur did to all those humans, either. It sucks that so many innocent people had to lose their lives, but I think it was a necessary evil for the immortals and witches who follow the High Council to see what was really going on. Or rather what the High Council is hiding from them. I haven't been a full immortal for long, but I really wanted to be a part of their world. I finally felt like I found where I belonged, and I desperately longed to believe that they had the best intentions for all kinds on earth. It turns out they only had themselves in mind. The High Council isn't doing everything they can to protect their people.

Our compound has become quite the busy hub. We now have eight witches and warlocks and forty-three immortals on our side. I've been trying to hone my gift to the best of my ability. Some days are better than others. A number of other immortals here have gifts as well, and I've been learning from them. It has been extremely hard to just sit back and wait for the right time to strike back when I know my parents' lives are at stake. Dante repeatedly reminds me we can't rush in, but I'm not sure how much longer I can wait.

"I can feel you watching me," Dante says in his husky, chest rumbling morning voice. Man, I love that sound. There's nothing like it. I wonder how long he's been awake just playing possum.

"I can't help that I love looking at your handsome face," I answer truthfully, and since he's awake now, there's no holding back my hand from caressing his stubbly cheek and jaw.

Eric has been gaining some useful information that has been helping us to shape our plan. He thinks that some of the guards and associates of Excalibur's are only helping because their minds are currently being controlled by him. If only there was a way to break that hold. Konstantina and Reid are both looking into some spells or potions that could help. There must be a way to reverse it, just like the pills that Eric gave my parents to cancel out the iron that was blocking their abilities. The next problem would be to actually get those being brainwashed to take the pills or potion.

He opens his deep emerald eyes and looks at me with that million-dollar smile. "I can look at your beautiful face all day."

He rolls over and puts his arm around me, pulling me closer. We stay like that for a little while, enjoying the comfort of being together like this offers. We don't have much downtime to just relax, so these sparse mornings have been very sacred to us. But of course, a loud rap on the door interrupts our peaceful serenity. I sigh inwardly.

My mom has supernatural swordsmanship, which is pretty badass, and my dad has visions of the future, though not all of them come true. Dante has been able to talk to them when he dreamwalks. I wish I could communicate with them for myself. I miss them like crazy. It feels like they're a whole other world away because so much has changed since I saw them last. It's only been about a month since they were taken by Excalibur and held against their will at the Murad-Janjira fort in India, but it feels like years have passed.

I'm sure the time is going by slowly for them also. Looking back on my childhood, I realize some things are starting to make sense. All the martial arts they made me do, their strange fear of having pictures of themselves on the internet or social media, and the obvious paranoia of somebody breaking into our home. I wish they would have trusted me with their knowledge. It hurts me to think they felt like they couldn't confide in their only daughter.

It's been nice to have Emma here with me. I couldn't imagine going through all the trauma without her. Emma's my best friend, and she's what's called a half-breed. Her dad, Raymond, is a full immortal, meaning he's gone through the transition like me, and her mom Charlotte is a human. Emma could go through the transition to become a full immortal if she wants to, but for her kind the risk of death is very high. As it is those that are born from two full immortals don't always survive the transition, I shiver as I recall my own.

Emma has been getting pretty close to Maverick lately as well. I can't blame her though. He's a very attractive man. At about six feet, with dark, disheveled hair and a smattering of stubble, he's a good catch. Not to mention he's kind of a badass himself. He's been in charge of combat training here at our compound. Between Carl breaking up with Emma because she couldn't tell him where she was and Vivian not willing to come with Maverick to the compound, they've both been brokenhearted. It's nice that they've been able to find comfort in each other. That is the crappy part about this life, we have to live in the shadows. No humans can ever know who we really are and what we do. It was just as much for Carl's safety as our own that she had to hide our location and her reasons for leaving Colorado.

I would love to say I've been spending some time by the ocean, but unfortunately, my free time has been minimal. The little bit of freedom I do get, I try to spend with Dante or Emma. Dante's been so stressed out that he barely sleeps, and I have to remind him to eat. I know he wants to save my parents and the other prisoners being held captive. But if he doesn't take care of himself, he won't be able to help when the day finally comes to rescue them.

We left Graystone about two weeks ago and have had to be very careful ever since. We received word from a source that all immortals who haven't reported to the High Council in the past week are now considered traitors. The orders from the High Council are to capture us alive if possible, and if not, dead would do as well. That's scary enough to have over our heads, let alone what Excalibur could be doing. We still don't know why he is drawing the blood of the immortal prisoners and cataloging their unique gifts, but it can't be good. Why am I so important to phase three? What prophecy was Eric referring to, and what on Earth does it have to do with me? God, I just want answers. It's so frustrating trying to guess everything, especially in a world that is still as foreign to me as Saturn.

Aunt Grace is in charge of all the humans and tasked with the day-to-day chores that need to be done for our compound to run smoothly, such as meals and housekeeping. Seeing her barking orders at the locals, we know we made a good choice. Maverick has been in charge of training and conditioning all the immortals. Uncle Joe is leading the recruitment side, and Dante is tasked with gathering and sharing information. Though all three switch roles occasionally, they excel in their chosen positions.

I've been looking forward to today, Sunday. Which is our one day off a week from training. It's the only day a week where I can actually sleep in and stay in bed with Dante for a little while. We've all been pushing ourselves so hard since we've come here to the island. There is no room for us to slack off. There's just too much at stake, too many lives at risk for us not to be at our absolute best.

"We can ignore it and pretend we're sleeping," he whispers as he yanks the covers up higher and tugs me in closer.

Another knock sounds. This time louder. Yeah, not going to happen.

"They're not going away," I say, disappointed our time is cut short.

I gently get out of bed, noting how sore my muscles are from all the extensive training I've been doing. I gingerly throw my purple plaid pajama bottoms with matching top on and head toward the door as Dante gets out of bed. As I walk across our hardwood floor, there's a twinge in the back of my thigh from a muscle I never knew was there. I blame Maverick for that; he's a ruthless opponent to spar with.

I open the door just a crack to see an anxious-looking Maverick. "Good morning, Maverick."

Speaking of the devil himself, as if my aching backside conjured him out of thin air just to torture me. Standing at about six feet, he towers over my five-and-a-half-foot frame. His black surfer boy hair feathering off to the side makes the gold flecks of his hazel eyes really pop. I have hazel eyes too, but unlike his, mine mostly have shades of green. He's wearing a pair of black cargo pants with a tear in the left knee and a long sleeve plain navy shirt. He's one of the few guardians that wear his weapons while walking around the compound. It would be odd to see him without them strapped to his sides.

"Morning, Sierra. Is Dante awake?" Right to business, so that can't be good. The furrowed brow and tight-lipped expression on his face doesn't bode well either.

"I'm right here. What's going on?" Dante asks as he comes up behind me and I step aside.

"Ruby was injured while she was gathering supplies in Germany. She was able to get to a safe house, but she isn't strong enough to create a portal."

My head snaps up, worry sinking its sharp claws into me. Creating a portal isn't as simple as pointing a wand and saying open says me. The action actually uses a lot of mental focus and takes energy from your body to invoke it. If Ruby's not able to make a portal, she must be in bad shape.

Ruby is one of the immortals that have joined us recently. I love her spunkiness. She reminds me of a punk rocker with her gothic style and devil-may-care attitude. I've always been envious of people who can pull off that look. I love spikes and chains, but they don't look right on me. I also envy her attitude; she doesn't care what people think or say. She's unapologetically herself. Me, I worry far too much about other people's thoughts and how they perceive me. I've held myself back on so many things because I fear what others would think of my actions.

"I'll grab my stuff, and we'll go get her." Dante reaches for his weapons on the small entryway table. Dante secures his sheaths for his daggers on his belt and pulls the black nylon shoulder strap attached to the wood scabbard holding his Katana over his head. The sword's length hits just below the dimples on his lower back, while the handle sticks up a few inches above his shoulder. "I'll be right back."

I hate it when he leaves like this. I always worry that one of these times he won't come back. I know that's a real possibility lately, not because of his lack of strength or fighting ability. No, my handsome protector is a ferocious soldier with an uncanny way of taking out his opponent during the exercises. I can only imagine how deadly he would be in an actual fight. "Okay, I love you. Be safe."

"I will. I love you too." He places a quick kiss on my forehead then he disappears into the portal Maverick creates in the hallway. I watch Dante's back slowly disappear as Maverick closes the portal behind him.

Sometimes I'm taken aback at how my life has turned out. I could never have imagined that the world I saw through my own eyes was hiding so much from me.

I thought fairies, vampires, and werewolves were only in fairytales. I don't even want to think about demons being real. My whole-body shudders at the thought. I really never gave much thought to immortals either.

I rub the back of my neck where my tattoo signifies I'm an immortal who's survived the transition. Mine is the hollow flaming sun, tattooed with black ink and transfused with a mix of gemstones that give it a shimmery look. The spell that's cast on the mixture before it's loaded into the tattoo gun hides the mark from those who don't know about the creatures that live in the shadows. That's why I never noticed my parents' mark on the back of their necks. I was unaware of who they really were.

Dante and the other immortal guardians have a star on the inside of the hollow sun, signifying their job, just like the immortal enforcers who carry out the High Council's justice have two large swords that make an x on the outside of the sun. According to my Uncle Joe, Excalibur wears the mark of an enforcer even though the High Council denies knowing him. I'm still living in a world full of secrets and lies.

I rub my temples, feeling a headache coming on. I snatch my cell phone from the small wooden nightstand on my side of the bed and head down to the kitchen to make myself a strong cup of coffee. I can't function properly until I've had my cup of joe. I also need to inform the others about Ruby. I really hope she's okay. My stomach is in knots just thinking about her. I don't think I'll ever be used to my friends and family going on dangerous missions like this. How will it be for Dante and I after we hopefully manage to capture Excalibur? Will he go back to being an immortal guardian risking his life daily? And what of me? Go back to school to become a guardian as well? Sometimes being an adult with real responsibilities sucks.

CHAPTER 2

DANTE

We step through the portal Maverick made into a densely wooded area. I'm on high alert, and I constantly survey my surroundings. The only source of noise is the slight wind rustling the leaves on the bushes that surround us. The moon's light doesn't trickle down much through the tree's thick canopies. We make our way to the small cottage located deep within the woods. We didn't know her exact location, so we had to guess where to create the portal. Ruby wasn't making much sense with the words she was telling Maverick; blood loss can mess with you like that. This is the second time one of the immortals from our team has been injured while outside the confines of our Caribbean compound.

I feel responsible if any of my teammates are hurt under my watch. They may have known the risks when joining our cause, but that doesn't make it any easier knowing they are following my lead. I never in my wildest dreams would imagine I would turn into a rogue immortal guardian. I've heard stories of other guardians going out on their own, and I thought they must've been insane. But here I am leading a relatively large group, defying the orders of the High Council that I have always sworn to uphold. I guess I was just naive to blindly trust them.

My right fist tightens on my dagger's rubber finger grips that were custom-made for me by the Holy Ones. The silver partially serrated blade forms a double-edged deadly point with perfect weight displacement. The knife is one of a pair that I never go without. Several years ago, I had another identical set forged for Sierra. I didn't know if she would choose the dangerous life led by an immortal guardian or even if she would choose me. There were a lot of sleepless nights spent wondering what would happen if she decided to stay the way she was and, if so, how we could make our relationship work. Luckily for me, she decided to go through with the transition and be with me. I couldn't imagine living my life without her.

We're careful to be mindful of the placement of our feet, not wanting to call attention to ourselves. Maverick cautiously surges forward with his own weapons out. I can only envision what my family thinks of me right now. They have always held the High Council up on a pedestal, and if anyone so much as breathed a word disagreeing with anything the High Council has said or done, my parents believed they were traitors. Since we left Graystone, I haven't spoken to them, my sister, Annalise, or my brother, Roman. I know they wouldn't understand. They live and breathe for the High Council, but I've always had a skeptical side, which made me question some of the High Council's actions. I didn't dare speak the words to them, though. I knew I was the outlier in my family. The black sheep.

But now, Sierra's my anima gemelli, and there's not a line I wouldn't cross for her. Helping her to rescue not only her parents but the others is the right thing to do. No matter if it goes against the High Council and what my family believes I should be doing. I know my moral compass is pointing in the right direction, which is more than I can say of those that govern us and dictate what we can and cannot do.

I knew Excalibur would be difficult to neutralize, but I didn't think I would have to deal with the High Council's hunters going after us as well. Andrew was spotted last week while he was gathering intel from a source. He managed to escape but not before he was shot in the leg. It could have been a lot worse, and he is recovering well, thankfully. I don't know how they're able to find us. It seems too much of a coincidence twice in a week or so. But I don't know if it's Excalibur tracking us or the High Council. In Graystone, we don't believe in using firearms to fight, which makes it more realistic to think Excalibur is behind the shootings.

Initially, we thought the sapphire rings that allow entry into Graystone could be tracked, so we locked them in a safety deposit box in Shanghai. We've all only used burner phones as well. None of my team would leak our locations to the High Council. Joseph, Maverick, and I all vetted each and every newcomer. We had to make sure that every candidate was on our side one hundred percent.

Maverick knocks on the scratched wooden door of the small stone cottage and waits. When nobody answers, he knocks again, louder this time. "Ruby, it's Maverick and Dante."

We hear slow-moving footsteps coming toward the door, and then the door slowly opens an inch and a sharp silver blade appears between the opening. Ruby must have seen us out here because she opens the door wide enough for us to slip through. As we step across the threshold, a branch snaps from behind me.

"Get down!" I yell as I slam the door shut behind us and cover Ruby. "Maverick, make that portal now!"

Bullets fly through the windows, shattering glass everywhere. We're pinned down. There's no way to tell how many are out there. It sounds like they're using automatic rifles as a barrage of bullets hit the cottage. They don't care who's inside; it's clear our only way out of here alive is by a portal. I duck as a bullet ricochets off a wall and whizzes by my ear. I grab the black backpack from Ruby and sling it over my shoulder. We can't leave the dragon's blood behind, or this will all have been for nothing. Maverick creates a portal to another country instead of the compound just in case one of them somehow follows us.

When the portal finally opens up large enough for us to fit through, I usher Ruby in first. I wrap an arm around her waist, holding up most of her weight as she leans heavily on me. As I go to step through the whirling mass, a stray bullet catches my arm. It tears my flesh apart as it travels through my left bicep, and I let out a curse through ground teeth. I quickly step through with Maverick on my heels. As soon as our boots land in whichever country he picked, he then selects another random country to portal to. I can feel the blood dripping down my arm, and it burns as if it's on fire, but I try my best to ignore the pain and stick to the task at hand. Ruby is too weak to stand on her own, and I will not let her down. I will get her back home to safety. Once we land in another territory, he creates the final portal to our compound.

We step through the portal, and most of our team on the other side greets us immediately. A look of shock crosses Sierra's face when she notices I'm bleeding. She runs to me, a frown marring her beautiful face.

"I'm okay, I promise," I say before she has time to say anything.

The portal Maverick created dumps us out in front of the medical ward. It's much easier to portal outside rather than inside a building. Plus, if the building is not one you own and maintain, there might be magical barriers that could severely harm you when you try to cross. Your body trying to get through a force field meant to keep you out can even trap you within the walls. Most are left in critical condition on the outside of the barrier.

Ralph reaches Ruby with a wheelchair. As Maverick and I help her onto the chair, I realize her paler and her blood-soaked clothes that look like they stem from her stomach. Ralph is an immortal doctor we were able to convince to join us. I was hoping we wouldn't have to utilize his skills but wanted to have him on our team just in case. We have a few nurses who are humans to help him out. Immortal doctors and nurses are extremely hard to find. The special healing ability and immunity to most diseases and infections don't warrant for much need of their expertise.

The nurse whose name is Claire asks me, "Can I see your arm, sir?"

"No, I want you to focus on Ruby. I'll follow you guys." I trail behind Ralph.

There is no way I'm going to take any medical staff away from helping Ruby. It struck me as odd that my blood wasn't clotting already. I follow Ralph and Ruby toward the infirmary on the left side of the building. It's not a huge space by any means, but there's a waiting room, a few patient rooms, and an operating room in the back.

We made sure we stocked up on any supplies or equipment we might need. We don't know how hard the battle is going to be to get Excalibur out of the picture. We had to prepare for the worst. I follow them to the operating room and stand outside the metal door while the medics evaluate Ruby's injuries. The smell of antiseptic turns my nose up.

"Are you sure you're, okay? Your wound is still bleeding." The worry in Sierra's wavering voice makes me even angrier for putting her in this position. We shouldn't have to go after Excalibur without the backing and the resources of the High Council.

"I'll be fine, I swear. It looks worse than it is," I say as I look down at my arm, which still hasn't stopped bleeding yet. Look at how bad Ruby is hurt. I have no room to complain. I lean my head against the cool stone wall, as I look up at the ceiling while my adrenaline slowly wanes.

"Anything yet?" Maverick asks as he and Joe join us in the brightly lit hallway.

"No, but they just got in there," I reply.

"You should get your arm looked at." Joe eyes my wound as his brow furrows.

I start pacing the small hallway. "I'm fine for now. I want to make sure Ruby is taken care of first. She didn't look good." I concentrate on each step I take, trying to drown out all the what if's blowing through my mind.

"Well, we should at least put a tourniquet on it to slow the bleeding," Maverick says as he ducks into one of the patient rooms. He comes back with one and wraps it around my arm. I clench my teeth and fists as he tightens the material until pain shoots down to my fingertips.

We all jump when the door from the operating room opens. Claire appears with her black curly hair hidden behind a pink and white surgical cap.

"She's lost a lot of blood, and there's a great deal of damage, but Ralph's optimistic Ruby will pull through. We're doing surgery to repair the damage and stop the bleeding."

"Thank you, Claire." Joe nods.

"He also instructed me to look at your arm since he has the other nurses in there with him, and they have everything under control." She looks pointedly at me, not giving me any leeway now. The bossy tone she uses reminds me of my mother.

"Okay, thank you." I follow her to one of the patient rooms. Joe and Maverick stay in the hall, but Sierra trails behind me into the small bright white room.

"Sit here and roll your sleeve up please," she instructs pointing to the blue chair next to the exam table.

I slowly do as she orders while trying not to scrape the wound too much with the bunched-up fabric as Sierra stands beside me. The nurse gathers some medical supplies and bandages out of the cupboard.

Claire grabs my arm and gently puts it on the exam table to get a good look at it. "This might sting a little." She pours a mixture of saline solution into the wound.

Sting was an understatement; it felt like I was being branded with a hot iron. I look to Sierra and hold my other hand out to her. She's biting her lip and picking at her nails. She takes my outstretched hand and puts her other hand on my back. I've been bit, scratched, stabbed and hit by numerous creatures and countless objects. Getting shot is a new one for me, though.

Immortal guardians don't typically use guns since we are in close range with our opponent most of the time. Guns can also draw the unwanted attention of humans since they're not the quietest form of combat. We usually try to capture our targets to bring them to justice, not kill them. If these are hunters working for the High Council, they appear to prefer to kill instead of capture.

Claire debrides the wound as gently as she can but it still stings as if my arm is in a wood stove. Minutes later, the wound is clean and bandaged.

"I removed all the debris, and it looks like it was only muscle the bullet went through, so it should heal just fine. I can't give you a time frame because I've only treated humans, and I'm told immortals heal much quicker. Just try not to use that arm if you can. The more you do, the longer the healing process will take." She narrows her eyes at the face I make. I can't be out of commission. I have too much to do. That isn't going to work for me.

"Thanks, Claire," I say as she walks back toward the operating room.

"You're welcome, sir." She quietly shuts the door behind her, but not before she gives me a stern look. She knows I'm going to continue to use it.

SIERRA

We wait for what seems like hours for an update on Ruby. When the tired-looking nurse finally comes out, we expect bad news.

Mackenzie says as she stifles a yawn, "We had some complications, but it looks like Ruby will be okay. She's stable now, and we will transfer her to a room shortly."

We all let out a collective sigh. The longer we waited in the hall, the grimmer the outcome seemed.

"Thank you, Mackenzie." Dante relaxes back against the cold concrete wall, the tension slowly dissipating from his body as he slides down to sit.

"If you could hang out here for a bit while we finish up, Ralph would like a word with all of you."

"Yes, of course," Maverick answers as he rubs at his messy ebony hair.

So, we wait some more on the floor of that empty hallway until Ralph's blond head appears in the doorway about twenty minutes later.

"Glad to see you waited for me." He twists his blue surgeon's cap in his hands as if wringing out a wet washcloth before tucking it into the pocket of his white lab coat.

"Thank you for saving Ruby." Dante slowly gets up off the cold white tiled floor.

"We were able to recover the bullet from Ruby's abdomen, but I would like to run some tests on it." The good doctor pulls out a small container from his pocket and rubs the scruff of his beard with his other hand.

"Okay, why's that?" Dante asks him.

"Well, it's not like any bullet I have ever seen. There is what looks like the typical lead you would normally have, but there was an unknown material inside the lead that broke apart. That could explain why both hers, Andrews, and your blood wasn't clotting. All of you could have easily bled out." He tilts his head while his gray eyes narrow at the container he holds up to the harsh fluorescent lights above him. If there's something out there that can pose this much of a risk to us, we need to know.

"Good catch. Do you have everything you need here, or do you need other equipment to figure out what the other substance is?" Uncle Joe wraps his fingers around the blue-green labradorite gemstone he wears for protection at the base of his neck.

"I believe so. I'll let you know as soon as I find out what the other materials are in the bullet," Ralph insists.

"Thank you, Ralph." Uncle Joe looks to Maverick as Ralph walks back into the operating room.

"That can't be good if they're creating bullets that can stop or slow our healing." Uncle Joe rubs a hand through his short brown hair.

"No, it's not. But who's the one creating such a weapon, the High Council or Excalibur?" Maverick adds, shrugging and shaking his head. "This just gets better and better."

"If I had to guess, I would say Excalibur. He's already cataloging immortals by their gifts. Maybe this is why. Maybe he's found a way to make us weaker." Dante speaks the truth we all didn't want to hear. "We should gather everybody and fill them in. I don't want anybody else leaving this compound until we know more."

"I agree. It's not safe for any of us to go out." Uncle Joe glances down to the floor with a look of defeat on his face, and his shoulders slump.

Uncle Joe and Maverick lead the way back to the dining hall, just as my cell phone goes off from the group text Uncle Joe just sent. "Critical meeting in the dining hall in ten minutes. All must attend."

I knew there was a possibility that we could get seriously hurt going up against Excalibur, but I didn't think Dante would be one of them. When I saw him come through that portal with blood dripping from his arm, I was so scared that I had to stop myself from questioning what we're doing. If it's all worth it? I know that sounds crappy to say, but I love my family, and I want to save them and the others more than anything, but what if we can't? How many could we lose, and it could be all for nothing? There's no guarantee we'll get any of them out of prison. This is all so stupid. Why couldn't the High Council do this? They literally have an army of trained guardians at their disposal who would be better suited for taking on Excalibur.

The walk back to the dining hall is quiet; we're all no doubt contemplating the fate of our team and how close we came to losing one or more of them today. We finally make it to the large rectangular dining hall, and each of us take our seats at the end of the longest table and wait for the other immortals and witches to arrive. This is a fairly big room with many tables, but when you have around fifty people in it, the room feels really cramped. Within a few minutes, the others start to trickle in. From the looks of it, other than Ralph and the nurses with Ruby, everybody is here.

Uncle Joe stands up and gazes around the room, making eye contact with every one of us. Maverick and Dante rise from their chairs as well. "Thank you all for meeting us on such short notice. As many of you are aware, Ruby was injured while she was out gathering the dragon's blood. She's in stable condition now. Ralph recovered the bullet that penetrated her abdomen, and he believes that this is a new type of weapon designed specifically for us immortals." Uncle Joe clears his throat, "He thinks that the unidentified substances within the bullet can cause our blood not to clot, which could cause greater damage than your normal round of ammunition. Because Andrew was attacked last week and now Ruby, unfortunately, we are asking everybody to stay within the compound's walls until we can assess this new threat."

"Do we know who attacked Ruby today?" Roger crosses his hairy arms over his broad chest, his eyes shrouded in anger creates wrinkles around his eyes.

"No, we don't. We were ambushed when we reached the cabin she'd escaped to. She was too weak to answer any questions. We plan on talking to her when she wakes up," Maverick answers him. His disheveled hair still looks as if he just climbed out of bed. At least it looks good on him. Mine would be a hot mess if I didn't brush it when I got up. Men have it so much easier than us ladies sometimes.

"How long until we know what the substance is?" Julian, a thinner older immortal with graying hair, speaks up with a sharp voice that cuts through the room like a samurai.

Julian doesn't speak much, but when he does talk, he carries an authoritative tone. Don't let the gray hair fool you; he's not an old man while training, I made that mistake, and he took advantage of it. I thought he'd be an easy match, but he left me bruised and sore for days.

Dante rubs at his arm before he speaks. "Ralph is running some tests on it and will let us know as soon as he figures out what it is. Once we have that knowledge, we will call another meeting." Dante cracks the knuckles of his fingers out of nervous habit.

I hand Dante a bottle of water Aunt Grace and a few others were passing out to all of those in the room. He's putting on a good show, but I can tell he's really worried about what this could mean for all of us. If they found a way to slow or stop the enhanced healing abilities immortals have, that adds another tally against us in this unyielding front that keeps looming larger and larger.

The room is quiet, and nobody else seems to want to ask any more questions. "Thank you all for your time. You may go back to your day. Please don't leave the compound without speaking to Dante, Maverick, or myself first." Uncle Joe dismisses them all with a sweep of his arm.

The group disperses from the large room until it's back to just us four again.

"I'm going to go check in on Emma. If you don't need me?" My gaze zooms in on Dante's arm where he was shot, the white gauze a menacing reminder.

The humans aren't included in the group text because most of the information doesn't apply to them. They can't leave the island without an immortal or witch anyway. Well, they could, but they wouldn't be able to come back without the black leather bracelet with an azurite stone. The stones were cast in a spell by Reid and Konstantina to allow passage through the magical wards that surround our island. Only witches, warlocks, and immortals have the bracelets. The humans are too easy a target for an enemy to take the stones from.

"Go ahead. I'm starting to feel better already." He gives me a reassuring smile that doesn't quite reach his eyes. I debate on staying beside him, but I feel he wants to talk privately with the other two.

I kiss him on the cheek before walking out of the dining hall. I cast another glance at him over my shoulder as he slumps in his seat and puts his head in his hands. Sometimes this place feels so small, and at other times it makes me feel so small. Such as now, it's as if the world is stacking up against us. We have not seen or heard from Excalibur directly, and we still don't know what he's planning. All we know for sure is that for phase three, Excalibur needs me and a full moon, I suspect my presence involves some sort of spell or ritual. Eric has to tread lightly otherwise they could find out he's helping us. He can't start prying information out of people there, or that would be too suspicious.

It came out that Eric can cloak himself and become invisible, and I can't help but be reminded of the time I closed the bookstore and sensed someone near me. Somebody chased me to the truck; I heard the footsteps. The hairs on the back of my neck stood up. I've been wanting to ask him about my suspicions, but I'm afraid of what the answer might be. What had he planned to do to me? Did he change his mind, or did he only stop advancing on me because I turned around? I know Dante is uncomfortable working with Eric; I would be too if I were him but we didn't do any more than kiss, and that's behind me now.

I can't imagine being with anybody other than Dante. I feel like he is home no matter where we are. I can't wait until all of this is over and we can just be together, not leading a group of rogue immortals and warlocks. I don't regret my decision to go through the transition. I just wish I had more time to be human, well, humanish. To be able to say goodbye to the ones I left behind. I can't help but wonder how Kayla, Amanda, and Cynthia are doing. Not only did I disappear, but Emma did too. I wish there was a way to let them know that we're okay, but I know they're probably being watched by Excalibur's acolytes or the High Council's goons.

I finally make it to Emma's room, and I peek my head through the open doorway. "Hey Emma, can I come in?"

"Duh, the door's open," she says sarcastically. Her tone changes when her eyes meet mine. "What happened?"

She scrambles out of the bed covered with several books, both open and closed, and wraps me in a tight hug. I hug her back even tighter, afraid if I let go, I just might fall apart. When her long straight blonde hair sticks to my face from the static, I gently brush it off. Emma's sweet-smelling honeysuckle perfume invades my nose, washing away the scent of the medical ward's disinfectants.

"Ruby was attacked this morning."

Emma steps back and her forehead wrinkles. "Oh no! Is she okay?"

"Ralph says she will be, but it was a close one. Dante was shot in the arm when he and Maverick went to help her, he's not bad though." I walk over to her light blue chaise lounge and plop down on it.

Her bedroom is slightly smaller than mine and Dante's but feels much cozier with her large Himalayan salt lamp in the corner throwing off a pinkish-red glow. The sofa I'm on is covered in white furry throw pillows, which would be the perfect spot on a day like today to curl up on and take a nap and forget our troubles. Unfortunately, we don't get that option, too many people are counting on us to save them.

"I'm sorry, are you okay?" She places her hand on my shoulder.

"I will be. How about you? You look like you're having a blast." I smirk as I point to her messy bed.

"Oh, you know. Trying to make up for what my dad is doing." Emma sits beside me and leans back into the cushions.

I know that burden all too well. I feel like I have to make up for being a part of Excalibur's plan. Emma's been busy studying medical books and journals. She planned to become a vet prior to our world crashing down around us. Now she's studying up on being a doctor who can treat immortals, witches, and the like.

Leaning her head on my arm we melt into each other. Serenity finally finding me after a long stressful day. Being around Emma calms me some; she's always had that effect on me. The weeks between Excalibur crashing the plane my family and I were on and coming to this compound were made even harder because I couldn't see or talk to my best friend about any of it.

"Their actions don't fall on you." I rest my head on hers, our hair blending together. My brown to her blonde. "I'm glad you're here with me, though."

"Where else would I be? Who would keep you out of trouble if not me?"

She's always been there for me, and I need her now more than ever. She's always been my person, my one truest friend that will be by my side no matter what. Furthermore, she's the only one who understands what I'm going through right now because her life was torn upside down too. We're both outsiders to this hidden side of Earth. We're doing the best we can by learning as we go.

CHAPTER 3

ERIC

I wake up early by my cell phone. Linkin Park's Papercut blares through the tiny speaker of the cell phone on the nightstand beside my bed. The verses of the song all but promise me today will be a shit show of a day. It's the ringtone I have set for Raymond. Well, good morning to me, not.

"Yeah?" I answer groggily, wiping the sleep from my eyes. What time is it anyway?

"Have you talked to your sister lately?" my dad barks out the question. There's no good morning son, how are you from this man.

"Uh, not recently, why?" Shit, is he onto me already? I blink the sunlight out of my eyes, trying to wake my sleepy brain that always seems to lag behind.

I sit up on the edge of the bed, and a wave of dizziness sets in. I reach a hand out to the top of the mattress covered with my dark red comforter to steady me. I drank far too much last night, but it's the only way I'm able to fall asleep lately. It's hard to play both sides without getting caught, and thoughts of Sierra have been invading my dreams far too often. I know I should leave it alone, but she's like a siren calling out to me in my dreams.

After all, she seems happy with Dante, and he's a good man. She deserves to be happy, and I can't give her the life she deserves. Even though I desperately wish

I could. That doesn't stop my fucked-up mind from coming up with all kinds of scenarios of me and her together. At least those are the good dreams. I won't even elaborate on what the bad ones have in store for me. I prefer the sweet seductive torture of her siren's call, begging me to go to her. I wonder if she dreams about me? I've heard that the person you're dreaming about can sometimes have the same dream as you. Wouldn't that be something?

"She's not answering her phone, and I can't find her." He actually sounds like he's concerned. What a liar.

"And you care what happens to her now because?" I roll my eyes and shake my head even though I know he can't see it. I do it often because I know he hates it when I roll my eyes.

"I've always cared what happens to both of you," Raymond snaps. "Maybe you're too naïve to see that right now, but later on you'll understand."

Slim chance of that happening, buddy.

"Last I knew she was 18 and could do what she wanted. Maybe the golden child has finally decided to live her own life. She's probably taken off with Carl." What else can I say to throw him off? I wasn't prepared for this conversation yet, though I should've been. I knew this would come up soon.

"No, she's not. He hasn't seen her in weeks. What do you know? You're hiding something. I can tell by your voice," he spits out.

That's it, I snap.

"I'm not hiding anything. Maybe you should ask that fucking boss of yours. Hasn't he threatened to hurt her several times? How soon you forget hanging Emma's safety over my head all these years!" I shout back at him, my muscles tense. I want to hit something, preferably his face.

Silence.

"Are you still there?" I huff out. The vein in my neck is pulsing hard against my skin. My hand is clenching the phone so tight I'm afraid I'll crack the screen. Maybe I should, then he won't be able to get a hold of me.

"Yes. Can you please try to find Emma for me?" Raymond's voice is hoarse as if trying to hold back from crying. Nice try, old man; your heart is filled with cement.

"I'll try to find her." Maybe he doesn't idolize Excalibur as much as I thought. It still doesn't change what he's done to us, though.

"Thanks, and I'll need you to swing by my office today." Of course, he would.

"Okay." This ought to be great with a hangover.

To be honest, I'm surprised we lasted this long with him not noticing that Emma's been gone. I think the only reason he hasn't noticed her absence before now is because Excalibur has had him working around the clock for phase three, whatever that is. Emma's an adult now, so it's not like he had to make sure she was taken care of. Not like he was a dependable father to me, either. I had to take care of myself. At least Emma had Charlotte. I was just her step-son, so I didn't hold the same needs as her own child. Gotta love step-parents.

I need to get into Excalibur's office to see that prophecy that he has. That would be the only place I think he'd stash it. The only other person that has a key to that room is Raymond, and he keeps it in his desk drawer. I've seen him take it out before when he had to grab something for Excalibur. I can only hope the key is where he left it. I take a quick shower while I try to think of a way to stall on Emma's whereabouts. I pound a blue Gatorade and a banana nut muffin, hoping the electrolytes and carbs will subdue the lingering effects from last night's excursions.

I take my blue benitoite stone out and create a portal to Raymond's office. Excalibur didn't put a magical ward around his fort like Dante did. Excalibur didn't have to do that; he puts the fear of death in everybody before they even think about double-crossing him. Nobody would be stupid enough to break into his fort, or so he thinks.

The coolness seeping from the stone into my hand reminds me of how cold my dad can be. A shiver runs up my spine from the memory that surfaces. I remember lying on the icy floor of a room down in the dungeon while I was transitioning into an immortal, all by myself and locked in a room where nobody could hear my screams of pain. The dread in my stomach is already weighing me down like a pair of concrete shoes in a lake. Saliva pools in my mouth as if I'm going to puke. I swallow it down. I don't have time for this shit right now. I step through and close the portal in time to have Raymond round the corner and walk in as I place my stone back in my jeans pocket and push the traumatic memory down with it.

"Any luck locating Emma's whereabouts?" His blue eyes that mirror my own bore into me. His good looks are one of the only good things he passed down to me.

"No, not yet. I've got some places I'm going to check when I get done here, though. Did you ask the big guy?" Looking at Raymond, I have a hard time shaking the memory off of the dungeon. I still couldn't shake the way his cold, calculating eyes regarded me as he locked me in the room as if I was no more than an unruly zoo animal he could shut away in a cage.

"No, and I'm not going to. If he's not the reason she disappeared, he'll think I had something to do with it, and I don't need that. I'm already on thin ice here." Raymond roughly rubs his face with his hands.

His stubble is longer than I've seen on him in a long while. It looks as though he hasn't shaved in a week. My father's usually meticulous about his looks. Something's not right here.

"Why, what happened?" I meet his gaze, curious on why he would be on bad terms with Excalibur.

"It's nothing for you to be concerned with. It's my burden to bear." He leans his hip against the wooden desk. "Listen, I have a pile of work to do, but Austin and Kairos would like to meet with you about locating Sierra. They have some ideas. They're down in the main dining room." He starts heading toward the door after grabbing a manilla file folder from the top of his desk. "And please don't be an asshole to them. It reflects badly on me."

"I'll do my best," I say flatly, deciding to leave it alone and not push my luck too much. Being an asshole is kind of in my nature, another thing I inherited from him, I guess. The fruit doesn't fall too far from the tree.

I wait a moment after he walks out, wondering if I have the time to grab the key. His footsteps are growing quieter and quieter. I walk to the backside of his desk, so I can access his drawers and pull open the top one. The drawer slides open easily enough. I gently lift the papers on top to reveal the small silver key hidden underneath. I grab it and tuck it into my pants pocket. That was the easy part.

I take a deep breath and let it out. Now it's time for my vanishing act. The vibrations start in my feet and make their way up to my face. I hold my hands out in front of me, but I can't see them, well, not exactly. The outline of my hands and arms are there but I can see it because I know my limbs are there. I should be invisible to anybody who isn't aware of my presence. I quietly walk through the open doorway and into the dim hallway. It's dark out because it's nighttime in India right now, which only makes this creepy old fort more horror movie-like. It's fitting for the shady shit they do here. The building is wired with electricity, but it's not well lit. Which actually helps me tonight. I never thought I'd be thankful for the darkness this place has.

I tiptoe down the hall, not wanting to alert anybody of my presence and freeze when I hear footsteps coming my way. I tuck myself as close to the wall as I can get. Fuck, it's Excalibur, of all people. He unlocks the door and waltzes right into the office I was making a beeline to. I silently keep walking closer and closer until the doorway is about five feet from me. The sound of a phone ringing breaks through the silence. The shrill sound echoes off the barren walls.

The enemy's deep gravelly voice answers the call. "Yeah. Again? You've got to be kidding me. I'll be right there."

Excalibur storms out of his office, slamming the door shut behind him as he barrels past me down the dimly lit corridor, mumbling profanities under his breath. I watch as he disappears around the corner at the end of the hallway. Now's my chance. I pull the key from the front pocket of my jeans and slide it into the keyhole. With a quick twist of the wrist, the lock breaks free, allowing me to gain entry. I shut the door behind me and relock it. The spicy, smokey scent of cigars greet me. His office is about twice the size of Raymond's, with many papers scattered across the top of his desk as if an open window did the decorating for him. Gently sliding the papers around to try to find what I'm looking for, I'm cautious of making them look rummaged through. It's not like they were organized to begin with.

The prophecy can be written on anything. None of the papers look as though they hold the clue. This is taking too long; Excalibur can come back at any moment. I pull the drawers open one by one, each slide having its own distinct screech. Every creak of the rollers makes me hold my breath and wait to see if I've been discovered. I open the bottom one next. That must be it—a glass framed yellowing paper with odd symbols that somewhat resemble letters. I dig my cell phone out of my back pocket and open the camera.

A door shutting echoes down the corridor. I snap a picture of the worn paper and close the drawer. I put my cell phone away just in time to hear a key being pushed into the lock of Excalibur's door. Shit. I start panicking inside. What the hell am I going to do? I'm a dead man if he catches me in here. I've heard rumors of those who crossed him; none of them lived to talk about it. We're so close to having answers. I tiptoe away from the desk to the wall on the other side of the room, where there's no furniture. The door swings wide open, and in comes Excalibur himself.

The fridge of a man is wearing his shoulder-length black locks down today, like some rough-cut Fabio. He's far from the pretty boy Italian model the ladies adored. The jagged white scar across his left cheekbone is like a beacon in the night sky. The light stemming from the bronze gooseneck desk lamp that was on when I came in highlights the rugged lines of his face. Excalibur's biceps must be the same size as my thighs, if not bigger. The hunter green long sleeve shirt he's wearing looks like it's ready to burst at the seams. I hold my breath, focusing all my energy on staying cloaked. I can't get caught now, not when I finally found this madman's bible.

He takes a few more steps in, barely reaching the large ugly brown oval carpet with the odd flower-like shapes. Not exactly the type of rug you would think to find in an evil villain's lair. His head swivels around as if sensing my presence. His blood-red eyes meet mine, and I think for sure he knows I'm here. My fists are clenched so hard my short stubby nails bite into my sweaty palms. I count to five in my head to try to remain calm. This would be a horrible time for my cloak to disappear because of my nerves.

"This god-forsaken place is haunted," he grumbles as he takes a seat in his large burgundy wingback chair, like a king at his throne, and shakes his head vigorously.

Realizing Excalibur left the door open, I cautiously take a step in that direction, watching to see if he notices. He doesn't; he's too occupied with shuffling his papers around as if looking for something important. I sneak out the door and back down to my dad's office. I quickly put the key back where I found it and uncloak myself. Now I'm off to meet with Kairos and Austin and get the hell out of this place.

DANTE

The afternoon sunlight glitters across the small table in my bedroom as I sit with a hot mug of coffee, feeling utterly exhausted. I had a hard time sleeping last night. I couldn't help but think of what could've happened if we hadn't gotten to Ruby when we did. Waiting on news from Ralph has been excruciating. I want more answers than a simple test can provide. I have to try to be patient, though. These things can take time. I checked in on Ruby later last night when she was awake, but she couldn't provide any information that we didn't already know. She wasn't close enough to any of the attackers to be able to ID them. Her body is starting to heal on its own, same as mine. At least we know once all of that substance from the bullets is removed from our bodies, we can heal like we normally would. Its effects aren't permanent. I've never heard of anything harming immortals like this before.

I crack my knuckles. I can't help but think of all the possibilities that Excalibur would need Sierra for a full moon. I keep getting stuck on sacrifice, though. I can't lose her. I've known that he's wanted Sierra since before the plane crash. Her dad told me as much. But the fact that he can't do phase three without her makes my stomach grow cold as ice. Sierra has only left the island a few times since we came here because we knew Excalibur would be after her. Her parents did say they were afraid she'd have a target on her back. But does that mean they knew about the prophecy too? Could they be withholding more information? It wouldn't be the first time they've hidden something from Sierra. My jaw clenches. I think they could have put their daughter at more risk from hiding Excalibur's interest in their family.

Having no one coming or going from the compound makes it harder for us to gain more allies. If we want to win this war that Excalibur has started, we will need more fighters. He has about at least a hundred fighters on his side, mind-controlled or not. Reid and Konstantina have been working diligently on a spell to reverse the effects he has over others, but they don't seem confident they will find an answer soon enough. I would rather we had a fix for his mind control abilities before we went there. I'd hate to think what could happen if he was able to manipulate us as well, turning us against one another. I couldn't live with myself if I hurt any of my teammates. I can't even fathom what it would feel like to be responsible for hurting Sierra.

I was exempt from today's training with Maverick and the others so my arm can heal properly. Not by my choice; Maverick made it very clear I wasn't welcome at the training arena. It's eerily quiet in the castle with everybody outside. Even the humans are out there tending to the many vegetable gardens and farm animals we have to help supply our food.

I take my amethyst and azurite stones out of the zippered pocket of my black tactical pants and sit on the bed. I lean heavily against the tall wooden headboard behind me.

These two small quarter-sized stones have been through a lot with me. I flip over the amethyst stone with a blend of dark and light purple and some white on the end. I rub the small crack that lines the bottom side, the only visible reminder of the night I almost lost my life.

The night that changed me was just over a hundred years ago when I was fresh out of the Guardian Academy and thought I was unstoppable. I graduated at the top of my class and had the ego to match. My unit had been hunting down a pack of werewolves for almost two weeks, but the pack was always a step ahead of us. They had ravaged several small towns across the Midwest, breaking down the doors of the houses that belonged to innocent humans. They would tear apart families limb from limb with no remorse.

The sights of the victims are still an image that haunts me now and again. The rusty scent of blood is forever burned into my brain. The worst casualties were the defenseless children. The youngest victim was just shy of his first birthday. The blond hair on his little head was plastered to the floor in a puddle of blood and guts, while his blue glassy, lifeless eyes stared up to the ceiling. The dried tears had stained trails down his plump little cheeks. An angel taken far too soon. I can't look at a cherub without thinking of him. Hell, I can't even look at a toddler without seeing his face. Women and children, the werewolves didn't discriminate. They killed them all.

That was my first violent case I'd been involved in, and it's not one I ever want to go through again. The wolves were attacking in a coordinated strike every two days and the most recent strike that occurred was in Williamsport, Indiana. Our team, made up of eight immortal guardians, was scattered in the neighboring towns. We each had a different location and were instructed if there was any sign of werewolf activity, to report it to the team and wait for backup to arrive before advancing on them.

I was positioned in Attica just east of Williamsport. Attica was a sleepy little town full of saw mill workers. I stopped at the only diner in the village to grab a coffee and a quick bite while I was poking around the town looking for anything that could place the werewolf pack in the area. The diner was nothing special. It had a long wooden bar with white bar stools pulled up, but their French fries were amazing. I remember sitting on a stool filling my face with those greasy potatoes, frustrated that I couldn't see out of the frosted glass windows. It would've been the perfect place to mingle with the townspeople to get information if not for those opaque panes.

While I was waiting for my cup to cool enough to drink, the radio in the diner had announced there was a break-in earlier at the old foreclosed farm just on the outskirts of town. That would be the perfect place to hide a pack of wolves, I radioed it to my team and was told to stand down until they arrived. All I could picture was that baby and his siblings with missing limbs and chunks of their flesh bitten off. His pale eyes begged me for help, but I was too late to save him. I couldn't let that happen to another family, not when I could stop it. I jumped into my dark blue Austro-Daimler and drove as fast as the car would go, hardly letting off the throttle enough to make the turns without causing the vehicle to skid around the corners of the narrow dirt road.

Once I was just down the road from the abandoned farm, I killed the engine and walked the rest of the way. Keeping my silver dagger embedded with moss agate stones in my hand, I stuck to the shadows of the trees lining the dirt road. Moss agate is a common stone to have attached to your weapons because of the natural ability to dull your fear. It was a dark night with the clouds obscuring much of the moon and stars. The scent of crisp fall leaves hung heavy in the air, a tease for what was to come. My enhanced sight allowed me to see even in the darkest of nights. I stopped at the end of the barn's driveway with nothing but an overgrown hayfield between the building and myself. There was an occupied house just a mile or so down the road, and I hoped they hadn't attacked them yet.

I inched closer and closer, waiting for any noises to carry over to me on the wind, but there was no sound. Not even the crickets or frogs were calling out. It looked like this was the right place after all. I left the safety of the tree's shadows to get a closer look. I moved toward a dirty window so I could peer inside of the rundown structure without being spotted before my team arrived. Five feet from the building, a low menacing growl emanated from behind me, instantly sending goosebumps up my spine.

I whipped around with my silver dagger and scraped the werewolf's chest as he howled in pain. He pulled away before I was able to slam the blade home in his heart. The large black wolf lunged at me, and I swung my blade out again, slicing a wide gash across his shoulder. He snarled at me as he showed his large mouth full of teeth and lunged for me again. This time he was able to grab my arm that held my dagger in between his sharp teeth.

Pain lanced through my arm like a rocket. I struggled to free my arm, but the wolf wasn't letting go anytime soon. I reached behind me with my free hand to grab my spare knife while he continued to clutch my arm between his teeth. Awkwardly, with my left arm, I jammed the razor-sharp blade through his thick mane, finding the sweet spot in between his ribs and pushing up at a 45-degree angle, just like we were taught in the academy. His bright orange eyes found mine as he let out one last growl before I shoved him off of me with a resounding thud that seemed to echo in the vast field. This was the first life that I ever took, and my adrenaline coursed through my veins like a lifeline engaging my fight instincts. Wolves always traveled in packs. There would be plenty of time to reflect on the monumental kill later if I survived this.

Another snarl came from the tree line as I spotted a smaller gray wolf barreling toward me at an astonishing speed. I ran to the building but the door wouldn't budge. I bolted in the opposite direction toward another stretch of woods. My arm screamed in pain as the wind cut through the wound like a blade. The gray wolf paused long enough to let out a long, loud mournful sounding howl, no doubt calling the other werewolves to our location.

I reached the dense forest, and the only option I could think of to survive the night was to climb one of the trees. As cocky as I was, I had limits too, and I couldn't outrun a pack of wolves. I slipped my daggers into my pants pocket and reached up to the nearest limb. As I grabbed hold of the thick branch and hoisted myself upward, I let out a curse as my arm buckled under the pressure of my weight. Limb after limb and branch after my branch, my arm held up, barely. I was about twelve feet off the ground when the wolf appeared below me, followed by several others.

I should have waited for backup to arrive. This was exactly the scenario the academy taught us not to put ourselves in. I was too arrogant and thought I alone could stop a pack of weres. Now, look at where I was. The wolves below me snarled and jumped at the tree, trying to climb it. The large lion-sized paws of one scraped at the bark, while others circled below, waiting for me to slip and fall. Suddenly from out of nowhere, a man appeared and walked right down the middle of them. The wolves parted down the center, creating an aisle for the newcomer. He reached the base of the tree.

His eyes met mine, and the familiar orange-yellow irises of a werewolf stared back. It seemed the werewolves outsmarted me after all. The man climbed toward me. I struggled to clamber up the tree, but my arm was so weak it wouldn't lift my heavy body. With dagger in hand, I waited for him to come closer. His bulky body, built much like mine, meant we would be closely matched, but I had a weakness, my forearm. We faced off in the air, balancing on the swaying limbs of the oak tree until another wolf joined us in his human form. The second man was taller and had broader shoulders than the first, but that was where their differences ended. The similar build of their facial features made me think they were brothers. They both came toward me, and there was nowhere to go but up or down.

Going up wasn't an option where I was; the next branch was too high for me to reach. I slipped down to the limb below and scooted to the other side of the trunk and out of their reach. I knew I was outnumbered and the odds weren't in my favor, but I wouldn't back down. I swiped my dagger toward the smaller guy, who managed to get closer, and he maneuvered away. The larger dark-haired werewolf did something I hadn't anticipated. He leapt from his branch onto me, taking me down with him. The heft of his weight was like an anchor driving me to the ground far too fast. I couldn't fight him off me quick enough.

I hit the ground with a loud thud that made stars dance in my eyes. As soon as the spots cleared, I was surrounded by wolves. The man quickly got off me, while a long-bodied dark gray wolf with plenty of muscle mass appeared to my left. He was the alpha. If I wasn't fighting for my life, I would've said he was beautiful. His long, almost black fur streaked with shades of gray, and his sharp orange eyes stood out in contrast to the dark fur around them. I reached for my silver dagger that fell out of my reach when I hit the ground, but the wolf pounced on me before I had a chance to grab it.

I clutched his coat just in time. He was snarling, spitting, and trying to snap his powerful jaw around my neck. His hot breath feathered my skin, making my muscles tense. All the other werewolves stood back. I was his to claim. Nobody would challenge their alpha without having to face the consequences. My arms shook against his brute strength as the wound on my forearm from his teeth streamed blood down my bicep. Just when I thought I was a goner, a well-placed arrow from Maverick's compound bow took the wolf in the side of his head, instantly stopping his assault. The signature blue and silver feather fletching on the arrow told me it was Maverick's arrow. I pushed my attacker's limp body off me and scrambled to get up, grabbing my knife as I did.

The other werewolves, after freezing briefly as if shocked at the death of their leader, took off as shouts from my unit surrounded the field. Most of the immortal guardians who ran after them were also armed with silver-tipped arrows and knives.

I owe my life to Maverick. If it wasn't for him, I wouldn't be here today. My outlook on life changed that night, as I was also responsible for my teammate Elliott's death. Elliott died from a werewolf attack as he tried to subdue a young wolf he cornered in the woods. If I had waited like I was instructed, he'd still be alive. After that, I realized how fragile life could be, even for one of us immortals. I learned to trust the process and wait for help before charging in like I did. My reckless side was left in that field that day like the blood that I lost, the life I took, and the life of my fellow brother. Or so I thought I left it there to stay.

The crack in my stone is from when I hit the ground. I landed on the small purple gem causing a nasty bruise on the backside of my leg, and the force of the impact created a reminder that I carry with me every day. I'm no longer the hothead who goes into battle unprepared. I can't help but feel like this mission we're on to save the prisoners is a lot like that memory, though. I don't want to take someone else's life unless it's them or me. Unfortunately, there's been more death than I can count on my two hands. The thought of being responsible for another teammate's demise is a heavy weight I've carried all this time.

I toss my azurite stone up in the air and catch it. The smooth dark blue rock speckled with blotches of shades of green carries a much lighter memory. My little sister Annalise gave me this as a gift when she got back from traveling to France. She knew of my troubles in the beginning stages of learning to channel the right person, and this stone has been a very useful tool with dreamwalking.

I craft a dream of Sierra's parents' house back in Colorado. I picture the small dining nook with the worn blue cushions that I often refer back to when I choose a dream with her parents. Any dream when I try to seek somebody out, I use a place that's familiar and comfortable to them. I try to relax my mind and think of Michael. Taking away any other thoughts from my brain besides Sierra's dad. I've learned over the years to clear my mind or I won't be able to find the correct person. It's not easy to block out everything else in my mind, especially lately, but I've found a way to put walls up around me. I finally see the thread of his subconscious. I grab on to it and pull him into the dream with me.

After we exchange pleasantries, I decide to get right to the point. "Do either of you know of any prophecies tied to you or Sierra?"

Unfortunately, I haven't figured out how to link more than one person in a dream yet. I never had a need to prior to Michael and Sophia's abduction. I know it would do Sierra and her parents some good to see each other. I really wish I could do that for them. I've tried unsuccessfully many times; I can't bear to see the sadness in Sierra's eyes at my failure to do so again. Not being able to do what she needs tears at my soul like nothing I've ever felt before.

"What do you mean prophecies?" Michael leans back in his chair with a puzzled look on his face.

"According to Eric, Excalibur said the prophecy must not be fulfilled at all costs directly referring to needing Sierra for that to happen?"

"I've never heard of any prophecies unless he's talking about my visions. Which I've told you before, some happen and some don't. I wouldn't exactly call those prophecies, though." Michael shrugs his shoulders.

I was afraid of that. "Is there anything in your visions where Sierra is involved in some type of ritual?" I ask.

"I haven't had one since last week when I saw us all die at Excalibur's hand." Michael looks away as he rubs at the large dark circles under his eyes. A haunted look crosses his face.

It must be hard to witness such awful visions. "Is there a way he could be manipulating your visions or getting in your head to see them?"

I've often thought of trying to contact Excalibur through the dream realm, but I disregard it just as fast. If I'm unable to erase the memory from his mind like I did with Sierra, the act could do more harm than good. Considering he's able to control others with his mind, I think his own mind would be hard to alter, and who knows if Excalibur could mind control me through a dream. It would be nice to get a peek into his thoughts, though. I can only imagine what goes on in that psychopath's gray matter.

"No, I don't believe so. I think I would know if he was rooting around in there." He taps the side of his head with his finger.

"Have you heard about any specially made bullets to slow immortals healing and clotting?"

Michael shakes his head. "No. I can't say that I have, why do you ask?"

"Two teammates and myself have been shot recently from ammunition with an unknown substance. Our blood wasn't able to clot until all the shards were removed."

His hazel eyes go wide as he leans forward on the table. "Are the others healing now?"

"Yes. Thankfully, they received medical attention in time." I twist my fingers until the pop off my knuckles releases some building tension.

"I wish I can help you Dante, but as it is Excalibur hasn't come down here in at least four days. If I was a betting man, I would say that he's the one creating the bullets."

I don't like the sound of that. "Are they still taking blood from you?"

"Every day like clockwork." Michael rotates his arm to reveal thin tubing taped to the inside of his forearm.

At least Excalibur is still using the prisoners for their vein, so that's something. If he has no use for them, he'll kill the prisoners.

"How are you two holding up?" His cheekbones are more prominent than before. I wish I could slip him some food or weapons but the guards check their cells frequently.

"We're doing the best we can in this situation. Do you know an ETA on when you guys are attacking this place yet?"

"If everything goes well, within a week." I hope my team is ready.

"We'll be waiting." Michael shrugs as if it's no big deal.

"I'll check in again tomorrow, stay safe."

"We will. Take care of my little girl."

I nod and end the dream with no more information than I started with. I lean my head back against the headboard and close my eyes.

As I sit on the bed, I take a minute to enjoy the calm. Since Sierra's 18th birthday, when I came to her in a dream that I did not remove her memories, it's been a constant roller coaster. Between waiting on her parents to tell her the truth about who she really is, then her parents getting kidnapped and now we're leading this group. It's hard to believe it's been two months since Sierra's birthday. It seems like a lifetime has passed. There hasn't been much time to do anything else but survive. At least for the moment, I don't have an immediate crisis. But thoughts of Elliott cloud my mind. The guilt still gnaws away at me all these years later.

My phone buzzes on the nightstand beside me, alerting me to a new message. I swipe its face to reveal a text and image from Eric. He managed to get into Excalibur's office and take a picture of what he believes to be the prophecy. At least one of us can do what Sierra needs. I run a shaking hand over my thigh as I look closer at the image. The only problem is the writing on the faded yellowing parchment paper looks like it was written in Greek. I thank him and forward the picture to Reid. The warlock is versed in many of the old languages, and if he can't translate it, he'll know someone who can. The history of us immortals' dates back to the ancient Greeks and Italians, so it makes sense that a prophecy might be in Greek.

Reid is one of the few we allowed to leave the compound since Ruby was shot. He's been trying to convince a few other warlocks to help us. Reid replies he knows of an interpreter. At least we have our hands on the prophecy now. Maybe it'll reveal why

Excalibur is trying to stop it from happening. I don't know if I believe in prophecies or not, but clearly Excalibur does, and he's willing to kill for it. At least we might learn what his motivations are and how Sierra fits into his plans. I stand up and stretch my tight muscles, hating that I'm benched from training with the others. I could really use the distraction.

Chapter 4

SIERRA

"You can do better than this."

I reach my arms up in an x to block Maverick's swing. Thwack, red-hot stinging shoots up to my shoulder and into my collarbone.

"I'm trying," I say as I pant, struggling to catch my breath.

"Come on, Sierra." Maverick taunts as he lands another blow to my side.

Maverick is no joke to train with. He knows his stuff, that's for sure. He has no reason to take it easy on me, and he hasn't. I've come back to our bedroom bruised and bloody more times than I can count. My body is so exhausted between fighting and healing that it's a constant battle to get through the day sometimes. In a moment of weakness, I broke down the other day with Dante, saying "I'm quitting. I can't do it anymore. I'm scared of failing everybody involved, and my body is nowhere near conditioned like theirs is, so how can I really fight somebody anyhow? Just like back on that plane, I'm a liability, not an asset."

He just looked at me and said, "No, you don't get to quit. If you give up, you're letting Excalibur and the High Council win. I'll be your crutch and help you stand, but I will not let you fall. You hear me? You can do this."

That alone has kept me going this past week.

The whistle blows letting me know this torture session is over. I head to my bedroom to get cleaned up from the combat training session with Maverick and the rest of the immortals, witches, and warlocks. I take a quick shower and change my clothes. Next on my list is to meet up with Konstantina to work on my hydrokinesis gift. We only have a little over two weeks before the next full moon.

I'm thankful for the extra time that we have to prepare to rescue the prisoners, but I also feel bad that my parents and the rest of the prisoners are still down in that dungeon. Even with the fifty or so we have willing to fight against Excalibur, we just don't have the numbers to go up against him yet. It would be like sending hens into the fox's den. I wonder how many he's captured and held against their will. My parents told Dante that there were at least ten of them locked up down there in the basement.

I step back outside into the warm sunshine with aching muscles and exhaustion wanting to consume me, I slowly walk to the far corner of the lawn where I've been practicing safely away from others and the buildings. I don't want to risk harming our friends, and my abilities don't always do what I want them to do. Today's combat training whooped me; Maverick was extra hard on us. To say I was glad when it was over would be an understatement. I was dragging half way through, which made it worse because Grant got in more hits than normal. Usually, I can hold my own with the young stocky warlock, but not today. I gently rub my chin. My jaw still hurts from that last punch he landed. Then I had to duel Maverick and obviously that didn't end well either.

This also happens to be the corner of the island where the wall is closest to the ocean. I take a cross-legged seat on the soft grass and try to calm my nerves. The ocean's so close I can taste the saltiness in my mouth. The sea's soft breeze brushes across my face and blows my long brown hair behind my shoulders. It brings me back to the last time I was able to be on the beach; it was the day before my transition. It seems so long ago now. The thought of relaxing on a sandy beach somewhere is just crazy now. No matter how much I crave that simplicity.

Dante did his best to make sure my last day as a somewhat normal teen was beautiful. It was hard to enjoy myself knowing that my parents were being held prisoner someplace but he tried so hard for it to be perfect. My cheeks warm with what happened later on that night. It was our first time together, and my first time going all the way with someone. He was gentle and slow, taking his time to make sure I was okay. I knew I loved him deep down the first time I met him, but after that night it was like our souls actually intertwined. Finally coming together, the way they were meant to all along.

Drawing myself away from fond memories, I try to focus on the task at hand. Water. It's subtle, but I can feel the water all around me, in the ocean close by, in the grass below me, even in the air that surrounds me. With my eyes closed, I silently call to the water, and I ask it to bend to my will. The rush of coolness that greets me in my veins is the element answering my plea.

I open my eyes and turn my palms up to the big blue sky and gently lift my hands from my lap to my shoulders. As my upturned hands raise up, so does the water around me. There's water droplets floating midair, frozen in time. My hands slowly lift higher and higher, and so do the droplets. Once my arms are stretched above me as far as they can, I quickly drop my arms to the ground. The precipitation around and high above falls to the ground like rain in a summer storm. The dampness of the drops coating my skin, cools it from the sun's hot rays.

I do the same thing again, except this time, I pause as high as my shoulder and turn my palms inward as if I'm holding onto a ball. The water swirls around and around in my hands as if trapped in a glass sphere. I spread my arms wider, and the sphere gains in size. I slowly pull my arms back over my shoulder and then fling my hands forward with as much force that my tired aching muscles can muster. A loud splash erupts as the water bomb hits the tall concrete wall surrounding the island, sending a small cascade of water flowing in every direction over the rough, bumpy exterior.

"Easy on the wall there, we still need that." Konstantina struts over to me in her signature blue stilettos that match the shade of her hair and the lipstick on her mouth. Her dark brown eyes crinkle at the edges. "You're improving more and more each day."

"Well, a lot of that's because of your help." I gently shake the rain from my wavy hair as I stand up.

"Let's work on some more rain. We'll see if you can make it downpour over there instead of on us. My hair doesn't do well in the rain." Konstantina pats down her curls.

The last time we practiced, I accidentally doused us both with a heavy sprinkle. She laughed it off but was quick to disappear soon after to change. I've never seen Konstantina look anything but perfectly polished. I'm envious of her beautiful sun-kissed skin and how flawlessly she looks no matter what. I wonder if she even sweats and if that's a witch thing. I can't remember the last time I put make-up on; there really is no sense in it with all the training and sweating I do. It would just get ruined anyway. Somehow Konstantina's doesn't, though. I'll have to find out her secret.

I pull the water from the earth and the ocean until it feels like a weight is pushing my arms down. Moving my arms in the direction of the sea's crashing waves, I drop my arms to my sides as rain pelts down a short distance away from Konstantina and me. Not as far out as I had wanted to go, but at least we didn't get wet this time.

"Focus harder and try again. Imagine Excalibur on the other side of that wall, and a torrent of rain will stop him." She nods enthusiastically as she points a delicate finger toward the ocean.

"But rain won't stop him." I raise my eyebrows at her as I put my left hand on my waist.

"For one, you don't know that it won't, and for two, think about the bigger picture. If you can make it rain, you can make it storm. A storm may be the perfect cover for when we sneak into the fort." She adjusts her black beaded bracelet with the large oval labradorite gemstone in the center. The metallic blue and green hues are luminous in the light of day.

"I never thought of that." It's actually a good idea.

I unconsciously reach for the emerald amulet Dante gave me on my 18th birthday, rubbing its smooth surface. Dante has a matching necklace. The only difference is that mine is on a silver chain and his has a black leather cord. The amulet is forged with magic, allowing each of us to know when the other is in danger of dark ones. Dark ones can be werewolves, vampires, demons, fairies, and other evil creatures. It's not necessarily the species that makes them a dark one, it's their intent. The necklace will heat up against our skin when dark ones are nearby. I've only felt it a very few times and I didn't realize what it meant until after.

Dante said he can also feel some of my emotions if they're strong enough, but I have yet to sense his through my necklace. I only take it off when I shower. I feel naked without the weight of it. Other than when I'm showering, since my birthday, I've only taken the amulet off once when I thought it was cursed. I was at war with myself, not knowing if Dante was real and if my parents were hiding things from me like Dante said they were. I really thought I was going crazy. I only saw Dante in my dreams, so that really didn't help the situation. It turns out that my parents were actually hiding things from me, lots of stuff. I was born from two full immortals which means I'm an immortal as well, but to become a full immortal like my parents and Dante, I had to go through the transition.

Just thinking about the transition makes me wrinkle my noise and pull my arms closer to my chest. The pain I went through after the ritual performed by the Holy Ones was indescribable. The Holy Ones are comprised of nine immortals and warlocks who perform the ceremonies as well as forge and enchant the weapons that the immortal guardians rely on. When I went through my transition, it felt like every bone in my body was shattering and every blood vessel was on fire. Immortals only have until their 20th birthday to go through the transition. After that, the transformation is too dangerous, where a small percentage of us die in the process of transitioning into a full immortal. The same night that I underwent the transition, a boy named Dion had died in the process.

"Try again." Konstantina puts a perfectly manicured hand on her slender waist, her long blue fingernails in contrast to her pretty pink knee-length dress.

I unconsciously rub the tattoo on the back of my neck. I never made it far enough to get the guardian mark added to my tattoo, which is a star in the center of the sun. The guardian mark represents their duty to keep the balance between the light and the dark, the sun and the stars.

My thoughts turn bitter as I recall why I couldn't go on with my training and why we had to leave Graystone. The High Council dropped the investigation into the kidnapping of my parents and the plane crash that Excalibur was responsible for. That meant if my parents were to be rescued, we were their only option. When my parents were captured, we weren't aware that Excalibur held other prisoners within his fortress' walls. Unfortunately, that meant I had to skip going to the Guardian Academy where I would train to become an immortal guardian and hopefully pass the rigorous test at the end.

I've only known about this secret society for about a month, so I'm astonished at how much getting the star added to the tattoo meant to me. I feel like that is what I was meant to be, to help protect the humans and the High Council just stole that away from me. My mother always told me that everything happens for a reason, that you can't truly appreciate the beauty of flowers without first enduring the rain. My parents didn't raise me religiously, and we never went to church. That just wasn't who we were. But she always believed in a higher purpose.

Pulling my brain out of the black hole of memories that keep surfacing, I again focus all of my energy and thoughts on making a rainstorm in the distance. I sigh and shake my hands out, releasing my cramped-up fingers.

I wring my hands with chewed fingernails out again and kneel down to the ground, putting my palms on the damp grass. I guess it wouldn't hurt to put some nail polish on my own nails. I'll make a note of that for later. I whisper to myself, "You can do this, you're their only hope." No pressure at all.

Palms pointed toward the cloudless sky; I slowly lift them from the ground until they're inches above my head. Again, I thrust them out to the sea. I slightly round my palms like a bowl and hold it. Off in the distance, a small dark cloud forms in the sky. I make the bowl shape larger, and the cloud gains in size. A bead of sweat drips down the right side of my face, over my top lip, and into my parted lips. The salty taste reminds me of what I'm fighting for, their freedom.

With the sphere growing larger and larger, I'm unable to stretch my arms any further. The ominous cloud blocks the sun's rays from reaching the water off in the distance. I swing my arms downward with all my strength and drop to my knees. My legs collide with the hard ground. The large dark cloud releases all the water it's collected through a torrential downpour. An excited squeal sneaks past my lips as I stand back up, and I can't control the happiness that bubbles up inside me. We might actually be able to pull this off.

"That's great, Sierra. I knew you could do it." Konstantina wraps her arms around me, sharing in the happiness. "Now, make it bigger!"

Of course, she wants it bigger. She's always pushing me to do more, which I guess is a good thing. Not that I'm unmotivated to excel, but the drive to impress her is huge. So, again I make another cloud, and another one, and another one after that. Practice makes perfect as the old saying goes. Each time I use my gift, I get more control over the element; it bends to my will, and becomes easier and easier each time, but my stamina is rapidly dwindling. Each manifestation is more challenging than the previous.

"I think that's enough for now, but you should practice some more after dinner once you've replenished your energy." She taps her index finger against her lips. "I want to take you somewhere tomorrow where water isn't as accessible as here. Just because Excalibur is surrounded by the sea right now doesn't mean you'll always have that luxury." Konstantina gives me a reassuring smile.

"But they said it's not safe off the island and don't want anybody leaving right now." I give her a blank expression. She was in the meeting yesterday so she should know this. But a gentle reminder never hurt anybody.

"Yes, I'm aware. I'll talk to Dante tonight about it. I believe he'll see it's worth the risk." She saunters back toward the compound. It amazes me that she can walk on the grass without the heels of her fancy stilettos digging into the ground. With more positive vibes than when I arrived at this spot, I take off in a jog toward the compound, my tired muscles begging me to slow down. I can't, though. I have to tell Dante what I was able to do.

DANTE

I've been pacing this room for a little while now, trying to shake the unease creeping in since I received that message from Eric. He came through for us by getting that prophecy, and I should be happy he got it. But I still don't trust him. The way his face lights up when he hears Sierra's voice or sees her beautiful face on his phone's when we video chat is like a gut punch. I can't blame him for being attracted to her, but I think it's more than that. I've felt like this for a while now.

Sierra's given me no reason to question her loyalty to me; she has been the perfect example of what a man needs beside him. Unfortunately, even so, my jealousy has been rearing its ugly head far too often. I do my best to hide it, to wear the guardian mask I've worked hard to achieve every time I have to deal with Eric. It's the bonded male coming out in me, the dangerous side of a soulmate that others warned me about.

Once two immortal anima gemella's come together in the most carnal way, the bond is sealed. The need to protect your mate is deeply ingrained into you, bringing out the primal beast that was at rest until you've been united. It's not like anything I've ever experienced, nor is it as simple as the meager teachings they did at the academy. Beings aren't property I know that, but she's mine, and God help the poor soul who dares to come between us. Things won't end well for him. I would fight to the death for her.

The bedroom door flings open so fast that I nearly jump out of my skin. Sierra comes through the doorway with a radiant smile that lights up the whole room, effectively burning away the thoughts of destroying another man.

"Guess what, handsome?" she says with a twinkle in her mesmerizing hazel eyes.

"What, beautiful?" I make quick work to close the distance between us.

"I made a dark cloud that created a downpour!" I don't think her smile can get any bigger. Seeing her happiness shine in the dark times we've been in has been a lifeline I cling to.

"That's awesome, babe. I'm so proud of you." Wrapping my arms around her amazing body, I lift Sierra up and spin her around in a circle and let my hungry lips find her soft, inviting mouth. Her kiss makes me forget about all the insecurities looming deep within my mind. It's just her and I.

I gently let her small body slide down the front of me until we're face to face. As her lips graze mine, the ache in my chest slowly dissipates. I've hardly seen her today, and I've yearned for her. Her kiss tells me she's missed me just as much. God, I love this woman. Her warm hands are running through my hair, gently tugging on the strands. I take a step toward our door, still holding her close to me, my hands just beneath her lush behind.

I kick the door closed with my right foot, and I'm instantly rewarded by her soft giggle and smile against my lips. I can never get enough of her; she's the drug that feeds my addiction. Every kiss, every touch, lights a wildfire within me.

The closeness I feel with her is like nothing I've ever had before. The women I've dated in the past just seem like friendships compared to what we have. I can't imagine my life without Sierra. There's no line I wouldn't cross to keep her safe. I don't know if that thought should scare me or not. It doesn't.

"My beautiful Sierra," I whisper as I nuzzle my face into her hair and leave a trail of kisses down to her collarbone. Her unique scent of rain and cherry blossoms create an irresistible magnet.

I carry her over to the bed and set her down on its edge. Sierra scoots backward to make room for me to climb in. Taking the invitation, I follow her up the mattress until we reach the headboard. My arms are holding most of my weight off from her. Sierra pulls off her damp t-shirt, and I let out a groan. She's wearing my favorite black lace bra. Her hazel eyes are always gorgeous, but in moments like this, they are truly captivating. They remind me of a sunflower; her black pupil is surrounded by petal-shaped gold hues encircled by a bright green field. I can't look away.

She tosses her shirt on the floor, and I follow it up with mine, enjoying the way Sierra's looking at me as if she's committing my image to her memory. She knows how to make a man feel wanted. She pulls me down, and our lips meet again as we hungrily kiss each other. Without crushing her small frame, I shift my weight to my forearm as I run a hand through her soft wavy hair. She never ceases to amaze me.

A loud rap sounds at the door. I reluctantly break away from our kiss.

"Yeah?" I answer harsher than I intend.

"Sorry to bother you, Dante, but Ralph was looking for you," Maverick says from the other side of the door.

"I'll be right there. Tell him to meet me in the dining hall." Of course, Ralph would choose now to have the information we need. At least that's the only reason I can think of right now.

I give a frustrated groan as I roll off of her. As I sit on the edge of the bed, my shoulders slump. It seems like we're always getting interrupted, not just times like this. Even a rare cuddle on the couch is hard to come by lately. I guess that's the price we have to pay to get through this stage.

"Hey, it's okay." Sierra's voice is far too husky to make me believe the words she's saying.

I look behind me to where she's still lying in our bed, still breathing heavily. Desire still burns in her eyes. "I promise I'll make it up to you."

"I'm counting on it." Sierra winks as she rises from the bed and starts rummaging through her clothing bureau.

"I'll see you down there?" I ask as I grab my discarded gray t-shirt from the floor and pull it back on over my head.

"I'll be right down." Her gaze still filled with longing lingers on me.

I leave our bedroom before I'm too tempted to stay. The urge to ignore everybody and everything else is far too strong. I try to clear my head as I walk down the long empty corridor leading to the dining hall. I step into the large room and pull out a wooden chair next to Ralph. I give Joe and Maverick, who are both sitting across from him, a nod as I take my seat.

"Now that you're all here, I found out the substances in the bullet we pulled from Ruby." Ralph meets my eyes with hesitation.

"Okay, what is it?" Maverick prompts the fair-haired doctor.

Sierra enters the hall and comes to sit on the other side of me, and I give her a grin when I notice that her eyes are still ablaze. She rests her hand on my thigh and my pants do little to block the current of electricity from flowing between us. I have to drag my gaze back to the reason I was called down here.

Maverick gives me a knowing smirk. Joe is raising his eyebrows at me, throwing a clear down boy my way. Obviously, what I'm thinking about is on display for everybody's humor. Great. That's just what I needed. I let out a breath and nod to Ralph for him to continue.

Ralph clears his throat. "Anyways, like I was saying the chemical make-up of the bullets is the usual lead but with crushed iron, orange calcite, and malachite in the mix." He sighs. "We already knew that iron interferes with our abilities. I've never heard of the other two stones having a reaction to us, but then again, I've also never heard of anyone doing experiments on immortals before either." Ralph leans back in his chair, his face weary. No doubt thinking of all the worst-case scenarios that concoction could do.

"Is there anything that might counter it or reverse its effects?" Joe asks.

"There's no reversal agent that I'm aware of yet, but I can run some tests on other materials. I can't promise anything, but it's worth a shot." Ralph shrugs his shoulders, his white lab coat moving stiffly as if he starches it.

"Well, that's all we can ask. Hopefully, there's something out there to counteract the mix. Eric has pills that he takes that cancels out the effects of iron, which means Excalibur has done some of his own research." I have a hard time thinking clearly with her so close. I can feel her watching me. The alluring scent of her perfume fills my nose and messes with my brain.

"I'd like to get my hands on some of those pills if that's possible. Then I might be able to narrow down some possibilities."

"We can make that happen. My guess is Excalibur's the one behind the ammo anyway." Maverick crosses his arms over his large muscled chest and as he leans back, the chair creaks.

Others start filtering into the hall for dinner. We take the opportunity to share the information that we just gained from Ralph to the crowd of people in the room. A tap on my shoulder draws my attention behind me to Konstantina.

"I have a request that I'd like to make, but I'm afraid you won't like it." Konstantina tosses her curly blue hair behind her shoulder with a flourish. The little witch doesn't ask for much, which automatically sets me on guard.

"What is it?" I ask warily, narrowing my eyes at her.

"I want to take Sierra away from the island- "

Oh, hell no. "I don't- "

"Wait, let me explain." Konstantina holds her hands up to stop me. "It's important that Sierra learns how to use her gift when she doesn't have an abundance of water nearby. I think that her gift will prove to be invaluable when we take out Excalibur, but that doesn't guarantee she'll have access to water. We might not be at the fort he's currently holding." She flashes a warm, convincing smile.

"Okay, say if I was to go along with this. Which I'm not saying I am. Where do you want to bring her?" I crack my knuckles as anxiety threatens to choke my breath away, and my knee starts to bounce involuntarily under the table.

I glance at Sierra, trying to gauge her feelings. I really don't like the thought of her outside these walls. My protective side wishes I could keep her here where she's safe forever, but I know I can't do that. She nods in agreement with Konstantina, shattering the thought of her being shielded behind these walls.

"Anywhere you would feel comfortable, as long as it's not close to a water source."

"When?" I sigh, knowing that her logic is sound. I'm already starting to think about some secure places. Having Sierra leave the island is terrible timing, what with learning about a type of bullet that's targeting us immortals.

"The sooner, the better. How about tomorrow?" She's practically bouncing with excitement like a puppy on those sky-scraper heels of hers.

"I tell you what, let's make it for the day after tomorrow so I can have a day to scope out a designated site."

"You won't be disappointed!" She gives Sierra a quick hug and then struts out of the hall.

What did I just agree to? I'm not able to eat much for dinner between thinking about how to keep Sierra safe and wanting to finish what we started earlier. She seems to want to get back to our room just as quickly. Every time our gazes meet, I go wild with the heated passion in her eyes and seductive smile that she gives me.

How I managed to live this long without Sierra and the fire coursing through my veins at every touch from her is beyond me. Each caress from her is like a volt of electricity that makes me feel more and more alive with each passing day.

CHAPTER 5

SIERRA

To say I'm nervous is an understatement. This is the first time I've left the safety of our island since Andrew was shot. Dante spent most of the day yesterday planning our little field trip today. I did my usual morning laps with the rest of our team, but that didn't help calm my nerves. Every few days, we add another loop around the makeshift track that Uncle Joe made down on the side lawn. Really, it's just a large oval outlined with bright orange spray paint and fence posts marking the starting line.

I was never one who liked cardio before, but as the days go by and my body gets stronger, it's not so bad. Every circuit is about a quarter mile, and today we hit 12 laps. I never thought the words I ran a 5K would ever come out of me, but that's what we're up to. I'm still more winded than the other immortal guardians who I practice with, but at least I beat almost all of the witches and warlocks on our team. It's quite the sight to see Konstantina in sneakers and jogging pants; they just seem so out of place on her. Of course, the sneakers are her favorite color blue.

The hot water coming down on me in the shower feels good on my aching leg muscles. I reluctantly get out of my own personal sauna and dry off. I pull on a plain dark purple ribbed tank top paired with black cargo pants that so many of us choose to wear here. At least my love for pockets can continue. With shaky hands, I brush my hair and reach for my emerald amulet, which goes over my head next, settling just under the scoop of my top. My aquamarine ring comes next, and then my black leather bracelet with an azurite stone, my key to our compound. I step out of our private bathroom attached to our bedroom and grab my sheaths containing my daggers. I attach one to each side, feeling awkward with the extra weight pulling at my waist.

Dante gifted me these daggers when we first came to the island, but I don't carry them around here, only when I leave. When I practice, they're usually in my duffle bag with the rest of my weapons. The roughly eight-inch blades of the daggers are made out of silver and come to a razor-sharp edge. The handles are made of stainless steel and carved into Celtic knots. There's a thin black rubber grip that curves around my fingers. The knot at the base of each handle has a large round moss agate stone set into the center.

My thumb rubs over the etched engraving at the butt of the handle. Dante had these engraved with my initials SW prior to giving them to me. I guess it's a good thing my initials didn't change when I found out my true last name of Walker. I've been Sierra Rose Wilson for my whole life, so Walker still feels foreign to me. Then again, Dante knew my real last name even though I didn't yet. He knew more about my life from standing on the sidelines than I did living it. I sigh as I grab three stakes from the small table by the door and put them in one of the larger pockets of my pants on my outer thigh.

Konstantina, Reid, and Maggie made us all black leather bracelets that hold our azurite stones. The rocks act as a key to portal back to the island. If you lose your bracelet, the magic wards surrounding this place won't let you in unless you're with someone who has one.

Maggie is another witch who joined us about two weeks ago and seems like she has her own agenda at getting close to Dante. She kind of irritates me, to be honest. She's always fluttering her overly long eyelashes and smiling up at him. I can't blame her for wanting him; he is hot. But he's mine, and she better back off before I'm forced to make her back off myself. I'm not usually possessive like this. I don't know what's come over me lately. Maybe the chronic exhaustion is eating away at my usually good-natured attitude.

I reach for my wand-shaped blue benitoite stone that allows me to create a portal, and hold it up to the sunlight trickling in through the small arched window in our bedroom. The intense blue of the stone is creating dancing reflections across the walls. I'm still learning to portal, practicing by traveling from one end of the island to the other or from inside our castle to outside on the lawn. I definitely wouldn't trust myself in an emergency or a stressful situation to create the portal I need, though. As I exhale a deep breath, I put the stone into the pocket that's not holding the wooden stakes.

Maverick has just started teaching us how to stake a vampire by using a dummy stake that bends and won't actually harm somebody. I still feel clumsy when I use a stake, but I've actually pierced the heart on rare occasions. I hope I don't have to use any of them today, I don't feel I'm ready. But is anybody really ready for taking another being's life, even if it's down to theirs or yours? I know Dante would do everything in his power to protect me, but this whole damsel in distress thing doesn't work for me. Don't get me wrong, I love how strong and capable he is, but I need to be able to hold my own too.

I walk past a few others on my way to the dining hall to meet Dante and the team going with us today. I don't personally know everybody who's come to help us, but I try to at least remember all the names. As I arrive at the dining hall, Dante's leaning over a large wooden table. I meet Dante's captivating deep emerald green eyes, and a smile comes easily to my face. I wish we could've met under different circumstances, be a normal couple who can actually go out to eat and watch movies together. Our dates are the small slivers of time we get before crashing every night due to being so tired. How romantic is that? Not like I have much experience with romance anyway. The boyfriends I had were just your typical high school teens; they couldn't care less about flowers and dates.

Looking away from me as I walk past them to the attached kitchen, Dante goes back to speaking to the others about where each person is going to be. Uncle Joe, Tony, Roger, Lucas, and Thomas are all seated around the table, taking in the large map spread across the wide slab with empty glasses holding down the corners. Dante is referring to specific people as he points to different places, but I can't quite hear the plan. I'm only about twenty feet away but the crunching of the breakfast bar I'm eating overpowers their voices.

Knowing Dante has to put in this much effort for me to be safe, so I can try out my gift in another landscape worries me. I get where Konstantina is coming from, but is it really worth the risk? I mean, what are the odds of us finding Excalibur elsewhere? We need to break into the fort to free the prisoners.

Dante rolls up the map, folds it into a square, and slips it into the back pocket of his black pants. As I walk up to him, the scent of sandalwood drifts toward me. Mmm, I love that smell.

Sometimes if Dante's away on a mission, I wear one of his shirts that smell like him, just to feel close to him. My favorite is a super-soft black t-shirt with his favorite band Metallica written across the front in silver. That shirt also holds fond memories of the beginning of our relationship.

"So, where are we going?" I rest my hand on Dante's shoulder, feeling the muscles ripple under my palm as he moves.

When he finally came to bed last night, talking was the last thing on our minds. I didn't get a chance to ask him before about where he was planning on taking me. I know he put a lot of work into making sure I was safe. I trust him with my life; it doesn't matter the location. As long as he's with me, I know I'm well protected.

"We're going to the Gobi Desert in Mongolia." Dante wraps his arm around me, pulling me close to him. His distinctive Dante scent invades my thoughts as his rock-hard body radiates heat, warming me up.

"Uh, where is that?" I'm sure I learned about this in school, but I'm drawing a blank. Could be because of Dante, or I just wasn't paying attention in school. Kind of a crapshoot which is the culprit here.

"Mongolia sits just above China." Dante smirks at me. "As soon as Konstantina gets down here, we'll leave." He draws me in tighter to his side as I put my other arm around his waist. I loop my thumb into the belt loop on the pants that sits just right on his hips.

"Are you ready, baby Poseidon?" Uncle Joe asks with a grin.

I shake my head in amusement and look up to the ceiling. The other guys chuckle. Uncle Joe gave me that nickname shortly after my gift manifested. At first, I was annoyed by the endearment, but it's grown on me. I won't tell him that, though.

"Ha-ha! I'll show you baby Poseidon. I'll throw a water bomb at you when you're not looking." I place my free hand on my hip and smile sweetly back.

"We're going to a desert that might be okay with me," he answers back with a laugh, mimicking my voice and pose.

The image of a grown man throwing sass like that makes me giggle. Uncle Joe reminds me of my dad when he's like this. Well, the way my dad used to be. This past summer he wasn't really himself. Looking back now, I wonder how many times his visions were what made him so quiet and reserved.

Konstantina arrives shortly after, and Dante creates the portals. We always travel through at least one or two other destinations before we reach where we want to go so nobody can easily track us back to our compound. He makes it look so easy to create a doorway to another place, but I know better. It actually takes a lot of focus and strength. It explains why Ruby couldn't make a portal after she was shot. She just didn't have the energy left in her to spend.

The last portal opens, and I follow Thomas into the vast hot sandy desert. The little breeze that's blowing my hair around is more like a hairdryer than anything refreshing. Konstantina follows after me. Then Dante is right behind her, waving his hands together to close up the portal. Once he slides his blue benitoite stone back into his pocket, he gives the other men a nod, and they all disperse. I wasn't really listening to the plan the guys were going over; I was too transfixed on how Dante's bicep moved underneath his snug-fitting black t-shirt as he pointed to various spots on the map.

It takes me by surprise when Uncle Joe shapeshifts, and I jump. I've seen him shapeshift a handful of times, but it never fails to leave me speechless watching his large, stocky body turn into a cloud of fog and emerge as a massive bald eagle. Uncle Joe looks toward Dante and me before taking flight. I watch until I can no longer see the brown of his wings as he circles high above us. He's our eyes in the sky. Who needs drones when you have a guy like that?

Turning my gaze back to the desert, I notice that all I can see is just sand for miles and miles. Tony, Roger, Lucas, and Thomas are all spread out, forming a huge square around Konstantina, Dante, and I. The guys are so far out there that I can barely see their tiny silhouettes in front of mountains of sand.

"Are you ready?" Konstantina asks me, gently nudging my arm.

"Yes." I hope so. I don't want to waste everybody's time when they could be doing something else. Something that actually might make a difference in the end.

I take a deep breath, close my eyes and tilt my head toward the sun. I exhale and open my eyes. I can't feel the water here like I can back home. It's here, but it feels so far away, like an echo in the forest. I lift my hands up like I usually do, but nothing happens. I try to pull an Elsa and just let it go, but it's easier said than done or sang rather. I silently count to ten and concentrate only on water. What it feels like to be in the rain, the smell of the ocean, the sounds of waves crashing, the taste of cool water on a hot summer's day, and the beautiful turquoise waters of an ocean beach.

I can feel the water far below me like the reverberation of a babbling stream off in the distance. Knuckles cracking draws my attention to where Dante is standing about six feet away. He only cracks his knuckles when he's nervous or antsy.

"I'm sorry." He glances at me sheepishly. "I didn't mean to distract you."

"It's okay. Anytime you're near, I'm distracted." I grin at Dante.

If he only knew how much time I spent watching him when he's not aware of it. To be fair, he admitted to, "keeping an eye on me" before I even knew him. So, in my defense, I have a lot to catch up on.

It's hard to concentrate on anything when he's this close. He shifts back and forth on his heels as if his tense body is ready to pounce on anything that moves. His eyes are scanning the open desert for any potential threats. There's a silver dagger in his right hand that's identical to mine, and his Katana is strapped onto his back. I know what power lurks beneath all that sun-tanned skin. Any type of confrontation with Dante would leave his opponent in great pain. He must be glorious in battle, like a sexy warrior god. Focus, Sierra! Ogle your man later!

Konstantina unrolls a yoga mat with a loud snap she had been carrying with her and sets it on the sandy ground. She takes a seat cross-legged and motions for me to sit across from her on the other end of the mat. I lower myself to the ground, and she lights a large white candle that she puts in the center between us on a small selenite plate. Vanilla fills the air as the wind flickers the small flame about. Konstantina reaches to the sides of the candle for my hands. I gently place them in the palms she offers. She closes her eyes and bows her head. I copy her motion and soon hear her casting a spell.

"Dear Ancient Ones, let us have the focus needed to guide this young woman. Mother Earth allow us to use your water freely and easily so that we may be able to defeat the evil that is Excalibur. I call on all of you to help Sierra move forward toward her destiny." Konstantina gives my hands a gentle squeeze, and I open my eyes. "Try it now."

I nod at her, take a deep breath, and close my eyes again. I'm thinking of just water, picturing the aquifer that's far below the surface of the desert, the moisture that's within the small grass-like vegetation that's the only plant life within our sights. A cooling sensation spreads through my body, and I open my eyes again, knowing that I can wield the element. Turning my palms upward and slowly bringing my arms above my head, tiny water droplets form and dot the air around me. The drops are much smaller than I'm used to seeing, but still magical nonetheless. They look like tiny flecks of floating glitter from the sun's bright rays.

As I continue to raise my arms, the tiny droplets gain in size until they are nearly the size of a dime. I stand and continue to lift my arms far above my head. The hot, dry air alters, slowly, unmistakably. Humidity is now heavy in the atmosphere. Sweat starts to bead on my forehead, and I have to fight the urge to wipe it off. The path it travels down my face makes my skin itch. Having to concentrate this hard to hold the element around me is taxing on my energy.

Inching my palms closer together creates a dark cloud that hovers above our heads. My breathing is labored, like I've run a marathon in the muggy Florida summer. My body is sweating profusely. Not able to hold the cloud any longer, I set it free. The precipitation drifts down like a slight mist around us. The cool dampness quickly dries on our skin.

"Good job!" Konstantina praises me. "When you can catch your breath, try it again."

I groan, knowing she would say that. Just that small cloud took a lot out of me, far more than back at the compound. But I guess I should've expected it to be more challenging with no water nearby. Dante is standing close to us, his head constantly swiveling, looking for anything that could be a threat to me. He eyes me briefly, looking for any signs that would alarm him. I nod, letting him know I'm okay. My silent words aren't reassuring enough because they don't help the creases forming on his forehead.

Finally able to breath normal, I take a drink off the water bottle Dante hands me. Setting the plastic bottle on the edge of the blue yoga mat, the condensation instantly draws the sand to stick to it and coats the bottom in a thin layer. I plant my feet shoulder-width apart and look up into the sun. Repeating the same process as before. By standing this time, I'm able to create a larger and stormier-looking cloud. A dark gray mass mixes with white and blue fog until an almost solid black cloud. The darkness swallows the light.

My throat hurts, and my head starts to pound, the beginning signs of a migraine. I've had these symptoms before, but only when I push my magic wielding really hard. I keep trudging through, making the cloud larger and angrier. The darkness in the sunny desert looks like something from an edited photo and completely fake. The world seems to start spinning; my head feels like it weighs too much. I let my arms fall to my sides, and I'm rewarded with a light rain. I go to sit on the yoga mat too fast and I lose my balance. The candle knocks over and the sand extinguishes the flame. Dante catches me by the waist and helps me slowly to the ground, his eyebrows drawn together with worry.

"Are you okay?" He kneels beside me in the sand, searching my face. Dante cups my cheek in his rough, calloused hand as his eyes darken with concern and bore into mine.

"Yeah, I just need to sit for a minute," I manage to say between haggard breaths. The heat of the desert is really not helping me out right now.

My breathing starts to even out a bit, and I take a sip from my water bottle, then lay back on the mat and close my eyes. The hot sun is almost blinding me through my closed eyelids. Dante's hand finds mine, and our fingers intertwine, the bottom of his calloused thumb rubbing the top of mine. He's letting me know he's there for me without having to say anything at all. I try to draw strength from his strong, silent presence.

"Here, try these." Konstantina hands me a medium-sized banana and a small bottle of apple juice. "Fruit always helps me restore my energy after a demanding spell."

I swear that blue backpack of hers holds all the wonders of the world. What will Konstantina pull out of there next? Ooh, I got one. How about she pulls out instructions to defeat Excalibur. That would be nice but not likely going to happen any time soon.

I take them both from her, eating the banana and washing it down with the juice. I don't feel an instant energy boost, but I trust her experience. Konstantina is wise beyond her years. I still don't know quite how old she is, but she was good friends with my parents when they were guardians. Witches and warlocks can live as long as immortals, but their bodies are more susceptible to damage and don't heal as fast as ours.

The hammer going to town on my head seems to have slowed its pounding. I stay sitting for several moments before I get up to try again. I close my eyes and whisper, "Please work."

I start by kneeling and focusing as hard as I can on making it storm. I can feel the faint whispers of water around me. I raise from my knees, bringing my arms as high as they can go, reaching for the stars that are hidden from view. The pounding starts again in the center of my forehead and radiates around to the sides. My throat is dry, my mouth feels as if it's full of cotton, and my muscles are straining and threatening to buckle under the pressure. The clouds start forming larger than before, the swirling of the white fog mixing with the black, creating an ominous sight as it rolls in on itself.

I continue to hold my hands skyward, making the rolling angry clouds choke out the sunlight and cast us in darkness. My arms shake from the force of holding the storm together. I feel light-headed, but I can't lose this. My parents need me to be strong. The clouds are darker than any I've ever created before. The migraine puts so much pressure in my eyes that I have to squint to keep them open. The wind begins to whip around us, tossing my hair about my face and blocking my sight. The ferocious force is threatening to knock me down too.

"That's enough -."

"No, let her keep going. She can do this," Konstantina says, but it sounds so far away, too far away.

"She's going to pass out," Dante insists as my world starts to spin as if I'm riding a tilt-a-whirl. Spinning faster and faster until I can't tell which way is up, and everything blurs together as if it's a paint spinner.

The loud crack of thunder is the last thing I remember before everything goes black. The darkness steals all sounds and sights from me, robbing me from seeing my most powerful storm yet.

DANTE

As Sierra's body sways back and forth, I know without a doubt what's going to happen next. She's going to faint. I step toward her when a sharp thunderclap cracks the sky above us, making me glance up and flinch. When I look back at her, she's on the ground, half of her small body on the yoga mat, the other half of her on the hot sand. I kneel down beside her and pull her onto my lap. Rain and hail start to pelt down around us. I shield her body the best I can with my own. I check her pulse, scared of what I might find. She's never pushed herself this hard.

Her pulse is there, weak but still beating. I sweep her long brown hair out of her face and attempt to brush the sand off of her. That's when I notice blood seeping from her nose. The sight of her blood nearly paralyzes me until I remember that I have to act. I pull my shirt away from my stomach and gently dab the blood with the black cotton.

"Sierra. Wake up." I gently shake her shoulders, trying to wake her. I hesitantly pull my gaze to quickly check our surroundings again. I'm not risking someone sneaking up on us while in a compromising situation.

I'm instantly brought back to when Excalibur took revenge on her parents. He overtook the commercial jet they were flying in on their way to Ireland to visit Sierra's Uncle Joe. Excalibur had ripped one of the wings off the airplane before it plummeted from the sky. I portaled to Sierra, getting to her just in time. Her parents and I scuffled a bit with Excalibur before he ultimately abducted both of her parents with the help of a warlock who sucked them both into a vortex caused from some strange gold and red box. Afraid that we'd be sucked into Pandora's box next, I tried to create a portal but failed.

With Sierra in my arms, I was forced to jump out the emergency door of the plane. The force from hitting the water was too much for her and she was knocked unconscious. I'm forever grateful I was able to swim to shore since we weren't too far out from land.

I was terrified when we reached land. I couldn't wake her then either. I brought her to her uncle's house, and we were able to have her come back to the realm of consciousness there. That was when she found out the truth of what her parents had been hiding from her, the moment her life was forever changed.

I know Konstantina is saying things to me, but I don't understand her. Bile starts to build in my throat, and I feel like I'm going to throw up. Sierra's limp body isn't fighting against my gentle rocking. I check around me again to make sure we're still safe. This is one scenario I didn't prepare for. Coming through my earpiece, I can vaguely hear the others asking if everything is alright. Because of my alarm for Sierra, I forgot they were there.

"We have to get back to the compound. Sierra passed out." Another clap of thunder sounds in the distance. This one is so loud I feel the boom of it deep in my chest.

I couldn't muster anything else. My focus was solely on Sierra and keeping her safe and alive. Only proving my point that I need to learn to be able to control myself out in the field with her. I really don't know how I'll ever be able to work side by side with her, I'm afraid I'll always be distracted by my need to keep her protected. Which in turn leaves us both in a compromising position.

"Sierra." I don't recognize my own voice. "My beautiful Sierra, please come back to me." I gently keep nudging her shoulders as I place a kiss on her forehead, but nothing is happening. She's far too pale, and her breathing is shallow.

Others arrive around that time, but what they're saying isn't registering. The storm is still raging, still pummeling us with rain and hail. The wind carries their voices away. The water is puddling around us; a strange sight for a desert. Somebody grabs my arm then, and I shout, "Don't touch me, stay away from her!"

I cradle her limp body closer to me. "I love you, Sierra. I need you to wake up now. I can't bear the thought of living in this world without you."

"Dante, we need to get her home to Ralph. Right now." Joe's voice is strained, but it sounds strong and steady. "Come on."

He reaches down to help me up. I won't loosen my grip on Sierra. As I stand with her in my arms, her head rolls off to the side. I adjust my grip on her, so her head nestles back against my chest. I blindly follow Joe. I don't even remember where or for how long until I realize we're in the clinic and Ralph is talking to me.

"What?" I try to think of what he could've said.

"Dante, I need you to put Sierra down on the bed so I can take a look at her." His kind gray eyes soften as he places a hand on her back.

I look down at Sierra, motionless in my arms, and I gently set her down on the black vinyl cushion of the gurney. I stand to the side of her, not taking my hand away from her arm. I need her to know I'm still here. There's a flurry of movement and machines shuffling around me, but I block everything out. All that matters is watching her breathing. If she's breathing, she's alive. A hand rests on my shoulder, and I flinch.

"Hey, it's just me." Joe stands beside me.

"What's wrong with her?" I dare to ask.

"Ralph's running some tests, but he thinks she just exerted herself too much. That was one hell of a storm she manifested. I've never seen anything like it." Her uncle looks down at her, his wide-toothed smile and gleaming eyes show the pride he has for her.

I glance around noting that while I was transfixed on her breathing, the med staff had hooked up Sierra to a bunch of machines that monitored her heart rate and vitals. The steady thrum of gentle beeping is a reassuring sound. There's an IV in her left arm with fluids being pumped into her. I don't recall seeing them put a needle in her. Everything that happened after she fell to the ground is a blur.

"What's in that?" I point to the IV bag hanging on a metal pole beside the bed.

"It's a lactated ringer. It'll give Sierra some extra electrolytes and fluids," one of the nurses explains.

"I'm sorry I broke protocol out there when I saw her fall..." I couldn't finish the sentence; I know I screwed up. I put us all at risk. I gently brush her hair, thick with sand, away from her face. Her color is coming back, thank heavens.

"It's alright. It's understandable. I don't know if I would've handled things differently if that were Grace." Joe rests a hand on Sierra's leg covered by the white cotton blanket. "That's what you have a good team for. We're a family, and we always look after each other. We're strongest when we stand together, a united front."

A gentle knock on the door causes both Joe and I to look in that direction as Ralph appears in the threshold in his white lab coat and holding onto a clipboard. He walks over to Sierra, who's still motionless on the bed, and puts his stethoscope on several places around her chest. The wait for him to say anything is agony. His expressionless face gives nothing away. He'd be one hell of a poker player.

"She just exhausted herself to the point where her energy stores weren't enough to keep her conscious anymore. Her body went into a protective state of sleep, almost like what happens when someone is going through the transition into a full immortal. She just needs time to heal," Ralph says.

The nurses carry in four large bloodstone obelisks. I track Mackenzie and Claire's movements as they put a tall green tower in each corner of the room to aid in healing. The red flecks speckled throughout the stones catch the bright lights overhead showing us why the crystal is aptly named bloodstone. The shade is eerily close to the crimson flowing in our veins.

A short time later, Emma barges into the room with tears in her eyes. She runs to the other side of Sierra and sits on the edge of the bed holding Sierra's delicate hand in hers. After I explain to Emma what happened in Mongolia and the prognosis, we sit in silence. Joe had left earlier after Ralph confirmed she was fine. He had to see to the others on our team. I'm struggling sitting here watching Sierra on that bed. I know she's okay, but seeing her unconscious doesn't help. The memories that spawn up from the recesses of my brain plague me. I pace the room until I'm convinced Sierra isn't going to wake up right off.

I leave Emma with Sierra. I don't want her to wake up without me, but I have some things I need to take care of. Emma will be there with her, and if all goes well, I'll be back within an hour or two. With the added threat of altered bullets looming over us, I want to be able to provide my team with Kevlar vests. The problem is all the more reliable ones have been taken up by law enforcement, and I won't chance my team with some knock-off wannabe version. The uptick in dark one activity has led to a spike in crime rate worldwide, causing the militaries and police forces to take more supplies than they previously used.

I don't like the option that I'm about to present to Joe and Maverick, but it seems to be our only one at this point. I send a text to them to meet me in the dining room in five minutes. I just have to run back to my room and grab the folder I've been working on in secret. I haven't told Sierra about it yet either; I know she won't be thrilled with the only recourse I have left. I don't like going against the boys in blue.

The bedrooms are on the opposite end of the castle, so I break into a light jog. I grab the papers I have stashed in my nightstand and rush back out the door. As soon as I enter the dining room, I get a text from Emma saying Sierra is awake. I groan. I really wanted to be there when she woke up. That figures right after I leave. I let her know I'll be there shortly. I was hoping to have this all done before she woke up. Maverick and Joe have already taken seats at the large rectangular table. I choose the chair opposite Maverick.

"Is everything okay with Sierra?" Joe asks.

"Yes, she actually just woke up when I came in," I reply.

"That's good news. That was one hell of a storm you missed, Maverick." He chuckles as he slaps a hand on Maverick's back.

"So, I've heard. That's all Thomas and Lucas could talk about when they came back. I'm not missing the next one." Maverick shakes his head.

"Anyway, gentlemen, ever since we found out about the bullet's new deadly elements, I've been racking my brain to find a way to protect us out in the field." I swallow the lump that's growing in my throat. "We need police-grade tactical vests." I hesitate to let that sink in.

"I agree," Joe says as Maverick nods his agreement.

"You're not going to like where we need to get them from, though." I lean forward on the table. Now for the main event.

"Oh boy, I'm almost afraid to ask." Maverick runs a hand through his inky black hair, making it even more mussed up than usual. I gotta get this guy a brush.

I let out a deep breath. "Trust me, I wouldn't suggest this if I thought we had another way. Unfortunately, we're short on time and don't have the right contacts when it comes to vests." We never had a need for them before. I flip open the manilla file folder to reveal a blueprint and point to the armory in the building. "We have to steal them from the FBI, and this one in Tucson, Arizona is the least guarded of them all."

Silence and blank stares greet me. A pin could drop several feet from us and it would be loud.

"Come on guys, say something," I say, shrugging my shoulders to release the bunching of my nerves.

"Oh, you're serious?" Joe asks, his eyebrows rising so high I'm afraid they'll recede into his dirty blonde hairline.

"Deadly." I meet his gaze straight-faced. I know it sounds crazy, but it's for the greater good.

"And how do you plan on breaking into one of the most secure buildings in the United States?" He crosses his arms on the table in front of him and leans in as if eager to hear my pitch.

"That, my friends, is where Eric comes in. We send Eric in while he cloaks himself while we wait a little ways from the building in a tractor-trailer truck. Eric will steal a keycard off of a guard to gain entry into the armory located in the basement. When Eric lets us know he's in we then can create a portal into the armory and have a small team constantly going in and out with the vests until we have what we need. I was aiming for at least sixty."

"Why do we need a key card if we can portal into the armory?" Maverick asks.

"Because there's infrared sensors that will detect us and set off an alarm if not deactivated by a key card at the door. Just like Tallahassee." I meet Maverick's brooding gaze.

Maverick and I had to break into the police headquarters in Florida's capital when the cops captured Isaac, an immortal guardian that was working a case. There were too many innocents who could've been harmed if he didn't go quietly. Most of the time, human minds are easily swayed, but Isaac couldn't change theirs for some reason. We had to scope out the place and try to impersonate another officer to gain access to Isaac's cell. This should be much easier and faster.

"You're putting a lot of faith into the enemy's son." Joe scratches at his scruffy beard.

He's not wrong. How do we know Eric is one hundred percent on our side? I've had my own doubts about him.

"I think his intentions are good, no matter his sparkly personality. He cares about Emma and Sierra's safety. I think he'll do what needs to be done." God, I hope so. This operation is dependent on him doing his part. The last thing we need is for us to be locked up as well.

"I'm in." Maverick cracks all of the knuckles in his fingers as he stretches his arms out in front of him in a backward bridge.

"I guess I'm in too." Joe shrugs his shoulders. This was an easier sell than I thought it was going to be.

"Joe, I think it would be best if you stayed behind to run things just in case. Maverick and I will run point on this one. We can have a few other immortals helping us transport the gear. I don't want to leave our home base without one of us three here." I didn't need to add if this should end badly; Joe's good at reading between the lines.

We all agree that it's our best option, and I dismiss myself. I want to go tend to my girl.

"No way, Ralph. I'm sorry but, I will not be treated like a sensitive little flower," Sierra huffs out.

"You need to rest. I know we all have a lot riding on the training and you using your gift. My main concern however, is your health. I'm suggesting you take two to three days off," Ralph insists.

I press my lips firmly together to hide my smirk as I round the corner and walk into the open doorway of her room. I'm relieved that Sierra is back to her stubborn feisty self. She gave me quite the scare earlier.

She's sitting up in the bed, arms crossed over her chest and scowling at the doctor. When her narrow eyes find me and light up, I bark out a laugh and try to cover it up with a cough. It doesn't work though; a flush turns her cheeks pink when Emma chokes on her own giggle next to her.

"I'm sorry I wasn't here when you woke up, beautiful." I place a kiss on her forehead and take the seat beside her.

"It's okay, handsome." She leans into my shoulder.

"Remember, Sierra. No magic or training for at least two days." Ralph cocks his head to the side as he glances at me.

He knows Sierra's not going to heed his advice. My chest expands as I'm finally able to take a full breath of air. She's okay that's all that matters to me.

As soon as Ralph exits and closes the door behind him, she twists her body toward me. "This is bullshit. I can't not train or use my hydrokinesis, is he crazy?"

I sigh. "He's right you need to recuperate. It's only two days, you won't miss much."

"I'm already farther behind than everybody else." Sierra picks at her fingernails.

"I'm going to get back to studying. If you need anything at all, let me know. Get some rest." Emma leans across and hugs Sierra.

"I will. Thank you."

We retire to our bedroom early so she can rest while I attempt to contact Eric in a dream. It's nighttime in Colorado right now, so he may be asleep. I try for a little while to catch him, and I'm almost ready to give up when I see a tiny thread of his subconscious. I grab on and pull it until he's in the dream I've crafted. I have to remind myself that he hasn't actually made a move on Sierra and for now he's useful to our cause. We have burner phones we could use to contact him, but I don't want to waste any more time, nor do I want to give him another excuse to talk to Sierra. I know it sounds selfish and possessive, but that woman is my weakness.

CHAPTER 6

RUBY

My already rampant heart beat speeds up as Ralph gently tugs away at the gauze to peek at the healing. I stare off to the side, not ready to see it for myself yet. The white walls of this tiny patient room are closing in on me. Slow, deep breaths. Inhale. Exhale.

"You're free to take the bandages off now."

Simple words that excite and terrify me at the same time.

"Thanks Doc, for everything." The shakiness in my voice matches my trembling knees.

"That's what I'm here for. Come back in a few days for me to check the wound and clear you for duty." Ralph's firm hand on my shoulder helps to ground me in the here and now.

Once he walks out of the room, I yank the hem of my red Henley back down. I won't take the bandages off in here. This part of the castle reminds me too much that I could've died the other day. I walk out and close the door quietly and walk in the direction of my bedroom. I have a chilled bottle of tonic and some vodka waiting for me for this reason.

The bullet hole should be mostly closed by now with my immortal healing ability speeding up the process. I've been dying to know if the Phoenix tattooed on my stomach has been affected by my injury, but I haven't dared to look. I swear to God if it's altered, I will hunt that shooter down and gut them like a fish, leaving them to fry on the asphalt in the morning sun. I still should either way, but the fiery Phoenix isn't just a tattoo to me. That bird represents all that I have overcome. I rose above the ashes of my past, and I will continue to come back stronger each time my life goes up in flames.

It's been three days since I was ambushed in Germany, and I'm feeling almost back to normal. I still have to be cautious with twisting, not really from the pain, but so I don't pop a stitch and be stuck on the sidelines for longer. I'm no stranger to pain; in fact, I crave it. Some days it's the only way I know I'm still alive.

We don't always get to grow up in happy little homes with parents that love us. Just like with humans, we have immortals who choose to be horrible individuals. My older sister Summer and I were orphaned when I was just five years old. Our parents were killed by a vampire clan they were hunting. It's a startling truth that we immortal children are four times more likely to grow up without at least one of our parents than humans. We have foster families who offer to help, or we have group homes too. I've been through a few of both, and they all sucked. Eventually we became wards of the Guardian Academy. Students stay Monday through Friday in the dorms anyway, so why not the other two days too.

The academy acts as a short-term group home when the kid's mom and dad are away on assignment, so it's not out of the ordinary for others to be there over the weekend on occasion. Immortal guardians don't have a cushy 9-5 schedule, and at least they know their kids will be safe at the school. They should have done a better job screening for foster parents. Maybe if they had just let Summer and I stay in the dorms instead of going through the fosters, I wouldn't be so messed up, or at least not put us with *him*.

Brooks seemed great in the beginning. He'd play dolls with us and make us pancakes loaded with chocolate chips and topped with whipped cream. The good times didn't last long, though. We were treated like unwanted pets soon after that, and we learned to walk on eggshells when we were around him and to only speak when being spoken to. He even had wire dog crates in the basement he'd lock us in when we didn't behave the way he wanted us to.

Our opinions and feelings didn't matter to him one bit. We stayed with him for close to a year before the counselors at the academy noticed all the bruising. He was smart in a way to only hit us in places that were easy to cover up with clothing until that last time Brooks abused us. He backhanded me hard enough for me to smash my head against the tile floor. The split lip and bruised cheek weren't something he could throw sleeves over and keep coasting along and cash in the foster system's checks.

After they took us from there and placed us with somebody else, we were already too far gone. Well, me more so. Summer was smart enough to shut her mouth, but I wasn't. I was a firecracker even as a five-year-old. I was too stubborn, and I argued with everything our foster parent said. I guess you could say I made it a lot worse for myself. But I just wanted my real mom and dad back. I thought if I pushed him too much, he'd return us and we'd magically be reunited with our parents. Kid logic right there.

We were never placed in another abusive household again, but after the trauma I was subjected to with *him,* it didn't matter. Some scars never heal, and most of mine are invisible. Nobody understood me back then. I didn't even understand myself most times. I knew I needed attention, and it didn't matter whether it was good or bad. In my early teens, I started cutting myself. I needed to feel the pain. I needed to know I wasn't locked in that crate in the basement, alone, scared, and so cold my limbs would go numb. The damp frigid air permeated the concrete below the plastic bottom of the crate. The cellar wasn't insulated or heated.

I hid the self-harming for a while, but Summer found out, and I again was forced into therapy that didn't help me. Drugged up with little happy pills that didn't do their job; the meds just made me feel like a zombie. I was me but not me at the same time. I started partying, but recreational drugs and alcohol didn't interest me much. They just made me think of Brooks since he was at his worst when he drank. The few times I did drink, I kept waiting for him to come around a corner.

I took myself off the pills because I didn't like how they made me feel. I wasn't depressed, and I didn't want to kill myself like they thought I did. I just needed the pain as a release. It was at one of those parties later on that I found my own custom-made escape. I was coming down the stairs that overlooked the living room when I froze halfway down. I spotted a dark-haired guy with a large pair of black plugs in his lobes. He was hunched over another chick with multiple facial piercings. Her face was scrunched up in a wince, but she looked engulfed in the moment with her head thrown back and her eyes closed. I took the last few steps, and when I came around the corner, I saw the tattoo gun in his hand. The buzzing noise coming from the tiny little machine was just barely audible over the loud music booming throughout the house.

Intrigued, I slowly sat next to the blonde woman on the black futon, but she didn't notice me. He did, though, and his striking amber eyes met mine for a split second before he went back to working on her forearm. I didn't know at the time that he was a werewolf, though I should have. As he went back and forth into the ink cups and wiped the surface of her skin, he would sneak glances at me. I watched him as he marked up her skin with a snake winding through a skull. His arms were a work of art; his left bicep had wings wrapped around an angel that merged with a wolf and a clock down on his forearm. His right arm contained mostly tribal designs.

"What do you say, you wanna try it?" His deep voice broke me out of my trance and made me look away from her work in progress.

"Does it hurt?" I couldn't stop watching this beautiful man. His mesmerizing yellow-orange eyes flicked to the scars on my forearm, and I quickly pulled them to my chest to hide them. My lighter skin tone usually hides the white marks.

"A little, but you look tough enough to handle it with ease." He smiled warmly at me. "I'm Alex by the way."

"Ruby."

"I'm almost done with hers if you wanna stick around," he said without looking up from blondie's serpent.

I completely lost track of Ella, the friend I came here with, but that's okay. He's done the woman's piece shortly and had me sit next to him on the other couch. My palms were sweaty and I bit my lip out of nervousness. He showed me quite a few of his tattoos on his arms and back. He was easy to talk to even though he's bad boy gorgeous. The smile he gave me with the twinkle in his mischievous eyes almost made me tell him he can put whatever art he'd like to on me just to feel his large warm hands on me.

In the end, I decided to go with a small black rose about the size of a half-dollar on my outer right shoulder. He walked me through everything, and I felt comfortable with him. My heart was hammering in my chest harder and harder as Alex set everything up. He was meticulous about the order in which his tools were placed. He pulled new needles out of his duffle bag next to him, tearing open the clear plastic packages and loading the first needle into the small hand-held machine.

"Are you ready, Ruby?" Alex asked one final time as he stretched a pair of black nitrile gloves over his large hands, snapping them in place like a doctor, and the sound made me flinch.

"Sure." What did I have to lose? He couldn't hurt me any more than what's already been done to me.

The moment the tattoo gun touched my skin, I was lit up from within. As he pulled the needle down to outline my favorite flower, it felt like little bee stings one right after the other. The more he outlined and shaded my skin, the more the pain and brokenness inside of me eased. It's as if he'd opened a fissure to my soul, and the hurt seeped out from the crack. The pain that he caused me wasn't a pain born out of hate or abuse; instead, it was a controlled ache that took something horrible and traumatic and created something beautiful from it.

In the end, the rose was puffy and raw but still the most beautiful thing I'd ever seen and the start of the most meaningful friendship that I've had. He saved me from myself in a way I thought I could never be saved. He gave me a safe way to channel everything that's trapped inside of me.

I need to get back to Alex soon. It's been several months since I had any tattoo work done, and I need the release. He's the only one that has tattooed my skin besides my immortal guardian mark. I didn't have a choice with that one. Even though he's hot as hell, he's my best friend, and I prefer it that way. I miss him so much.

I finally reach the door to my room and I step inside and immediately go to the mini fridge in the corner. I fix myself a glass with some ice, tonic and vodka. Taking a few sips before setting the cold drink on my small nightstand. I sit on the edge of my bed, sinking down into the fluffy comforter on top.

Pulling the white tape off the edges of the bandage and unrolling the wrap, I manage to get the gauze off of me, and I close my eyes and take a deep breath before I dare to look down at my belly. Three, two, one. My eyes desperately scan my abdomen. The scar from the gunshot wound and where Ralph had to open me up is about an inch and a half away from the wings. The healed wound is an angry pink color, and the stitch marks have a reddish tint. Thank fuck! I think I would have lost my shit if my beautiful mythical creature was scarred like me.

Alex taught me to find the beauty in everything, and if I couldn't do that, then to create my own. I really wish he wasn't a werewolf. Our species are constantly at war, mine always trying to control theirs. He's like many other werewolves and not as vicious as they make them out to be. But of course, there are the ones that are bad, just like every species. I mean come on, look at Excalibur; he's an immortal too. Alex is aware of what I'm doing, but he doesn't want to get involved for fear of being exiled from his pack. Maybe someday it won't be taboo to have multi-species relationships. What really matters is what's on the inside and not their armor for the world to see or in his case, gloriously soft dark gray fur.

I slowly trace the orange, red and yellow flames surrounding the Phoenix with my index finger. Alex has been good at covering my other scars; this one shouldn't be too difficult for him. I wonder what he'll come up with for a design.

SIERRA

I wake up and find Dante isn't in bed with me. He must be up and about already. The sunlight weaving through the narrow gaps of the thick gray curtain make me wonder if I've overslept. I've been so tired since I woke up yesterday afternoon in the infirmary. Rolling over on the large queen mattress, I grab my cell phone from the nightstand and glance at the time. It's still early. I have about an hour before I have to be on the track for our morning run. I decide to stay in the warmth of my bed for just a little longer. I pull Dante's pillow close and inhale his manly scent that is strictly alpha male. I wrap my arms around the fluffy cushion and relax my head against it wishing it were him.

Tomorrow night Dante and a few of the others are raiding an FBI compound to get Kevlar vests to help protect us from all the enemies that we seem to keep gaining. I hate that he has to do that, but I get why. I just really hope it goes off without a hitch. I wouldn't want anybody getting hurt on either side. We all want the same thing in the end. I'm curious how well Dante and Eric will work together, though. Every time we video chat with Eric or his name gets brought up, Dante seems to get tense.

Dante should know by now that I'm in love with him and not Eric. I don't know how else to show him that he's the only man for me. Of course, I still have feelings for Eric. I can't just turn them off with a flick of a switch like a light bulb, though I wish it were that easy. The more time I spend with Dante, the more my feelings for Eric dull. When Dante's away, I feel like a piece of me is missing.

I'm starting to understand that anima gemella bond Dante and I share. I've also been reading about it in one of the books we have in our massive library. I kind of feel like Belle in the Beast's castle. The library here has large floor-to-ceiling bookcases filled to the brink with all kinds of genres. I let out a sigh. Maybe someday I can find the time to curl up on the couch and just read a book that's only purpose is to steal me away from reality for a little while. There's a tapestry hanging on my bedroom wall back in Colorado that says, "Into the pages I disappear, only to find myself in a world far from here." I try to study while I have breaks in between training with Maverick and working with Konstantina, but those texts are just informative, not the story telling I could desperately use right now.

I toss the thick gray comforter with its matching sheet back and climb out of bed. The wood planks of the floor are cold on the bottom of my feet. I really need to get a pair of slippers. After grabbing some clothes out of my bureau on my way to the bathroom, I turn on the light. Its reflection bounces off the mirror and nearly blinds me. My eyes finally adjust to the harsh lighting. I dress, brush my teeth and put my long brown hair into a ponytail. After throwing some flowery scented deodorant on, I grab my small black duffle bag for training, and I'm out the door.

The mouthwatering scent of coffee and buttered toast tease my nose before I enter the kitchen. I toss my bag down on the white tile floor in the corner and head straight for the coffee machine.

"Good morning, beautiful," Dante's husky voice startles me out of my tunnel vision of java.

"Good morning, handsome. You're up early." I remember falling asleep in his arms last night, but I'm not sure how long he was able to sleep.

"I'm just working out some of the final details for tomorrow." Dante glances at the bag I threw in the corner. "You know, you don't have to train today. Maverick would understand." I catch the hint in his voice. He puts the scattered papers into the manilla folder and slides it out of the way on the table, clearing a spot for me to sit beside him on his right.

"I'm okay, I promise. I just need coffee," I say as I take the steaming coffee pot and pour the miracle liquid into a large blue mug, I had pulled down from the cabinet above.

"Will you at least take it easy then?" His concern is etched in the lines on his gorgeous face. A face that handsome shouldn't wrinkle with worry as often as his has been lately.

"Not a chance," I scoff as I toast myself some bread, slathering them with butter, before sitting with him. I told him last night I was still going to train; I don't care what the doctor said. Obviously, he didn't take me seriously, and that's on him.

"Of course, not." Dante sighs as he leans back in his chair. The old chair creaks in response.

If we're going to end up staying here after all is said and done, we can use some new furniture. This place was built for normal humans, not for all these bulky men testing the strength of the furnishings. I wonder if Dante misses the peacefulness of his beautiful picturesque log home. I know I miss home; I really miss my parents. I wish I was able to dreamwalk like Dante. He tells me how they're doing, but it's not the same as seeing them for myself. There's so much I want to tell them, so many things I want to ask my mom and dad. However, the most important questions are ones they won't have the answers to. What if we don't pull this off? What does Excalibur want with them? Why does he need me? All of these questions are like a thorn in my side that never goes away. The little barb slowly inching its way deeper and deeper into me until it's all I can think about.

I blow on the top of my coffee before taking a sip, the hot liquid bringing me out of the thoughts bouncing around in my head that I can't find an easy answer to. I finish my breakfast in silence, all the while Dante is watching me. I know he means well and he cares deeply about me, but really, I'm fine. The training is too important for me to skip. I'm so far behind the others because I didn't attend the Guardian Academy like they did. Although my gift may help me tremendously in combat, if yesterday proved anything it's that if I don't have a ready source of water, I need to be able to fight hand to hand.

Dante disappears to stash his work in our room before we head out to the track for our morning run together. Others are trickling out as well and chatting with each other. I'm surprised to see Emma coming down the lawn in jogging pants and a teal racerback tank top, her straight platinum locks tied up high on her head in a ponytail.

"Hey Emma, are you running with us today?"

"It beats sitting around all day and studying." Emma gives Maverick a lingering look.

So, that's what brought her down here. I snicker.

"It wouldn't have anything to do with tall, dark and handsome over there, would it?" I smirk at her after glancing at Maverick. I'm not blind I've seen the way she eyes him and the way he looks at her.

"I don't know what you're talking about." She purses her lips, shiny from her pink lip gloss.

I let out a laugh at her obvious attraction to Maverick, and she narrows those icy blue eyes at me proving me right. A whistle sounds out, letting us know we're ready to begin as Maverick takes his place at the front. We don't race against each other, but he goes first to keep us at a good pace. He does a double-take as he walks by Emma, and we both throw Emma a grin.

I elbow her in the side to break her out of her trance, and she winces from the jab as I whisper, "Don't forget to pick your jaw up off the ground."

She answers me back with a scowl. We start off slow and steadily increase our tempo. I slow my pace to keep in step with Emma. These runs are to build stamina, not for speed anyway. I can converse with Emma easily, but she's having a hard time doing both. If I thought I despised running, Emma truly hates it. That's another reason I knew she had ulterior motives for joining us. She's never been one to do any strenuous activities.

We split ways once we've finished our laps. She no doubt goes off to shower and study, and I go to another section of the lawn where we break off into teams. Maverick selects random people to spar so we don't always go against the same opponent. I don't know how he remembers who he's previously paired together, but somehow, I haven't fought the same person more than once yet. After he announces several pairs, he finally reaches my name.

"Sierra, you will be paired with Roger," his clear voice cuts through the talking.

I nod and head over to where Roger is standing. He doesn't look at me in the face but stares down at the grass. This'll be interesting. Roger's a nice guy and all but his awkwardness around women is palpable. From what I've seen, when he's paired with other men, he fights fiercely. I don't recall him having a female opponent before, though. I think I'm the first.

"Hi, Roger." I smile at him.

"Hello, Sierra." Still no eye contact.

The whistle sounds again, meaning it's go time. I plant my feet a shoulder width apart and lift my fists in front of me, waiting for his first hit, but nothing comes.

"I'm sorry, I can't hit a woman," Roger says with a shrug.

"Okay, pretend I'm not a woman then." Well, duh, didn't he have to fight the ladies in the academy?

"Not likely."

"How about a sister?" All siblings fight no matter the gender.

"I only had a brother," he says quietly.

That figures.

I take a jab at him, but he maneuvers out of the way. We go back and forth for a few minutes, me attacking, Roger effectively dodging my fists. Once I understand he won't advance on me, I swipe my leg out, hooking his foot and taking him down by surprise. The guys always underestimate me because of my size. He grunts as his body hits the hard ground, his eyes flying wide open.

After Roger jumps back up to his feet, he stretches his shoulders out with a shake and takes a long deep breath, and on an exhale, he narrows his eyes that are gleaming with determination. His fist comes at me so fast; I don't have time to react. The impact of his unforgiving knuckles hitting my stomach's left side sends me backward, but I catch my footing before I fall to the grass. The adrenaline pumping through my veins dulls the ache, but I'm sure I'll pay for it later. I always do.

I swing my leg at him again, this time toward his thigh. His strong, oddly hairy arms block me before I can land the blow. Bouncing back and forth on the balls of my feet like a drug addict jonesing for their next fix, I wait impatiently for his next move. He swings his arm out in the direction of my face. I duck and land a hard punch on his muscular abdomen before jumping to the side to miss his next one. I needed this today.

He lands a few good ones on me, but nothing comes close to his last one. He pulls the same move I did to him in the beginning. I'm so razor focused on his hands that keep coming at me at an increasingly fast speed, I forget to watch for his feet. Almost in slow motion, a navy-blue shoe comes from the side and takes my feet right out from under me. The hard landing bouncing my head off the unforgiving ground causes pain to lance through my head as stars dance in my vision. He reaches a hand down to help me up, and I take it.

"I'm sorry, I didn't mean to kick that hard." His lips form a straight thin line as I rub the egg forming on the back of my melon.

"I'm good, Roger. You did what you should be doing." I laugh at his sudden white face when he notices Dante watching us. "Hey, you wouldn't teach me anything if you took it easy on me. Don't worry about Dante," I say as I brush the grass and dirt off my pants.

Another whistle signals the end of our sparring matches with that person. I take a glance at Dante and notice the hard set of his jaw. I knew he wouldn't be happy with me taking part today, but he shouldn't be angry at Roger. Dante must have said something to Maverick because I get paired with Dante next. Sighing as my overprotective stud walks in my direction, no doubt to make sure I take it easy. I chug some water down, trying to swallow the retort on the tip of my tongue with it.

We wait for the whistle signaling go time. As soon as it's blown, I come at him. I've watched him spar so many times I know his tricks. He smirks after I miss blocking one of his kicks. He's not putting much force into it; he's taking it easy on me. Just as I suspected he would. He's so quick dodging my swings.

I'm starting to be able to notice the differences in my body since I went through the transition. I'm faster, stronger, more agile, and I heal quicker, thankfully. I do enjoy having the gift of manipulating water. It has been both a fun and frustrating process learning to use it. I can feel the water in the ocean like a thrum in my veins. I wonder if that's why I've always had a love for the water, or is it because of my love for the ocean that I was given this gift?

I land only three hits on him before my last try when he wraps his hand around my fist and spins me around so fast, I can't focus on anything. He pulls me in tight, my back to his chest, and he covers my arms with his own and hugs me, effectively pinning me to his body. The only thing I can do is swing my legs and try to kick him.

His nearness is affecting my ability to fight him off. I don't really want to hurt him, but he's so good it's frustrating.

Dante laughs as he nips my earlobe and whispers only loud enough for me to hear, "I told you that you should've sat out today, my feisty little woman. This is what you get for being stubborn." He lifts me up off the ground against my protests. It gives him the upper hand, yet again.

"You're not the boss of me, you know." I struggle in his strong grip, trying to break free.

"Sierra, nobody can control you. We both know that. Doctor's orders were for you to take it easy for your own good. Are you forgetting I had to sit out not long ago too?"

"I know," I growl.

I hate that he's right. Dante did have to take it easy when he got shot. He listened to Ralph's advice. But there's a difference I don't have a hole in me. He finally frees me from his hold.

Even though I clearly lose this round, I'm just warming up. I'm not going to let him take my size for granted again. We go at it a second time, and he's still holding back. I fake a side jab toward him and instead kick my left foot out, catching the back of his knee. He buckles at the attack and reaches for me a second too late. I'm already out of his reach. I wipe the sweat off my forehead with my forearm, and he takes advantage of the opening and whacks me in the side. The blow sends pain shooting through me before he swipes his leg under my feet. Unable to right my footing in time, his inhuman reflexes has him throw a hand out to catch me before I hit the grass. The grin on his face is contagious.

We take a short fifteen-minute break before we dive into weapon techniques. Thankful for the recess, I flop back into the soft grass and relax. Maybe I am a little more tired today than I like to admit. It takes longer than usual to catch my breath. But I'm not going to stop. The only way to get better is to keep plugging along. I won't give up; I've come too far. I want to prove them all wrong that I'm stronger than they

think I am.

CHAPTER 7

ERIC

I portaled to the coordinates they gave me. I couldn't believe the plan that Dante and his team came up with last night. I understand why they need the vests but damn. I never thought Mr. Perfect would be one to attack any form of authority. There's a lot riding on us getting this shit done right. I meet the team in a local freight truck about a mile out from our target. This is the first time I have ever met them face to face. Well, I've seen Dante in my dreams—shit, that didn't sound right, but oh well. Yes, I dream of the man who's with the girl I'm in love with. I really should go see a therapist.

I gotta say I'm a little unnerved by Maverick and Dante; they both seem like they're on edge more from being around me than the heist they planned out to a T. Maverick explained in detail exactly what they need me to do.

"We can count on you, right?" Dante's voice is low enough that the other men don't hear him questioning my abilities.

"Yeah, why wouldn't you be able to?" I snap back at him, offended that he thinks I can't pull this off. He has no idea what I've been able to accomplish by going invisible.

"I'm just double-checking. There's a lot of lives relying on this to go smoothly, and I'm not just talking about the ones that are here." He looks me pointedly in the eye.

Ah, I see it. He's worried I could jeopardize this whole operation. He's crazy if he thinks dangling my sister's safety as leverage is a good idea.

"I would do anything to make sure Emma's safe." I glare back at him. Man, what I wouldn't give to punch him in that pretty boy face he has right now.

"The question is, is that with us? Or them?"

Are you fucking serious man? I bite back a few choice words. "I don't want Emma anywhere near Excalibur, so obviously, she's safer with you guys. What, you don't trust me?" I cross my arms over my chest, the universal sign of back the fuck up.

"I don't know you." Dante crosses his arms too.

"Fair point, but Sierra does. And I bet she trusts me to do it right." Yup, I went there. He wants to dick around with me, then I'll give him what he wants, a reason not to trust me.

His eyes narrow as he presses his lips into a firm line. Good, he's at least worried about me in that regard. He's not the only one that loves her, and he knows it. My fucked-up mind has been telling me to go after her for some time now. Maybe I should. It turns out he may not be as good of a man as I thought if he can put this plan together so easily and have no compunction about stealing from the police. Maybe we're not so different after all.

"We're on the same team here. We both want to be able to go on with our lives once this mess with Excalibur is dealt with. I can go back to being a guardian and you can go back to doing whatever the hell it is you do."

"Deal."

He reaches a hand out to me, and I take it. There's two other men besides us three. The odds aren't great with five immortals against a whole building full of FBI agents. Especially since we're not bringing any weapons. After all they are on the same side as us, whether they know it or not. It doesn't really bother me to steal from the police. They've hassled me plenty of times. I've been on the other side of the law on more than one occasion.

All of us put our tiny plastic earpieces in so we can communicate during the raid. It's my turn to do my ghosting act. The adrenaline pumping through me is making it hard to focus on vanishing. After a minute or so, the vibrations start in the soles of my sneakers and slowly crawl up my body. Reaching in front of me, I see the outline of my arms and hands, which lets me know my transformation worked. I step out of the open doorway and start walking toward the building.

It's about 10:30 at night, and with the shift change at eleven, that should allow me time to sneak in the entrance on the heels of another undetected. I'm sure seeing a door open and close on its own would draw some unwanted attention to us. I can't say I haven't screwed around with some people with that before. It's amazing how freaked out some people get thinking places are haunted.

I forgot how much hotter Tucson is than Colorado Springs. After just a few minutes, my t-shirt sticks to my sweaty skin. I swear it feels like the rubber of my shoes is melting to the pavement. Even with it being pitch black outside, it's still scorching. The entire walk to the building takes me about fifteen minutes. The only thing that masks my footsteps is a light hand-dryer-like breeze ruffling the nearby trees. I come to a tree that's about twelve feet from the front door and lean against the rough bark, waiting for an agent to lead the way inside.

This place looks much bigger in person than what the blueprints indicated. The brownish concrete walls must go up at least a dozen or so floors. At this time of night, most of the lights are off because they don't have much staff on the third shift, lucky for us. A middle-aged man in a light blue button-down shirt steps out of his silver Honda and starts walking this way. Once he's close enough to the building, I take my place behind him and time my steps with his. Being this close to him, the scent of his menthol scented aftershave is overwhelming; I'll be glad to break away from him. He must've put the whole damn bottle on.

He pulls open the glass-paneled door and steps into the building. I'm right on his heels; otherwise, the door will swing back and take me out. I hold my breath so he won't feel it, and as soon as I clear the door, I back off a few feet. Then I continue to follow him past the large metal secretary desk with an older brunette sitting behind it and about thirty feet down the hall until we come to a T. He takes a left, and I take a right. The goal is to get a key card from an agent leaving for the night, so he wouldn't work for that part.

I lean against the smooth white wall and try to calm my mind down. My thoughts are scattered all over the place, and I could really go for a drink right about now. I'm used to numbing the cluster fuck of my life with alcohol. New footsteps come from the hall menthol man went down. Two older men appear around the corner. Instead of heading toward the exit, they keep walking in my direction. I quietly take a few steps back to gauge how close they'll walk by me.

I don't see a black key card on either of them, so I decide to let them keep walking by. I hope this doesn't take too long. I've only ghosted myself for about an hour straight before. I'm not sure how long I can hold it together. As I wait for another person to come along, my thoughts drift back to the last time I saw Sierra, where my guard slipped and I kissed her. I knew she wanted me, but I waited too long to act on it. Maybe if I'd been able to find a way out of this mess with Excalibur, things wouldn't be so complicated between us.

I'll never forget her face when I waited for her outside of the bookstore she worked at. She was closing up by herself, and I was supposed to abduct her for Excalibur, but I couldn't do it. I was so close, right on her heels, but the moment she turned around and I saw sheer terror on her face, I froze. I didn't care what happened to me. There was no way I'd hand her over to them.

I haven't been able to talk or video chat with her on the phone during the meetings without picturing her face later at night. Knowing I was the one that caused her to feel such terror nearly broke me, even if she doesn't know it was me, I do. It's just karma that Dante fell into her life at that exact time just to punish me. To take her away before I told her the truth about everything. He gets to be her knight in shining armor, not me. I shake my head to clear her sweet face from my mind.

Another set of footsteps come toward my hall. From how quickly the shuffling of the feet is, I would say this person is in a rush to get out of work. Perfect distraction. Louder and louder and then the person mutters, "Damn. I'm late."

A short red-haired woman with a scrunched-up face barrels down the walkway. I make my move, reaching for the key card dangling from a lanyard on top of her stack of files she's juggling. As I pull the black cord free, her files fall from her grip and crash to the floor.

She lets out a curse as she squats down to grab all of her belongings. I back away slowly, hoping she won't notice what's missing. Sure enough, she's too distracted by the mess and grabs all of her stuff while talking on her cell phone and rushes toward the exit. I sigh in relief as I make my way to the stairs leading to the armory located in the basement. I still walk quietly even though nobody is around to hear me.

Leaving all the lights off helps to hide my location as well. The lights are on a sensor, so that would be a red flag to the security guards on duty if they came on. Lucky for me, in my translucent state, the sensors are able to pass through me. Two flights left, and I'm glad this building's air-conditioned. These stairs would suck in the 95 degrees plus like it is outside.

Time to see if my work has paid off. According to Dante, any black key card should open the door to the armory. Only time will tell. I was half expecting a bank vault door. But, nope just another plain steel one. I take a deep breath and slowly let it out. If I'm caught breaking into a federal building, jail time is all but a promised outcome. Ah, screw it. I press the key card into the large slot of the silver handle and wait. The light flashes green and the handle unlocks with a click. I slowly open it and step inside. The door closes softly behind me as I let my eyes adjust to the complete darkness.

Well, armory is definitely the right word for this room. Behind caged walls, there are so many guns, ammo boxes, and other weapons it's hard to imagine needing them all at once. The police are definitely prepared for an apocalypse. On the wall to the right are the racks that hold what we came here for, bulletproof vests.

"We're good to go," I tell the other guys waiting back in the tractor-trailer truck.

Too bad we couldn't just skip my part and portal into it. Without using a key card on the outside door, a portal would make the sensors go off and this place would go into lockdown. Almost immediately, a portal opens up a few feet away from me and the four men come through it. Grabbing as many vests as we can manage, we start traveling through the doorway Maverick created to their base camp. A constant flow of back and forth happens for about five minutes. We're on the last pass when all hell breaks loose.

I don't know how they knew, but the FBI agents swarm the room. The confusion about what is really happening is the only thing that saves us.

"Forget about the rest," Dante shouts as we all dart for the open portal.

Maverick and the two other men are able to get through, but an agent tackles Dante before he gets a chance to get to it. I'm safe standing on the edge of the portal. I can get out and leave Dante behind. It should be a no brainer. That would take him out of the equation for Sierra. But can I face her after if I do it? Can I be the reason for her heartbreak?

DANTE

I see him hesitate. It isn't hard to figure out what's going on in his mind. If he leaves me here, I'll be out of his way to get to Sierra. I'm not stupid. He probably alerted the FBI somehow.

I struggle against three agents pulling me back farther and farther from my escape. It's chaos inside the small room: the yelling, the flash bangs going off, and about fifteen FBI agents fighting to get to the portal they know nothing about. I try to fight my way through them without hurting them too badly, which is actually pretty hard to do. I could've easily taken a few of them out, but I don't want that on my conscious. It's bad enough that I'm stealing gear that they need to protect themselves.

Against all odds, Eric steps in and helps me pry away from them. We both lunge for the portal, and Maverick closes it the instant that we're through. Seconds later, we're back on our private island in the Caribbean, and Eric's in deep shit. As soon as I can stand, I charge for him and wrap my hands around his throat.

"What the fuck were you thinking? Did you really think you could just leave me there like that?" I have never been so angry in my life. The veins are bulging in my forearms from the amount of pressure I'm applying to Eric's jugular.

"I didn't leave you there, did I?" Eric struggles to talk as my hand clenches tighter and tighter around his neck. His fingernails claw at my grip as he struggles to break free.

"I knew we shouldn't trust you. You alerted them somehow, didn't you?" I spit the words out.

People are shouting at me to let him go. But they didn't know what he did. Without warning, his knuckles meet the side of my face, and pain explodes in my jaw, making me loosen my hold on his neck. He takes the opening to knee me hard in the stomach, knocking the wind right out of me with a whoosh. I swing my fist forcefully and hit him in the center of his face giving him an instant nose bleed. That felt pretty gratifying. Watching Eric's blood trickle down his chin is the icing on the cake.

As he wipes the blood away from his nose with the back of his hand, I punch him again in the side. My arm where I was shot is on fire. It isn't fully healed yet. I'm not holding back like I did with the agents. I don't care if I seriously hurt him.

He deserves it. Putting his petty jealously over Sierra being with me jeopardizes our whole operation.

He rights himself and takes another swipe at me, landing his fist again on the left of my face with a cracking sound just below my eye. I'm vaguely aware of others trying to pull us off from each other. The fight rages on, blow by blow, we each take more and more hits. The metallic taste of my blood fills my mouth. I try to block his hits. I hate to admit it, but for not having any formal training at the academy, he's a good fighter. Not as good as me, though. I have years of experience on this prick.

I put as much force as I can into my next swing and hook him under the chin, snapping his jaw shut and sending him off balance. Eric hits the ground hard with a loud thud. I pounce on him while he's down. I continue swinging at him, my arm screaming in pain for me to stop the whole time. Each strike reverberates in shock waves up to my shoulder, then to my scalp as it tingles.

All of a sudden, it's as if a blimp full of water pops above us. The pressure from the water coming down on top of us breaks us apart and sends us in opposite directions.

"Enough! We're on the same team!" Sierra screams above the raging river of water rushing across the grass-covered lawn and crashing against the concrete walls.

Eric and I are both panting from exertion, and as the rush of adrenaline leaves me, the reality sets in. How can we work together after this? I can never trust him again.

"What the hell is going on here?" Joe's loud voice fills the silent void left by Sierra's angry plea.

"Eric must've alerted them. They we're on us within minutes. And worse yet, he was going to leave me there!" I glare at Eric while I point a finger at him as if they would think I was referring to anybody else.

"Like hell I did. I didn't do anything wrong, and I helped you escape!" He shouts back as he stands up, brushing the dirt off his faded blue jeans.

His face and hands are a bloody mess. I'm sure I look just as rough; my knuckles are split open and a red disaster as well. I didn't notice before, but the whole compound witnessed me going ballistic. I'm usually level-headed, but I'm always antsy when it comes to Eric. The onlookers are all keeping a safe distance from us. They all wear shocked faces as they take in what just happened. Looking around me, I then notice a stowaway. Somehow an agent came through the portal with us. By the look on his face, he's clearly suffering from a case of WTFs.

Thomas was on one side of him and Lucas on the other. They weren't going to let him get away. Both immortals are taller and wider than the agent, but he wasn't a small guy by any means. From his alert gaze, he's taking in every detail around him. No doubt because of his training as an agent.

"Shit." I rub my hand across my face, and it comes away bloody; I wipe the remains on my wet pants.

"You're telling me," Joe says, throwing his hands up in disgust. "You two get cleaned up, and then we're going to sit down like civilized people and sort this shit out. Maverick and Sierra, please go with them and make sure they don't do anything stupid."

I meet Sierra's gaze briefly before heading to the castle to wash up. She shakes her head and walks behind me with Maverick. Emma is up ahead with her brother, and Ralph walks up alongside me. Nobody says a word the entire time. Since it's clear Emma's leading Eric to the kitchen to clean up, I head for the bedroom I share with Sierra.

"I'll grab some medical supplies and meet you guys in the dining room," Ralph says, but no one answers him. Whatever minor physical damage we caused each other should heal on its own. That's one of the perks of being an immortal; we heal really quick from most things. I think the doctor just wants a way to help, or he's afraid we'll attack each other again. With just the girls and Maverick to intervene, they wouldn't be able to do much. Hell, I don't know how many were trying to pry us off each other earlier.

I continue walking in silence with Sierra and Maverick trailing behind me. The weight of her disappointment in me silences anything I might say. In a moment like this, sorry isn't enough. Eric may have been jealous and thought about leaving me behind, but he did end up helping me. And how did I repay him? By attacking him because of my own insecurities. Sierra may be my anima gemelli, and I know she loves me, but I can't stand the thought of another man putting his hands on her. Not even his eyes. Every time I think of Eric, I picture that time he kissed her, and all I see is red. I want to pummel him until he doesn't resemble the man she was attracted to. What does that say about me? What kind of monster thinks like that? I shake my own head, disgusted with myself and the possessive man I'm turning into.

I walk into our bedroom, leaving the door open behind me, but Maverick and Sierra stay out in the hall. I look in the mirror, and I'm shocked to see the number of cuts and bruises on my face and body. He did do a number on me; not like I'd ever admit that to anybody else. Most should be healed within a day or two. I scrub my face and hands, then find some clean clothes to throw on. Just another pair of black tactical pants and a black t-shirt, my usual go to. Black hides blood fairly well, and in this line of work, bleeding or causing bloodshed is almost a requirement. It's the way we pay our dues to stay in the club of guardians.

When I step out into the hall, it's just Sierra waiting. She's sitting on the floor leaning against the wall, her knees pulled into her chest, and her arms wrapped around her long legs. She quickly wipes at her eyes and looks in the opposite direction from me. Her tears make my heart ache for the sadness I'm causing her. My throat is hot with my own unshed tears of shame.

"I'm sorry." I offer a hand to help her up, but she doesn't take it.

"Save it," she says, her voice raw with emotion.

Sierra pushes herself up from the floor and walks beside me, not saying a single word or glancing in my direction the entire walk. Her presence fills the entire hall, and I feel as if I'm being smothered by it.

Walking into the dining room, I instantly spot Eric across the room leaning against the large wooden table. Emma and Eric are having a hushed conversation and they both stop talking as soon as they see us come in. They both look away from us.

Maverick strolls in right after and hands Eric a change of clothes. Eric saunters past me and gives Sierra a slight smile. Involuntarily my knuckles clench by my sides. Sierra notices and shakes her head and also walks out of the room. This day is just going great, isn't it?

I take a seat and rest my arms on the table, letting my head fall into my open palms. Lost in my own thoughts, I'm unaware of anybody coming in the room until the chair next to me lets out an angry screech as someone pulls it back from the table. Joe sits next to me while Maverick and Eric take their places across from me. Maverick makes sure to be the one directly in my line of sight. Eric is dressed in Maverick's clothes that he brought in earlier for him.

"Eric, I'm sorry. I know it doesn't make up for my actions. I shouldn't have assumed you alerted them." I rest my hands on the table in front of me.

"And I'm sorry for hesitating. I was worried if I tried to help you, I would get stuck behind too. I guess you could say it was fight or flight and, in that moment, I chose flight."

Joe clears his throat. "We also have years of training that help us to act the way we expected Eric to act with no formal training. That's on us. No offense, Eric."

"It's okay I get it. I'm just a stray dog you took in." He shrugs like it doesn't matter.

"I think what Joe is trying to say is that we're too used to working with other guardians. Our training program is so ingrained into us at a young age that we expect the same behaviors to be an automatic reflex for any of our team," Maverick adds.

"I think it would be best if we make sure that Eric isn't in that position again, until he's been trained." Joe raises his eyebrows in a question.

"If you think I want to train to become an immortal guardian, I'm afraid you got me pegged wrong. I'm just doing what I have to do to keep Emma safe. After this is over." He swallows. "Well, to be honest I haven't really thought that far ahead."

"Understandable," I reply.

We agreed that it wouldn't happen again, though I doubt that. I still don't trust him. With their powers of persuasion, Lucas and Thomas were able to make the FBI agent forget, and they deposited him about a half hour away from the FBI building we raided earlier. He's going to have a serious case of amnesia.

We end up talking in the dining room for a few hours. It's almost dawn, and the sun will be coming up shortly. Eric leaves to go back home to Colorado, and I retire to my bedroom. I was expecting Sierra to already be there, but she isn't. I haven't seen her since she walked out of the dining room. I try to go to sleep but find I'm too restless with her not in bed with me. Not to mention the reason why. I barely fell asleep when I wake up by a knock on the door.

CHAPTER 8

EMMA

Out on the front lawn, I can't seem to pull my eyes away from Maverick's tall, muscular body as he helps the others retrieve the vests through multiple portals. His strong arms fill out the sleeves of his black t-shirt until it looks like the cotton will split if he flexes too hard. All that hot hard muscle doesn't usually attract me, but it's all I can think about when it comes to him. What would it be like to be wrapped up in those set of arms?

I smile as Eric helps them out. It's about time something goes right for him. I understand now why he was so closed off to many people. I wish I could've helped him. We've always been close growing up, but these past few years he's tried to shut me out. Always the protective older brother.

A commotion draws me from Maverick's intense hazel eyes and that smile. Phew! That smile melts me every time, turning all my limbs into jelly. I haven't been around Maverick very often, but each time, I can't help but feel like maybe he's drawn to me as much as I am to him. Unfortunately, just like the rest of the fighters here, he's busy far too often to allow time for anything to bloom between us. Hopefully, that will change soon.

The next thing I know Dante is choking Eric. Fists and feet are flying everywhere until both guys are on the ground. Several men surround them while trying to pull Dante off Eric to no avail. The frightening look on Dante's face gives little to the imagination of his thoughts. I don't know what Eric did to deserve a face and body pummeling, but I've never seen Dante show much of any emotion until now. And holy hell, is he scary when he's mad.

A huge water balloon-like shape pops above them, finally getting Eric free from Dante's attack. Once they disperse, I jog to catch up with my brother.

"Are you okay?" I ask as I fall in step beside him.

"Yup, I'm fine," Eric clips out. His hands are still clenched into fists like he's going to throw another punch.

"What the hell happened Eric?" I hiss.

"I don't know." He stalks off toward the building.

Eric has never been to the castle before, I show him the way to the kitchen to clean himself up. My hands are shaking. I've never seen Eric in a fight like that before. Sure, he's been in other fights, but only a few hits were taken before they stopped. Not this time, though. He has a gash above his right eye that's trickling blood down the side of his face. I think his nose is broken; it's sitting at a weird angle, with its own trail bleeding down onto his chin.

I turn the faucet on warm water and watch the rusty color going down the drain as he scrubs his hands and face. His hands are torn up as well, my poor brother.

"Talk to me, Eric. What was all that about?" Then it dawns on me, when I remember the look he sent Sierra several days ago. I'd never seen anything like that on his handsome face before. "Are you trying to take Sierra from him?" I seethe.

He cranks the dial on the sink hard, shutting the water off. "No, but I'm starting to think I should."

"Why?"

No answer.

He leaves the kitchen, and I follow him.

"Why Eric?"

"It doesn't matter, Emma." He leans against the table in the dining room.

"It matters to me. Do you love her?" I ask quietly, not wanting the immortals with enhanced hearing to catch the words.

"Leave it alone, Emma!" Eric snaps, but the fire burning in his eyes tells me I'm right about this.

"Oh, Eric." I sigh as I rest my head on his shoulder, not caring if it's dirty and wet.

I do what he asks and I leave it alone. After all the years of trying to get him to date her, he waits until now? Men! I mentally slam my head against a wall. When will they learn to stop being so stubborn about hiding their feelings? The thud of boots entering makes us snap our heads in that direction. Maverick hands Eric a change of clothes, and I can't help but notice how close he's standing to me. His thick, heady cologne makes my brain synapses fire.

Eric's gaze meets Sierra's sad eyes. The anguished face Eric makes before quickly hiding it is like a gut punch to me. I've never seen him look so emotionally hurt before. Eric bolts straight to the exit, and I follow close behind, realizing we have walk past Dante and Sierra. I see the exchange between the two of them, and I feel bad for the awkward position this puts Sierra in. She's done nothing wrong.

Sierra walks out just after us and calls for Eric to stop.

"I can't right now, Sierra," Eric says, his voice straining as if he's swallowed shards of glass. He tries to turn away from her.

"Eric, please. I'm so sorry, I don't know what came over him. I-" Sierra begins as she reaches a hand toward him.

Tears glitter in the corners of her eyes. Eric spins around, causing her hand to drop in the air before she gets a chance to touch his arm. He hangs his head, his shoulders drooping.

His voice is thick with an emotion I've never heard from him. "This isn't on you, Sierra. I gotta go."

He's got it bad for her. I can't believe I didn't see it before. It's written all over his face. I give Sierra a shrug as I shake my head before we walk away and leave her standing there confused and hurt. I bring Eric to a bathroom around the corner so he can change. Uncle Joe stops us before he goes in to tell him to head back into the war zone of a room so they can all talk once he changes.

I take that as my cue. The guys need to talk this through without us girls being there impeding them. I find Sierra where we left her, grab her by the arm, and head to my own room. I won't tell her what I just gathered from Eric. If he loves her like I suspect he does, it should come from him, not his sister. Should he ever decide to tell her.... I'm a terrible liar, but I hope I can keep his secret buried within me. After everything he's done for me, it's the least I can do.

SIERRA

I can't believe how Dante attacked Eric last night. I knew it would be hard for him to work with Eric, but I thought he was able to put that aside. I love Dante with everything I have, but I can't be around him after his crazy outburst. I've never been afraid of him before but seeing him last night, all that anger that came out of him genuinely terrified me. I've never seen him lose his temper before; he's always been calm and collected. Dante's always the steady one. He never acts on impulse, and he's been riding me about not running into the fort that's holding my parents blind. He keeps telling me every action has a consequence and that we need to wait for the right time. I know he would never hurt me physically, but seeing all that raw power come from him because of his jealousy was something else.

I stayed with Emma last night in her room. I needed some time away from Dante. I still don't know what went on in the dining room after I left or when Dante came back to our room.

I quietly open our bedroom door and see Dante is asleep in our bed. I almost go to him; I really, really wanted to. I crave his touch. It was hard sleeping last night without being wrapped up in his arms. I desperately need him to tell me that everything will be okay like he usually does. But I don't know if it will be okay this time. He crossed a line I don't think can be fixed.

His hair is all rumpled, and his face looks peaceful. He has cuts and bruises on his gorgeous features. Grabbing a change of clothes from my dresser, I step into the bathroom and shut the door softly behind me. I undress and discard my yesterday's clothing into the small white hamper in the corner of the room. After throwing some dark purple jogging pants on with a matching tank top, I tiptoe toward the bed and take my earbuds from my nightstand. I steal one last glance at Dante before heading to the track to run my heart out. Maybe if I run fast enough, I can outrun the memory of last night and the strange mix of feelings it stirred within me.

I don't see anybody else in the castle on my way out. I shut the large wooden door as quietly as I can. I don't feel like talking to anybody or dealing with anything else right now. I can't handle much more. We don't lock up the castle since there's a magical barrier surrounding the island. You need to have one of the azurite stones Konstantina and Reid enchanted to be able to pass through the ward. Looking down at my still unpainted nails, I think I wear more jewelry now than ever before.

My emerald amulet is always around my neck, and I find myself reaching for the smooth stone and remembering the day Dante gave it to me. I also wear a small aquamarine ring on my right ring finger that Konstantina made for me to help me focus and manipulate my element better, and finally, the quarter-sized blue and green azurite stone wrapped in a black leather cord rests on my left wrist.

I find the grass still damp, their blades freckled from overnight dew drops. The droplets splash onto the thin stretch of skin between my socks and pants.

I toss my large blue water bottle into the tuft of grass next to the starting line stake and put my black wireless earbuds in my ears, pressing play on my playlist without looking at the list about to play. After some basic stretching, I break into a light jog for a couple laps to warm up. It seems the shuffle of my playlist only wants to play songs that remind me of Dante. Faith Hill's beautiful voice threatens to bring tears to my eyes. Of course, it would be our song that played, just my luck. Nope, I can't listen to country right now. Pausing on the track halfway between laps to pull my phone out of my arm pocket, I switch to something fitting my mood. Breaking Benjamin. Perfect.

I slowly increase my pace until I'm running so fast, that I struggle to breathe, my feet pounding hard into the ground to match the beat of the song. I don't know how long I run at that pace. I lose count of how many laps I make around that dirt track. Several songs have passed. Nobody is out here this early besides me. I don't even think anybody else is awake. There aren't any lights coming from the castle windows. I just had to get out of there. I felt like I was drowning and trapped inside. My legs are burning and begging me to stop, but the pain is a good distraction from the aching in my heart. Every time I close my eyes, I see the two men I love fighting because of me. Should I be angry or happy that Dante would hurt another man over me? I'm so confused by all the emotions swirling around inside me right now.

I don't care that Ralph said I should take it easy for a few days. I'm stronger than he thinks. I don't feel any different from before I passed out, and I only fainted because I was in the desert with no water source. I know my limits, and I pushed too far that day. I'm not a delicate little princess they need to take care of, and it's about time they realize that. I won't be that girl anymore. The sunlight is just barely peeking above the tall concrete wall that surrounds the compound in pale pink, tinged with shades of oranges and yellows.

Under other circumstances, the sunrise would be beautiful, but it's tainted by why I'm out here so early. Bitterly looking away from the pretty sky, I'm surprised to spot a dark figure leaning against the trunk of the small mango tree between the track and the castle. My pace falters a little. I'd know that silhouette anywhere. My traitorous heart calls out for me to go to him, but I'm still mad at him for hurting Eric. Dante doesn't come any closer, and I wonder how long he's been out here. Maybe he wasn't really asleep when I went into our room.

After I do another lap around, he's still standing there, his back to the tree and his folded hands coming to rest at the top of his powerful thighs. I can feel him watching me like a fire coating my skin, but he stays back. I think of just ignoring him and continuing my workout, but I know my legs can't keep going for much longer. I'm going to have to walk by him to get back inside. I slow down into a jog for a cool down. Once I reach the little wooden fence posts marking the finish line, I pick up my bottle of water and take a nice long swig off it, letting the cool water lessen the ache in my throat from running so hard, and I slowly make my way to the tree. Each footstep I take cranks my anxiety up a little higher.

"Hey, beautiful." His voice thick with remorse sounds deep and raspy, no doubt from a lack of sleep.

"Hey," I reply hoarsely. I'm still trying to catch my breath from my run and now trying not to cry.

His bloodshot green eyes meet mine hesitantly, and I immediately feel kind of guilty for not seeing him last night. My last words to him were 'save it,' when he was trying to apologize for being an idiot. He straightens and reaches a hand out to me.

I don't take it. He's not in the clear yet. I'm furious at him. Once he realizes I'm not going to hold his hand, his arm falls to his side. He drops his chin to his chest as he stares at the ground. Dante begins his therapeutic cracking of the knuckles as he turns away from me before he advances to the castle.

I follow but stop walking when we're halfway there. I can't take this anymore. Sensing my stop, he stills his pace and waits without turning around.

"About last night-"

"-I'm sorry I overreacted. It won't happen again." He gives me a sheepish smile when he turns his body toward me.

"I've never seen you so..." What's the right word? "Unhinged. It scared me." I avoid looking at him.

His trembling hand cups my chin and gently pulls it up so we're face to face even though he's half a foot taller than I. "Sierra, I could never hurt you. I'm sorry that I frightened you."

He tugs me closer and wraps his strong arms around me. The same arms that I witnessed hurting somebody hours before. But I'll be damned if my body doesn't start to melt into his embrace.

"I'm all sweaty and gross," I say as I reluctantly pull away from him.

"I don't care." He pulls me back into his arms and places a kiss on my perspiration-drenched forehead. Dante takes a few shallow breaths.

I wrap my arms around him and hold him tight, my head on his chest. Even when I'm angry at him, his arms have always felt like home. When I'm in his embrace, it feels like there's nothing we can't accomplish when we're together. That we really can save my mom and dad. God, I miss them so much. My heart breaks a little more every day that they're gone. I try to hide the pain and channel it into my training. I think I've been getting pretty good at putting the mask on, but I know Dante can still see it.

Dante's chest expands in a deep breath. "I love you so much, Sierra." He pauses. "It scares me that he might love you just as much as I do," he says quietly, almost whispering it.

"For one, I'm in love with you. You're my anima gemella. And for two, he doesn't love me," I say, shaking my head.

Dante sighs. "You really don't see it, do you? I can tell every time he looks at you."

I look up into his deep emerald eyes and see the vulnerability hidden behind the calm exterior he wears like a shield. The early morning sun makes his eyes glitter with wetness. I stand on my tiptoes, pressing a kiss on his soft but fierce lips. He relaxes and kisses me back, making the butterflies in my stomach flutter. We'll get through this storm just like everything else before it, side by side. I'm still mad, though. He pulls his mouth away but rests his forehead against mine, his eyes closed.

"I'm still really angry with you." My voice breaks and I blink my eyes rapidly to stop the tears from falling.

"I know, and you should be. We need to get inside. Reid was able to decipher Excalibur's prophecy, and he's waiting for us."

So that's what brought him out here so early. I'm surprised he was able to wait patiently while I ran my frustrations out. He doesn't offer his hand this time and we walk in silence until we get to the large wooden door. He steps ahead and opens the door for me to go through before following me inside. In the dining room, Maverick, Uncle Joe, and Reid are all at the table picking at a loaf of Aunt Grace's sweet bread. I'm not usually involved in running things here, so them waiting on me to arrive instantly sets me on edge. The delicious cinnamon scent of the bread makes my stomach growl in protest at me for not eating before punishing my body for what my heart is feeling.

Reid is always dressed so formally that it makes me feel inadequate around him. I know that's not his intent or how he acts to any of us less dressed people. It's just his style. I can't see anything below the table, but I'm sure he's wearing slacks and dress shoes that match the coat and red button-up shirt perfectly. Reid has black hair slightly darker than Maverick's, but his is always perfectly styled to just below his shoulders.

I take the seat next to Uncle Joe, and Dante sits beside me.

"How bad is it?" Dante's knee is bouncing up and down so much that I'm surprised it didn't make his voice waver.

"Well, that depends on how you look at it." Reid reaches into his black blazer pocket and pulls out a folded piece of paper and snaps it open. "Are we ready?"

Everyone at the table nods for him to proceed. We're all exhausted from everything that happened last night.

"He who calls upon the darkness to do his bidding will seek the power he was not given. With eyes that match the blood he has shed; he shall only have one true adversary. She is born of sword and sybil of mine own blood thirteen descendants down on the tree of life. It is she that is destined to be the Immortal Savior." Reid clears his throat. *"The maker of rain who calls on dark skies will extinguish the flames he has brought forth to scorch the Earth to ash. It is she who was gifted by the ancestors to wield water as a weapon more potent than his fire. The one with hair the color of rich earth and eyes the colors of sun and grass. Only her light can keep the darkness away, for without it, there is no hope."*

What. The. Hell.

Wow, I don't know what I was expecting, but it certainly wasn't that. All eyes shift to me as Reid sets the paper on the table in front of him. My eyes are burning a hole into the prophecy, trying to reread it and have it make some sort of sense. Surely, they're not suggesting I'm the savior. I can't be. I'm only eighteen and I've barely made the transition. I'm still learning to use my gift.

My world starts to spin. Nausea roils through my stomach. I feel like I'm about to embarrass myself and upchuck everywhere.

"Sierra, are you alright?" Uncle Joe asks kindly.

I manage to nod my head. Dante's leg stills. I take a peek at him, and he is ramrod straight in his chair. It's clear he's thinking the same thing as me. This can't really be happening. Maybe I'm still asleep in Emma's room. That would make so much more sense than what Reid just said.

"I'm just going to say it, so we're all on the same page. It's obvious Sierra is the Immortal Savior the prophecy is referring to," Reid says nonchalantly.

As if my world could crash any harder around me.

"Why me?" I cross my arms over my chest and rub the outsides of my arms. I'm suddenly freezing.

"Well, why not you?" Reid answers as he cocks his head to the side, his brown eyes begging me to understand.

I rush my words to get them all out there, my high-pitched tone on the verge of hysteria. "I'm only eighteen! I can't do this. I'm not strong enough. I'm barely able to create a large enough storm to cause rain and a little thunder. How can I put out a wildfire that's turning the Earth to ash?"

"The ancestors chose you for a reason, Sierra. They know you can do it, and so do I. You are smarter and more powerful than you give yourself credit for." Dante rests his hand on the top of my thigh and gives me one of those million-dollar smiles he shares with only me.

"He's right, Sierra. At least now we know what his motivations are. He wanted to take out the only immortal who could rival his power," Uncle Joe says with a huge smile, puffing his chest out. "I knew my niece was destined to bring good things to this world. I just knew it."

DANTE

I wasn't lying when I said she was smart and powerful because she is, but my stomach feels as if it's in a vise-like grip. I try to hide how uneasy I am with a smile, but I think she can see through it. I guess I should have known that Sierra would be in the prophecy. Excalibur has wanted to take her captive for a while, and now we know why. He no doubt wants to end her life, so she can't stop him from building his so-called Revolution.

He can't kill her; I won't let him. I'll do anything in my power to protect her. Why couldn't it be me. I would gladly lay down my life so that she may survive. The world needs her light. There's a goodness in her that's so rare to find in today's world. There are far too many people who have been touched by the darkness and allowed it to sway their soul. She's young, and as much as it pains me, she could probably move on easier without me than I could without her. I can't lose her now. Not after waiting for her for so long. What would be left of my soul if she dies? If she's gone, I'll go too. There won't be anything left for me in this world.

Holding her delicate hand in mine as we walk back to our bedroom, I try to hide my feelings like I've been trained to do. It's not an easy feat to accomplish when you find out your girl is the only one that can take out the worst immortal there is. Her silence is making these cold stone walls close in all around me. I feel like I'm in one of those creepy fun houses, everywhere I look is another barrier.

We arrive at our door, and I open it to allow her in first, softly closing the door behind us. It's still early, but others will be waking up soon to start their day of training. The bomb that just landed doesn't change the fact that we need to continue to train our team. In fact, it means we need to train harder.

"Are you okay?" I search her beautiful face looking for some way to help her through all of this. She's barely said anything since we heard those prophetic words.

"I'm fine," she says quietly. "I just have to grab my stuff."

She reaches for the small black duffle bag by her bureau and unzips it roughly, making the metal grind together. Sierra places it on the bed and starts to rummage through the bag. She puts her water bottle into it as well as her stakes and daggers that were left on top of the bureau from when she took them off after her last training session. I know she's not fine. How could she be after last night and now this? It seems as though something is always trying to tear us apart.

I can't help but think that she's closing herself off to me because of the fight I had with Eric last night. It kills me that she doesn't want to talk to me, even worse, that she might be afraid of me. I have to find a way to fix this. I didn't mean to hurt her. That's the last thing I wanted to do. I'm getting strange emotions through our magically bound emerald amulets. The feelings radiating off from mine are as clear as a muddy river. I don't know where she's at and what to do to even begin mending the mess I made, and man, did I ever create a mess. What the hell was I thinking? I screwed everything up.

The only time I've ever let emotions cloud my judgement before was that horrible night in Attica. I still carry the guilt of Elliott's death like a weight trying to pull me into the dark depths of despair. I've found ways to cope with what I've done, but I won't make the same mistake again. I have to make sure everything I do; I do with a clear head. I walk up behind her and wrap my arms around her slender waist and pull her to my chest, my head resting beside hers. The warmth of her body is a calming presence against me.

"I'm here when you're ready to talk," I whisper. "I'm sorry I was an ass last night. If there's anything I can do, will you let me know?" I hold her a little tighter, wishing I was a better man for her.

Sierra nods in reply but places her arms over mine, entwining her fingers in mine, and leans into my embrace. Holding her like this makes all the other stuff fall away, like all that matters is just us here in this moment.

Sierra slowly turns her head to face me, her long silky hair catching the scruff of my beard. "I love you so much, Dante." Her eyes are glassy with unshed tears.

My heart swells at those six small words. They hold the power of the universe to me. "I love you more than anything, Sierra," I say before placing a sweet kiss on her lips.

Without another word, we grab our things and head down the hall to start another day. I vow to myself to be the man she deserves; I need to earn her love. I have to learn to collar the beast within me. That green monster will cost me everything if I let it. I won't allow that to happen.

CHAPTER 9

DANTE

Sierra was still sleeping when I came down to the kitchen to make myself some coffee and grab one of Grace's blueberry muffins. Her soft snoring is evidence of how exhausted she's been. She's never snored before. I barely see her anymore. We run and train together but other than that, maybe a quick dinner and then when we go to bed. The loss of her presence has made me short-tempered lately. Simple things make me so angry now. I think that's mainly because I can't help but wonder if she still wants to be with me or not. She's hardly kissed me since I fought with Eric. I feel like she's slipping away through my fingers. I only have myself to blame for that.

I sit at one of the tables in the dining room to eat. Nobody else is in here yet. It's been two days since Sierra and I had our first argument, if you can call it that. Things have been better between us, but I'm still carrying the guilt of disappointing her. The cuts and bruises have faded but not the ache in my chest. Sierra has been razor-focused on her training and using her gift more so since we found out the weight of her role in the prophecy. She refused any rebuttal any of us gave her about Ralph wanting her to rest a few days. If I was in her shoes, I would probably do the same, but it's different for me because I should be the one protecting her from all of this. She should not have to bear the weight of being the sole person with the ability to take Excalibur out. The universe is expecting far too much from her.

We have close to sixty immortals, witches, and warlocks willing to take a stand against Excalibur's so-called Revolution. Believe it or not, we have a werewolf as well, the only dark one, so to speak, in our group. I can't help but see my past when I see those orange eyes staring back at me. It's not his fault, and I know not all werewolves are bad. I just have flashbacks to the darkest time of my life when he's around.

We may not have Excalibur matched person to person, but what we lack in numbers, we outweigh him in purpose. We found out why there was such an uptick among dark ones during the last couple of years. Excalibur has had them cause unrest with the humans so we immortal guardians would be spread thin and not realize his activities. He's also been empowering them to want to be free from the arrangement made centuries ago between the High Council and the leaders of each species.

The werewolf also confirmed what we have been told by Joe and Michael. Excalibur wants a world where all creatures come out of hiding, which may sound tempting. It's too dangerous, though. Humans when frightened by something or someone different, they lash out and destroy them. The dark ones do deserve to be treated fairly, just like immortals. I've always wished that we could all live in a world where we can coexist, but rules and laws need to be followed. They don't exactly have a good track record for rule-abiding.

There has been a shift in Sierra that worries me; she's more distant and closed off. I don't know if it's because of what happened after the raid or the weight that now rests on her shoulders, but I fear the responsibility is eating away at her. She's not the bright light in the darkness anymore. She's starting to blend in with it. The prophecy said only her light can keep the darkness away. I have to do everything I can to make sure the glimmer of her soul remains bright. Last night when she came back to our room, she'd cut about 8 inches off her hair. She said she needed a change and that it gets in the way when she uses her magic. She's beautiful no matter what, short hair or long hair, but I think there's more to it than simply being in the way.

I rest my head on my palms and rub my eyes. We're slowly piecing together how we plan on breaching the fort. We'll be attacking the night of September 13th, just a few days shy of the full moon. We have about twelve days left. Not enough to make sure everything we have worked so hard for pays off. I'd love to move the date up and get it done and over with, but each day we've been gaining more and more immortals on our side. When the sheep finally realize that they're just sheep following orders of a decrepit system, it tends to work in favor of the opposing force.

I don't care how we're gaining allies as long as they're true to their vow of doing what's right. I haven't been able to reach Michael or Sophia these last few days, which raises the hairs on the back of my neck. Eric says Excalibur has been putting more pressure on the prisoners lately to give up information, and one of his tactics is sleep deprivation. I actually think things have been going better between Eric and I since we had that long talk. I still don't trust him to not try to steal Sierra away from me. I just have to make sure I don't give her a reason to walk away. She needs to know she's everything to me.

Footsteps echo in the hallway coming into the kitchen, and I glance up, hoping Sierra will appear, but it's just Lucas, so I rest my head in my hands again. Her alarm should have gone off by now. I finish my muffin and second cup of coffee and head out to the track to get some fresh air before everyone shows up. I need to let some of my frustration out before I snap.

The rest of our group arrives down at the track a short time later, and Sierra is one of the last to arrive. She's usually one of the early ones. Her strides are uneven as she comes up beside Emma. All the muscles in her face are relaxed, there's no expression. Not even a half smile for Emma's sake. Emma tries to engage her in conversation, but Sierra just shrugs and chews at the inside of her cheek. Those two are usually joined at the hip with secrets and giggles.

Once the team starts running around the track, she lags behind. I slow my pace to stick with her.

"How are you feeling this morning?"

"Fine, just tired," Sierra says quietly.

I open my mouth to call her bluff on being fine, but decide against it. I don't buy it. I know her more than she realizes. She can use her words to lie to me all she wants, but I know her heart and soul. I'd be a fool of a man if I believed her. Her pace is faltering and slowing even more. She's not doing herself any favors by exhausting herself to the point that she can't participate the way she needs to. She needs to be able to give her all in these practices.

After our run, I pull Maverick off to the side. "Hey, man. Would you mind covering for me for a few days?"

"Yeah. Of course. Everything okay?" His dark brows knit together.

"I just need to get Sierra out of here for a couple days whether she likes it or not. I'm going to do what I swore I never would and take her out of the safety of our compound. She needs to remember what she's fighting for. She's no good to anybody being shut down like this. And she sure is in no condition to take on Excalibur."

I search among the sea of bodies on the lawn until I find her. Her head is hung and she's fidgeting with her fingers.

Maverick nods. "I got you. Go take care of your girl."

"Thanks, man." I slap him on the back.

There's a place I thought of bringing her on vacation once all of this blows over. So, while Sierra thinks she's going to the next training session, I'm going to sneak her away to a secluded beach back in the states on the east coast. I don't know how else to pull her out of this funk she's been in the last few days. A few days of rest and relaxation will do her some good.

"Hey, beautiful." I reach for her hand, stopping her from joining the sparring group.

"Hey, handsome," she replies automatically.

"There's a new plan for you and me today and tomorrow. Can you follow me?" I start walking back to the castle, but she stays planted where she is.

"What's going on? What's wrong?" Fear clouds her eyes as she looks around at everybody else.

"Nothing is wrong, I promise," I reassure her with a smile.

She walks quietly beside me until we're in our bedroom. "Dante, you're scaring me. What's happened?"

I sit on the bed and pull her down next to me. "I know the past few days have been rough, well, the past few months to be honest." I scrub at the stubble on my beard. I might as well just spit it out already. "I'm getting you out of here for a few days to reset."

"We can't leave, I have to train!" Her beautiful eyes snap wide with shock.

"I know, but you're not exactly in the best shape to train right now. The best thing you can do is take a step back and regroup. Trust me, you'll be much better off." I knew she would be against it. "I know first-hand that sometimes you have to take a break to be able to come back stronger."

"But it's not safe. I thought you didn't want anybody leaving?" she asks warily, using my own words against me.

"That may be true, but sometimes the risk is worth taking. I won't let anybody or anything hurt you." I draw her against my side and hold her close. "I will protect you until my last breath, Sierra."

"Where are we going?" She rests her head on my shoulder, nuzzling into me, caving in like I hoped she would.

"It's a surprise."

"Really? How am I supposed to know what to pack then?" She lifts her halo of brown hair off from me and defiantly raises her chin in the air. There's the feisty woman I love so much.

"You'll need to wear hiking clothes, but pack a bathing suit and maybe another outfit." When she gives me a puzzled look, I rise from the bed and she follows. I really hope I'm not making a terrible mistake. "Let's start packing, shall we?"

"If you say so." She grabs an empty duffle bag from the closet, throws it on the empty bed, and starts to put some clothes in there.

I get what I need out of my drawers and toss them in the same bag with hers. Next, I make my way to the bathroom collecting toothbrushes and other toiletries. I'm sure she'll want to spend most of our time in the ocean or on the beach, but we'll still need to get cleaned up. I pack a few elixirs and some spare weapons just in case. The thought of not being safe within a barrier spell is sobering. It's just going to be her and I. With that being said, I reach into the closet and swipe two baseball hats and two pairs of sunglasses to help mask our appearances.

"Are you ready to go?" I ask her as I sling the bag over my shoulder.

She nods as I pull out my smooth blue stone and create a portal. Slowly our bedroom warps in a circular motion until a narrow alleyway lined with brick buildings appears on the other side. I extend my hand for her to hold, and our fingers intertwine. Stepping through the doorway, I'm assaulted by cars honking and sputtering their exhausts, humans chattering among themselves or on cell phones, and all imaginable jarring sounds from a busy city. The noise makes me miss my cabin in the woods even more.

I reluctantly let go of her to close the portal by drawing my hands together in a typical praying pose. I place my benitoite stone back in the zippered pocket of my tactical pants before reaching out to her again. Luckily there are no humans in the alley, or I would've had to glamour them to forget seeing us poof out of nowhere. We're about a half-hour from our destination. There's a few things we have to pick up at the sporting goods store first.

With us being in a bigger city, the stores are also larger. One mega retail outlet comes into view. The multi-floored dark green structure with floor-to-ceiling windows in the front promises to deliver on everything we need. I grab a small shopping cart from the entrance as we walk in and put the duffle bag in the bottom.

"Now that's a sight to see," Sierra laughs, and it's as if the angels are singing above. It seems like forever since I've heard that sound.

"What's so funny?"

"Look at you, all domesticated and pushing a shopping cart." She grins.

I raise my eyebrows at her. I can't help but laugh as well. I'm glad to see her mood is improving. "I have to shop too, you know?".

I lead us to the camping section and choose a sturdy-looking three-person tent, an air mattress with a battery-operated pump. No foot jacking this mattress all the way. I've been there and made that mistake before. It takes far too long to inflate that way.

"I take it we're going camping?"

"We are. You want to find some pillows and a sleeping bag?" No sooner are the words out of my mouth, than she tosses a red plaid jack and jill in the basket.

We meander around the store picking up just a few more items. I have all this stuff back home in Graystone, but it's not like I can just pop in there to get it. Once we're back outside in the sweltering heat of the Carolina sun, I flag a taxi down. I put all of our belongings in the trunk and instruct the driver where to drop us off. The closer we get, the more I'm excited instead of anxious for this trip. Maybe we both needed this in a way.

SIERRA

Camping was definitely not on the list of places I imagined Dante would take me, but I guess it should have been. He loves the wilderness. We've been trekking along in the heavily wooded forest for at least an hour to God only knows where. I only know we're in South Carolina because I saw the license plates on the cars back in the city. There's not much sunlight poking through the canopy of leaves high above us.

"Are we lost?" I've heard the sayings of men not wanting to admit their lost or willing to ask for directions. I hope I'm wrong. The last thing I need is to be attacked by a bear or whatever kind of predators they have around here.

"Are you doubting my boy scout skills?" Dante places a hand over his heart as if he's offended by that notion.

"Were you a boy scout?" I smile sweetly, knowing he wasn't. I switch the duffle bag I'm carrying from one shoulder to the other. He refused to let me carry anything else. He has the tent strapped to his back, the other large bag on his other shoulder, and a cooler in his hand.

"No, but that's beside the point. I can find my way out of anywhere." He tilts his head to the side as if hearing something in the distance.

Great, here comes the bear, I think darkly. "Can't we just portal there?"

"It's all part of the experience, beautiful." He flashes me a devilish grin, the fluttering feeling in my stomach returns from a long lumbering sleep.

I huff out a sigh as I continue to walk alongside him. There's no trail to follow, just leaves, dead tree limbs, and some moss. I'm grateful that I happened to have a pair of hiking boots back at the castle. This would probably be a bit harder in my normal boots or sneakers. After what seems like ages, waves crashing in the distance drown out the sounds of birds and other critters hiding amid the trees.

Could that be what I think it is? Sure enough, the trees start to thin and reveal a beach on the other side of some downed logs. I walk faster to get out of the woods and make sure it's not a mirage. The light tan sand is barren of any other visitors. Driftwood and seaweed dot the coast from where high tide deposited them. The familiar scent of saltwater invades my nostrils.

"Do you like it?" Dante asks me, cracking his knuckles and biting his lower lip. Awe, he's nervous.

"I love it." I drop my bag in the sand, run up, wrap my arms around him and cover his face and neck with kisses. Yet again, my sweet man delivered on his promise to always take care of me.

After I let him go so he can put his stuff down, he picks me up against his hard body and kisses me deeply before setting me back down all too soon to start putting the tent together.

The remainder of our day is spent in and out of the water, our dinner consists of some hotdogs from the cooler we brought and s'mores. Even though we're alone in the wilderness, I feel safer than I have in a long while. Waking up in the morning on his chest to squawking gulls is a welcome alarm, as annoying as the pesky birds are.

We stay another day and still see no sign of another person the entire time. The only time we leave the beach is to shower in a coin-operated unit about a mile north from our tent and to get more food and ice for our cooler. I find it hard to enjoy myself knowing what I was leaving behind, but Dante was right; I really needed to reset. This whole Immortal Savior crap has been so overwhelming. My fear of failure is carried on my sleeve just like my heart.

Now I know why people often use those sound machines to fall asleep and set the dial to crashing waves. I don't think I've had such a peaceful sleep in I don't even know how long. We can't hear the waves back at the compound. The walls are too thick, and even with the windows open. I think sounds beyond the border wall are blocked somehow.

"Sierra! Wake up, grab your daggers and stay behind me." Dante grabs my shoulder and jostles me by shoving my shoulders roughly.

I shiver as I blindly reach for my knives that are on the other side of the tent. It's unnaturally cold, and the smell of rotting meat makes me want to gag.

"What is it?" I whisper to Dante, already fearing the answer I know is coming. Only one thing can cause a temperature drop and that nauseating odor. Please don't say that I'm right.

"There's a demon out there. You have to do exactly as I say, do you understand me?"

Of course, I'm right.

Dante's eyes hold a hardened glint I've never seen in him before. I just nod, uneasiness choking the words from coming out of my throat.

Dante pulls his katana out of its wooden sheath with a swoosh and slashes a large gash through our tent wall and surveys the area just outside. He slowly steps out onto the beach, looking glorious in nothing but a pair of navy-blue boxer briefs and holding his weapon in front of him. Dante motions for me to follow him. "Stick to my back and cover my six, you see anything, and I mean anything out of place, you tell me."

I swallow the saliva pooling in my mouth as I try to stop myself from puking. "Okay."

Shrill barking draws our attention to the water's edge where a woman resembling a mermaid with six serpent-like appendages protruding from her abdomen is creeping out of the darkness of the sea.

"What the fuck is that?" I hiss. I don't recall seeing a mermaid in the book of demons and dark ones.

"It's a Scylla. The only way to kill her is to cut off the head of each of her snakes and stake her through the heart with a charmed dagger or sword." Dante speaks the words fast as he holds his free hand to the side to keep me behind him.

More ear-piercing barking cuts through the night as the moon above casts an eerie glow over the creature. The eel-like bodies coming from her stomach are about six feet in length with a head at each end. Yuck. It looks like all six heads have a mouth full of razor-sharp teeth. That's what's making that awful sound.

"What can I do?" My palms are sweaty against the grips of my knives.

"Stay behind me. They typically travel alone, but I've never heard of one even being in the western hemisphere before." Dante holds his katana in front of him.

Dressed in a thin tank top, I press against his tense bare back. I scan the tree line and hope that nothing else decides to make a surprise visit. Icy air surrounds us and soaks deep into my bones, making my teeth chatter against each other. I'm holding my two daggers in front of me, but I don't see how I can help Dante unless I turn around and get within striking distance of her.

The closer the demon walks toward us on two green scaly legs, the harder it is to fight off the vomit from coming up. The stench radiating from her is what I can only describe as a month-old rotting carcass on the hottest day you can imagine. Breathing through my mouth doesn't make it any better; it just makes me taste the nastiness in the air. Dry heaves start to rack my body, and I worry I won't be of any assistance to Dante.

"Give me the girl, and you may live, immortal." A guttural voice that seems as if it's born from the depths of hell booms across the short distance, instantly raising the hairs on the back of my neck like a porcupine's quills.

"Never. You want her. You'll have to kill me first." Dante plants his shoeless feet in the sand, sword raised and waiting to strike.

"My pleasure."

My breathing quickens as I try to find a way to help him. She lives in water so I doubt my magic will do anything to the beast. There's no other threats between us and the woods that I can tell. "I can help, Dante. Nothing is back here."

His jaw clenches till I can hear his teeth grinding. His voice is pained. "You're not ready, Sierra. You have to work your way up to demons like this. I'm sorry, you haven't had enough training."

I know he didn't want to say it, but it's the truth. I'm yet again a liability to those I love. "How many have you killed?"

Silence.

"Dante, how many?" The longer he remains silent, the deeper my anxiety builds until it feels like a hand is wrapped around my neck, depriving me of oxygen, cutting off my brain's ability to think clearly.

He gulps loudly. "None."

Well, that's not good.

Dante and the other guys said I created lightning during my last storm in Mongolia. I don't remember because I fainted before it happened. If I can do that again, maybe we'll stand a chance against her.

"Then let me help you!" I whisper. "I may not be able to fight like a guardian yet but I have something you don't." I will not be a damsel in distress or put those who love and want to protect me in danger.

I love Dante and the fearless way he's willing to protect me, but I need to learn to protect myself too. I know he'll be angry but I can't take a chance of him getting hurt too because of me. Not waiting for him to say no I take a step back from him to face the ocean and the evil that's crawled out of it. I tuck my daggers into the side of my sleep shorts, the cold metal like ice against my thighs. Putting my hands out to my side, I start drawing the water from the sea. As I lift my arms palms up toward the starry sky a large cloud forms above the Scylla.

Her dark eyes dart to me as she realizes I'm responsible for the storm. "An elemental?" Her eerie voice grates on my nerves. "This will be fun." Her oddly greenish-hued skin stretches into a smile.

Her and her pack of snake dogs lunge in my direction. Finally, at least somebody perceives me as a threat. The silver moonlight glints off of the steel edge of Dante's katana as it glides through the air, timed perfectly to slice the head off one of six serpents that thought to attack me. Thick dark blue blood spurts from the opening in an arc. The others hiss and shrink away, and the mermaid thing wraps her teal-tinged arms around them as if comforting a hurt pet. She glares at Dante before rushing toward him next and bellowing out a warrior's call.

"Get back, Sierra!" Dane shouts.

I run about ten feet away then I fling my hands toward the ground, and a crack of thunder vibrates around them. The sound distracts the creature, giving Dante another opening to decapitate another head. Two of six now gone. The evil woman shrieks in her strangely gruff voice. Dante lunges forward as I throw water bombs at her, but they don't seem to divert her attention as she rushes toward Dante. The snake-like animals from the Scylla's stomach swirl left, then right, before surging forward. Their sharp teeth snap inches from Dante's leg, and he swings but the heads veer to the side, narrowly missing his blade. They're catching on to our distraction tactics.

I make another dark cloud, and this time I try to think back to when I learned about weather. Lightning is created when positive and negative charges start to go haywire, if I remember right. I make the black cloud that's sputtering rain here and there and continuing to roll in on itself to shake the static charges from inside.

Crack! The shockwave of heated air from the lightning bolt illuminates the sky without warning. The white light grabs hold of the creature, and she convulses before falling onto the sand. Dante rushes her as soon as she stops jumping. Like a warrior, he swings his katana again and again, taking all of the remaining serpent heads off before she rises again to fight him off.

She's larger than I thought and towers over Dante as she strikes her hand out and wraps her long bony fingers around his throat and her other hand around the handle of the sword. She lifts him up. I can't hit her with lightning when she's touching him and his body is blocking her heart from my dagger. I run toward them; my legs seem to be moving painfully slow. The short distance takes me far too long to reach them as he struggles for control of his blade. He's only wearing boxer briefs, so it's not like he had another dagger stashed in his belt, but I have one. Because his arms are too short to reach her, he tries to pry her scaly digits from his throat.

After what seems like hours but really only mere seconds, I drive the sharp end of my dagger hard into her left side, her scales creating a friction against the blade. I have to push with all my strength to ram it into her body. I yank it free as she hisses and stab again where her kidneys would be if the Scylla were human. Finally, she loosens her hold on Dante. As soon as his sword is free from her grasp, he drives the blade up into her chest cavity, eliciting an eardrum popping shriek. She falls to her knees in front of Dante, and he thrusts his foot into her chest, pushing her down as he frees his long sword from her scale-covered body.

Cobalt blood flows from beneath the demon, soaking into the sand surrounding her. What's left of her writhing body turns into a cloud of smoke until it slowly dissipates from a gentle sea breeze. The repulsive stench drifts away with it.

With my chest still heaving violently, I run into Dante's arms and hold on tight. After he drops his sword at his feet, he embraces me and kisses my forehead. Nothing but the sounds of the waves and our labored breathing remain. I swipe away the tear that managed to escape from my left eye.

"Are you okay, beautiful?" He tucks my hair behind my ear and studies my face.

"Yeah, are you?" That was intense. I don't think I'll enjoy the beach as much as I did before.

"I am. What do you say we get dressed and get the hell out of here?" He chuckles.

"I thought you'd never ask." I laugh back at him.

And so, we did just that. Our relaxing little getaway comes to an end all too soon. We leave most of the stuff sitting there on the beach. I'm sure some unsuspecting human will find them useful, because I for sure will not be camping again for a very long time, if ever. I'm instantly relieved when we cross the threshold of the portal into our highly guarded compound.

Chapter 10

SIERRA

I haven't seen Eric since the night of the raid and the fight between him and Dante. I'm surprised when Emma tells me that Eric wants to see me. I would think I'd be the last person he'd want to be around. He wouldn't even look at me after what happened. Emma said that Eric will be out by the barn to tend to the animals and the gardens.

It feels odd keeping this from Dante, but with how he was last week I don't want to upset him. Dante's busy right now with Uncle Joe and Maverick anyway, and I've hardly seen him since we got back from our camping trip. I wait until five minutes before Eric wants to meet me to head in the direction of the barn. The afternoon sun is shining and raising the humidity up a few notches. My hair is starting to frizz from all the moisture in the late summer air. You would think if water is my gift, I should be immune to its effects, but nope.

I walk around the backside of the faded brown building, where the paint is chipped and peeling in many places. I find Eric pacing in the small space between the back of the building and the concrete barrier that surrounds the island. He's wearing loose-fitting faded blue jeans and a dark gray t-shirt. He looks good. Though, I shouldn't be surprised he always looks gorgeous. I pat my hair down, hoping I don't look too poofy. Eric hesitates when he sees me, and then gives me one of his trademark bad boy grins that he wears so well. I can't help but smile back. I can't remember when he and Emma weren't an important part of my life, even if that's been strained lately.

He walks confidently toward me, wraps his arms around me in a hug, and lifts me off the ground. Eric spins me around in a circle before setting me down and releasing me. That small act reminds me of my birthday when he did the same. It also the day we had our first and only kiss. I thought the kiss would have felt better than it did. I think my body already knew that I was meant for Dante, my soulmate, my anima gemella. But that hasn't stopped me from still loving Eric. He'll always have a place in my heart even though I'm not in love with him. There was a time, though, not long ago when I thought I couldn't love anybody else but Eric.

"How are you doing?" Eric asks as he puts his hands in the front pockets of his worn jeans.

"A little overwhelmed to be honest. How about you?" I cross my arms over my chest.

He sighs. "I'm doing okay, but I'll be glad when this mess is over."

"You and me both."

"Oh, that's right. Pardon me Miss Immortal Savior." He bows in front of me with a smirk.

Laughing, I slap his shoulder as he rights himself. "Please, don't."

He gazes down at me with a strange wistful expression.

"What?" I dare to ask him, nervously fidgeting with my burgundy painted finger nails. I finally decided when I got back from dealing with the mess on the beach, I needed some me time. In the world of chaos in which we live, I have to remember to carve out some down time or I won't be of any help to those that need me. I can't be at my best if I don't put myself first once in a while.

"Can I ask you something?" His cocky smile falters as he looks off in the distance to sights unknown.

"Of course, is everything okay?" His serious face worries me.

"Are you happy here? I mean with Dante; does he make you happy?" He meets my gaze then, and there's something in his eyes that I've never noticed before.

"Yes, he does. I mean, he was an idiot the other day with you and I'm really sorry about that. But yes, he does make me happy. Why?"

Eric looks down to the ground before answering, "I just wanted to make sure you were okay and that he treats you the way he should be treating you."

"Dante's a good man and he treats me better than I could've imagined." I wonder where all this is really stemming from. He's never really shown much interest in my previous boyfriends. "Are you happy, Eric?"

He hesitates before his piercing blue eyes look back into mine, and he lets out a deep breath. "I'm working on it. If he ever hurts you, let me know. I'll see to it that he never hurts you again." His eyes flash with anger. "And don't let him treat you any less than the queen you deserve to be treated as."

"What's really going on, Eric?" I try to swallow down my nervousness. He's acting so strange.

"I haven't always been the man I want to be. I thought I lost him a long time ago but he's still in there." He pauses before whispering, "I'm trying to do the right thing by you, even if it kills me."

"You are a good man, Eric. That's easy for anyone to see. I understand now why you've had to build that wall up and not let anyone in. You've been carrying your family's secret for far too long and that wasn't fair of your dad to ask of you."

As I say the words his actions in the past start to make more and more sense to me: the drinking, the shutting people out, not keeping a girlfriend for long, even the moodiness and the trouble he would cause. It was all to protect himself from the truth of what his father was doing to and expecting of him. There's a question I've wanted to ask him but was too afraid of the answer. I need to know the truth, though; I've had enough with secrets and lies. I steel myself before I ask, squaring my shoulders.

"A while back, when I was closing the bookstore, I felt like I was being chased on my way to my truck. Was that you?" I ask even though I think I already know the answer; I hope I'm wrong.

Eric looks away from me, his gaze caught by the grass. I bite my lip nervously, waiting for the answer that I know is coming.

"Please, Eric, tell me the truth." I reach over and rest a hand on his shoulder. His muscles stiffen under my palm as his eyes flash to meet mine.

"It wasn't one of my finest moments, I'm sorry." His voice is thick with emotion as he leans against the barn for support, looking away from me again. His truth's too emotionally draining for him.

"What were you there to do?" I try to keep the wavering out of my voice but fail. He looks up at me with a vulnerability I've never seen in him.

"Do you really want the truth, Sierra?" When I nod, he keeps going. "I was supposed to kidnap you and bring you to Excalibur."

Oh, crap. "But you didn't, why?"

"I didn't think I could do it to begin with, but when you turned around..." He takes a deep labored breath before starting again. "When you turned around, and I saw the fear on your face, the fear that I caused, well, it broke something inside of me." He runs a shaky hand through his short dark hair. The humidity sticks his hair up like hairspray.

"Thank you for telling me. Once we get through this chaos and you don't have to hide anymore, you should come stay with us. It would be nice to have you around again. I've missed you."

"I don't think that's a good idea." His eyes darken as he looks at me with a you've-got-to-be-kidding-me look.

"You're welcome here anytime, Eric, regardless of what happened between you and Dante." I walk over and lean against the building beside him, but as soon as I do, he pushes off from the wall like he's trying to get away from me.

"I should get going. I'll see you soon, take care of yourself, Sierra." He hugs me so fast I don't have time to hug him back before he walks away without a second glance in my direction, leaving me even more confused than when Emma told me he wanted to talk to me.

"Be safe Eric," I say before he disappears into the portal he creates. I stand there stock still and stare into the spot he vanished into.

I walk back to where I was practicing my hydrokinesis gift. I keep replaying our conversation over and over in my head. I'm starting to get really worried about Eric. It seems like he's in a dark place. I have to help him, but I don't know how.

I find it harder and harder to control the water as the day progresses. My thoughts and emotions are clouding my ability to focus. Was Dante right about Eric loving me? Could that be what I saw in his eyes earlier? If he does, why is he waiting until now to express that to me?

I decide to call it a day and go see Emma. Maybe she knows what's going on with Eric.

ERIC

It was a lot harder for me than I expected to walk away from Sierra. Every step I took after I turned away from her broke my heart even more. She's happy, and that's all that matters. I need to keep reminding myself that. I told her the truth; I am trying to be a better man. I know I can never fully be able to make up for what I've done and the people I've hurt. And I can never be the man she deserves. But when I look at her, nothing else matters—there's only her. She's the only person who's been able to silence the madness in my head. When we're together anyway. When we're apart, she only adds to it.

As much as I want to be there with Sierra and Emma after all this shit goes down, I can't. I won't be able to stay away from Sierra, no matter how much I try to tell myself she's happy, and I don't want to be that guy to get in between her and Dante. He loves her too, but he's also her anima gemella. I don't have any experience with immortal soulmates other than what Raymond said about it just being a fairytale the elders passed down so you would feel important. But Raymond has fed me so many lies in the past, I don't believe him. I also don't know what to believe anymore.

She's where she belongs, and I'm where I belong, for now at least. After we attack Excalibur's fort, I don't know what I want to do yet. The appeal is there to go to Graystone. I wouldn't have to hide the real me, and I'd be surrounded by more immortals and witches. I've only ever been around the scum who work for Excalibur. There's got to be something I could do there instead of drowning myself in a bottle of Jack every night. Speaking of which, I need to stop by the liquor store and pick some up.

Once I finally return to my empty house in Colorado with my favorite choice of poison, I start to flick through the channels on the tube. There has to be something on that will provide a distraction strong enough to keep me here. Everything in me is screaming at me to portal back to Sierra, drop to my knees, and tell her how much I love her. To beg her to give me a chance. To spare her all the details of my past but to promise her from this day forward, I will do better. For her, I would do anything.

I go back to the kitchen and take a clean crystal tumbler from the cupboard and fill it with about a third of ice. I set my glass on the wooden coffee table in front of the couch and pour the familiar amber liquid over the rocks. Sitting back into the black leather cushions, I swirl the liquid around the glass before bringing it to my lips.

The banana-like smell tinged with wood undertones goes down smooth. The smoky-sweet mixture is a perfect match for me. Too bad it doesn't numb the pain as much as it used to. I can't stop picturing Sierra's pretty face, the wind ruffling her soft chestnut hair that I once was able to run my fingers through. Her luscious lips that burned an imprint into my own from that one kiss we shared. Her enchanting hazel eyes as she flirts with me, which has been painfully absent since she met Dante. She's a good woman; she'd never stray. Sierra only gives her heart away to one man, and that one man, is not me.

I thought I'd feel better knowing that she's happy and that I'm doing the right thing, but it's tearing me to pieces. One week left. I just have to hold it for that long, and then I can disappear into my sorrows if I need to. Is it possible for two immortals to have the same anima gemelli? I don't think I can live without her; this past summer has been a new form of torture. I was used to seeing her frequently for the past fourteen or so years, so to go months without her has been agony. I don't know which is worse, not seeing her, or witnessing Dante being with Sierra in a way I can't be.

I sit on the sofa, downing glass after glass with the television drowning out the silence. The alcohol isn't doing its job today, and soon enough, the bottle is empty. With a frustrated yell, I throw the bottle across the room. The glass shatters on impact creating a rain of shards flying in every direction. The gaping hole in the drywall is calling to me to tear it all down. To take out all my anger on this house that seems more like a prison than ever before. Chaining me in, so I don't leave and do what I desperately want to do, which is to profess my love to Sierra. To beg her to give me a chance to be the man she deserves. To prove to her I have what it takes to be by her side.

The house wins. I give in to the beast that lurks beneath the surface, and unleash my rage on the pale blue painted walls. I pulverize the sheetrock into small chunks by repeatedly punching and kicking it until it feels as if there's nothing left of me but a hollow shell of a man, just like the wall standing there with nothing but two by fours.

My black soled boots crunching on the glass and grinding what's left of the drywall into a fine dust, I collapse back on the sofa. My heart feels as if it's slowly being torn apart layer by layer, valve by valve, until all that remains is despair pumping through my veins.

My second bottle proves to be useful by taking the edge off or at least allows me to fall into a deep sleep. For once, my mind does me a solid and doesn't conjure up any images of Sierra or glimpses from my past. The alcohol burning through my veins is singing me a lullaby I can't resist.

RUBY

S ince the raid on the FBI building and then the meaning behind the prophecy that's been guiding us, there's been a different air around the compound. We've still been training hard and trying to make sure all the newbies are taught well. Mav, Dante, and Joe finally decided that it's okay to start allowing us to leave the safety of the magic barrier surrounding us now that we have Kevlar vests.

The roughly six extra pounds of weight have been odd to train with, more so because I feel like my moves are being constricted. I don't like feeling like I'm caged or being held down; it brings up too many bad memories. This leads me to act more forcefully toward my opponents who I train with. I can't help that it triggers my fight or flight response. I feel bad for hurting my teammates, but what doesn't kill you makes you stronger. I'm doing them a service. Excalibur and his merry-men will not care if they hurt us and won't be holding back at all. It's best they realize that now and adapt.

I was able to sneak in a visit with Alex yesterday. I didn't get to spend nowhere near the amount of time I wanted with him, though. His presence has always calmed the demons that lurk below my skin that try to claw their way out. And boy have I needed him lately. One of the new recruits looks so much like Brooks that I had to do a double-take when he first appeared. I was afraid my past and present were meshing together. For many years I used to keep tabs on him once he was released from prison.

Child abuse doesn't carry nearly enough of the jail time that he deserves. After all, I'm still this screwed up several decades later. I can't look at another man without distrust clouding my judgment. My feeling of them always having ulterior motives has not helped me find love, that's for sure. I've cemented walls up around my heart to protect myself from feeling anything more than lust. I don't lead them on; they know my heart's not in it.

Simon seems like a decent guy, but then again, so did Brooks. I've asked Mav not to pair me with him. He's not somebody I want to go toe to toe with. I'm not sure if I would shut down or murder him. Both are real possibilities that he doesn't deserve. It's not his fault he resembles a monster. Mav is one of very few who knows my troubled past and what I've suffered, so he understands.

I have yet to find a man I'm willing to allow to chip away at the armor that coats my beating heart like a second skin. I know there are good men out there like many of them here at the castle. Maybe my heart is just too numb to feel anything that resembles love when it comes to the other sex. I've thought about finding that asshole and putting a bullet between his eyes. My heart might have room for love if it wasn't filled to the brim with so much pain and anger. Offing him may take that away. I hate that he still has power over me so many years later.

I'm jealous Dante and Sierra got to fight a Scylla a few days ago. I've heard they're a beast of a demon, and to be honest, at this point, I could fight anything. I'm wound up so tight from essentially being on lockdown for so long that I'm itching to get my hands dirty. I need to feel powerful and let my own demon out. Sitting here keeping it caged within my skin makes me feel helpless. I don't handle helpless well.

I'm paired with Sierra for my next match. She's come a long way with her combat training, but she really is no match for me. Her gift, now that is something she has over every single person here. She's the Immortal Savior, the only one gifted by the ancestors to be enough to outweigh Excalibur. It's hard to believe that this sweet, innocent girl holds that kind of power inside her. It's only right that it would be her, though. We wouldn't want somebody who's been changed by this evil world able to harness that level of destruction. My body goosebumps at the thought of somebody less pure having that ability.

Sierra takes her place across from me, planting her feet firmly in the grass. The whistle blows, and I attack her. Sierra blocks quite a few of my swings but not enough of them. I strike her abdomen with my foot, and she tumbles hard to the ground with a wince. She jumps back up and brushes herself off, squaring her shoulders as I give her an apologetic grin. She smiles sweetly back at me as I lunge toward her again but I don't make it to her. The ground suddenly becomes too slippery. I lose my footing and fall into a puddle, splashing water all over me.

"Really?" I ask her, laughing. "That was a cheap shot."

"I gotta use what I got." Sierra laughs as she reaches a hand down to help me up.

"Touché." So much for innocent. This chick is going to fight dirty. "No kid gloves?"

Sierra takes a step back and strikes a pose as she builds a water bomb in her hands. There's my answer. I walk a little farther away from the others sparring on the lawn close by. I watch as her pretty eyes light up. This is where Sierra shines, and I may eat my words at itching for a real fight.

She throws that large swirling ball of water at me, and I dodge it just in the nick of time. The sounds of splashing erupt behind me. As she tries to prepare for another, I swing a leg out and catch her shin. Sierra rights herself this time and blocks my next kick with her arms forming an x. She twists her fingers, and another puddle appears. This time, I go slow as I advance on her.

Sierra swings and lands her own kick on my thigh, and white-hot pain bolts down into my calf. We're drawing a crowd around us to watch our little showdown. I sneak a glance at Mav, who's standing to the right of Sierra and wearing a devilish smirk. I bet he knew this was going to happen. Hell, he probably even told her to use her magic. The fact that she needs to use her gift to fight me makes my ego swell. At least she knows I'm a worthy adversary.

To the chorus of cheers and clapping, I fake a punch to her left and then swing my fist and make contact with her jaw a little too hard. She stumbles back, putting a hand to her chin and rubbing the spot that no doubt hurts like hell. I didn't mean to put that much swing into it. I blame the vest. She creates another water bomb and tosses it at me. As I dart to my right away from it, I'm taken by surprise as a blast of cold water drenches the front of me. She just used my own faking trick on me. She's a quick learner. I like it. It seems I may have found a match for me after all.

We go back and forth like this for a bit until we're both worn and soaked to the bone. The ground below us is so saturated with water that the grass acts as if it's the plastic of a slip and slide doused in dish soap. Her last sphere knocks me on my ass from the force of it, my feet unable to find stable ground. I decide to just stay down this time. Sierra comes over and flops onto to grass beside me and is just as winded as I am.

"That was fun," she says between haggard breaths, her eyes sparkling like a kid in a candy store.

I've never seen her use her gift against another here, and I know she wasn't trying to actually hurt me. I've seen what she can do with her magic. If harming me was what she intended, I wouldn't have stood a chance against her. This was indeed just fun. And was it ever, I can't remember the last time I felt this light.

"Hell, yeah it was," I reply once I'm able to calm my breathing.

Chapter 11

DANTE

I take a step back from Maverick's instruction to admire how far our team has come. I lean against a large beam and take in all of our fighters. Tony and Ari are squaring off a short distance away. Some of our group members have never been in combat before or trained for it. Ari is one of them. He may not have qualified before to be a guardian but he's well on his way. Tony grunts as Ari's fist meets his chin. A smile tilts my lips up. That was a nice punch, Ari has good form.

All of the grueling hours we've all spent planning and training for the takedown of Excalibur and his group are showing. They've all put in so much effort, and I'm proud to call them my teammates and friends. A wave of sadness threatens to darken my moment of pride by reminding me that they may not all make it out alive.

We'll be striking the fort tomorrow. The plan is to get in undetected, get the prisoners out safely, and then the part that terrifies me to no end, the actual takedown of Excalibur. Knowing Sierra is the Immortal Savior and the only being capable of rivaling his power is almost enough to paralyze me with fear. We worked good together as a team back in South Carolina, but that Scylla is no comparison to what we're going to be facing. I've hand-picked a few fighters to stay beside Sierra and I when we face off with Excalibur. The rest will have to fight whatever army he has on his side.

As important as it is to get the hostages out alive, it won't do any good if we don't succeed in capturing the man behind it all. He'll just do it again, and the next time we may not be so lucky with gaining a team this size so fast that's willing to sacrifice everything to stop Excalibur. All of our lives will be on the line tomorrow night, but if we don't do this and succeed, the world is in grave danger. Excalibur plans to unleash hell on Earth literally by not only taking control of the immortal country Graystone, but also reigning over any humans they decide to let live to be their slaves.

My gaze is drawn to Sierra. She's off in the corner with Amelia. I wince as a foot smashes into Sierra's stomach. She stumbles back a step before dodging the next blow. After faking a punch to Amelia's left side, she swipes her foot out and Amelia falls to the mat below. Sierra gasps and covers her mouth before reaching a hand down to help Amelia back up to her feet.

Sometimes it's a struggle for me to try to stay professional when we're around others under my command. When I watch her during combat training, I have all I can do to stay focused. My sparring partners have noticed my weakness and continue to take cheap shots at me. I have to learn to quell the desire for my girl and the need to protect her that's so deeply ingrained into me, or I won't do us any favors in the field. I never thought my focus could be ruined by a tiny brunette. But she's no ordinary woman. She's my anima gemelli.

Sierra's been quiet these past few days, but I'm not worried about her as I was when I took her to the East coast. I can understand having everything feel like it's all on you. She's been working so hard at manipulating her gift, and it truly amazes me how far she's come in such a short time. Her control of water has started to morph into controlling the weather, like rain, wind, thunder, and now lightning. To be honest, I'm surprised all of the storms she's created haven't drawn anyone's attention to our little island.

A high pitch whistle cuts through the fighting.

"Well done, everybody. You can take the rest of the day off," Maverick says as cheers erupt. "We'll meet up again tomorrow at two in the great hall. Have a good night."

Maverick, Joe, and I decided to cut training short today. We not only want everybody at their best tomorrow evening, but we also want to give them some free time to remind them what we're all fighting for. It's hard constantly training, especially since most of us left our families behind. Some of us don't have anybody that was a big part of our lives here with us. But we're not alone, we've created a new kind of family here, and I hope everyone feels that way.

The uncertainty of what will happen to all of us afterward has been keeping me up at night. I want, no, I need to go back to being an immortal guardian. That's my duty to my country and what I was born to do. Fighting that Scylla last week gave me the adrenaline rush that I've lived on since graduating from the academy. As much as I've enjoyed my time here at our compound, my body's been itching to get back out in the field and fight beings that I can and actually want to hurt.

I'm hoping after we capture Excalibur and break whatever hold he has on the High Council, that we'll all be reinstated to the positions we held prior to leaving Graystone. If not, the men and women on the council could charge us for treason. That can be long jail time or even death. My wish is that they show leniency. Surely, they can't prosecute all of us and get away with it?

We're having Ember and Finnley, two of our newer warlocks that Reid was able to bring aboard, put up an additional barrier spell around just the castle itself. That way if any of our azurite stones are compromised, the humans and those who remain behind to protect them are safe. I don't want to take any chances, so the two warlocks and the few immortals that stay behind will be the only ones who can crossover that magical ward. I wouldn't put it past Excalibur to try to come after them if he makes it through us.

I'm looking forward to finally having a night with Sierra that somewhat resembles a date. I want to get back to our room before she has a chance to. I would hate for her to walk in on my surprise and me not be there. I have white lilies- her favorite- in a crystal vase with candles placed around to give it that romantic ambiance. I already stocked the log rack with plenty of dry wood to keep us warm through the night. I have popcorn, a box of expensive chocolate with a movie of her choosing to win her over. It's not a lot, and she deserves so much more, but it's all the situation will allow for.

I vow that once we get through this rough patch, she will be my primary focus. I'll give her all the love and affection in the world. Nobody is guaranteed a tomorrow in this life; you have to live each day as if it could be your last. If tomorrow is my final day on this Earth, I'm going to make damn sure she knows how much I love her.

SIERRA

Aunt Grace went all out on what could be our very last meal alive. I know it's morbid, but it's a real possibility. She made a few lasagnas, a huge pot of beef stew, and an enormous amount of spaghetti and meatballs. It's as if she's fattening us up to use our own bodies for a stew next. Not to mention her homemade honey cornbread to go along with it. My mouth water's just thinking about her secret recipe that she uses. Her cornbread is hands down the best I've ever had.

Today's been flying by nauseatingly fast. For the most part, spirits are high with the rest of the group. Me on the other hand, I can't get Eric and my conversation from the other day out of my head. Obviously, I don't want to be with him, but I want to help him in some way; I just don't know how to do that. I'm nervous about seeing him tomorrow. Emma assured me he's okay, but the look of utter sadness I saw on his face before he walked away from me is burned into my brain. I don't know what he wants from me that I can give him other than my friendship.

Dante eats his meal so fast I'm not even halfway done with my lasagna. He acts as if he's a starved animal.

"Are we not feeding you enough?" I raise my eye brows as he shovels another heaping forkful into his mouth.

"I just have some things I have to take care of."

"And it can't wait ten minutes?" I ask.

He shakes his head no before finishing the last bite. "See you back in our room in a little bit?"

"I'll be there in a few minutes."

Dante unfolds his large body from the chair and brings his empty plate back into the kitchen and disappears without looking back. He's acting suspicious. I think he's planning something for our night off. I don't push it. If he wants to surprise me, then he can. We don't get anywhere near enough time to just be us. I finish my plate while visiting with Emma before the curiosity gets the best of me, and I leave the dining room.

I try to walk normally, but everything in me is telling me to go faster. I finally arrive outside our room after what seems like a mile long hike. I stall for a minute before reaching for the silver handle. A twist of the wrist is all it takes to crack the door open. Pushing the door wider, I'm enveloped with the sweet, delicate fragrance of lavender. Candlelight flickers in the room, and the large stone fireplace beckons me closer with its heat. It's not very cold here at night, but I can't resist a fireplace. The crackling of the fire holds my attention.

There's a vase of white lilies on our small round table, and I rub their velvety smooth petals with my fingers. My eyes find an unmistakable pair of deep emerald eyes in the dim lighting, and the scorching look he gives me makes me forget about everything else in the world but him. He's dressed in a button-down navy dress shirt paired with a flattering pair of jeans that fit just right on him, his hands clasped behind his back.

I'm thankful I at least took a shower and got into some clean clothes after training earlier. I'm still underdressed compared to him. I'm just wearing a plain white t-shirt and a pair of blue jean capris. I tuck my hair behind my ears before walking to him.

"Hey, handsome." I swallow thickly.

"Hey, beautiful," he says in his husky voice as he steps toward me until inches separate us.

"You did all of this for me?" I ask even though, duh, come on, who else did it? I'm not used to any type of romantic gesture, so I'm not sure what to say.

"Anything for you." Dante nuzzles his face into my hair in the crook of my neck.

The intoxicating scent of sandalwood, cedar, and pure Dante invades my nose making it hard to concentrate on anything other than the sound of our breaths mingling and the snapping of the fire. He reaches into his back pocket and presses a button on his phone. The little silver Bluetooth speaker on the table roars to life and starts playing our song.

"May I have this dance?" he whispers against my ear, his hot breath against my skin making me shiver.

"You may," I answer as I wrap my arms above his broad shoulders and around his neck, pulling him closer to me.

We slow dance barefoot on the hardwood floor of our room through several songs in silence, lost in the moment of being in each other's arms. It's nice to ignore the rest of the world for a change. He chose a playlist of sweet country songs, causing my heart to flutter. The lyrics serenading us in the candlelight says everything he feels without him having to utter a word. My head rests on his hard chest, and I swear the thud of our heartbeats are in harmony with each other. There's a red-hot air popcorn popper, a miniature version of those big carts they push around at fairs sitting on my bureau.

A large plastic jug of popcorn kernels sits beside it with a few bottles of seasonings and a large bowl.

A small flat screen T.V. sits on Dante's nightstand. The simple act of watching a movie and eating popcorn is like something out of this world for us. The fact that he thought to do all of this for me makes me love him more than I ever thought possible. I can't imagine a life without a love like ours. It wouldn't be a life worth living. I'm dreading what tomorrow will bring, and I can't bear the thought of Dante getting hurt. His death would be like a stake through my heart. I know he'd protect me until the last beat of his heart. I hope it doesn't ever come to that.

Dante must've felt the change in my thoughts. He stops dancing and cups both of my cheeks in his warm palms and my mouth parts automatically. Our lips touch, and Dante gives me the most tender kiss he's ever given me. He pulls back and rests his forehead on mine while we both reign in our ragged breaths. Every time we kiss, it's like a wildfire in my veins that can never be smothered.

"Are you ready for a movie?" he asks with desire burning in his eyes and voice.

I don't trust my voice enough to speak, so I nod instead. He holds his rough hand out for me to take as we move toward the looming bed in the center of our bedroom. Once we're both seated next to each other on top of the gray comforter, we find something we like.

I can't help the huge smile that forms at his back as he fires up the popcorn machine. How in the world is this sweet, gorgeous man the same person who can cut off the heads of a demon without breaking a sweat? Dante turns and meets my gaze and flashes me that sexy smile that makes all the butterflies somersault inside me. Thoughts of tomorrow and every other horrible thing that's happened recently disappears from my mind to allow me to have possibly the best night of my entire life.

EMMA

The meal we had was somber but delicious. It's no wonder with everyone thinking this might be the last one before many of them might die. Not me, I'm staying behind since I'm practically just a human. Ralph, the nurses and I will tend to any who comes back hurt.

Dante is stealing Sierra for a date tonight, so I'm left by myself and end up alone in my room. I don't really know many of the others here that well and most seem to have vanished for their own plans. I slam the medical journal shut with a loud clap. I've been rereading the same page for the last half hour, but I can't even recall what it's about. My nerves are a mess, and I try to pace in my little bedroom to relieve some of it, but all that does is manage to make it worse.

I throw my thin sandals on and step into the empty hall. Nothing but closed doors greet me. I sigh and keep walking to the front entrance of the building. I quietly shut the thick door behind me as I venture out into the night. The dark sky is crystal clear and filled with twinkling stars. The moon casting its illumination over me is fairly bright- just a few days away from being a full moon.

The dewy blades of grass tickle my toes and sides of my feet as I walk through them. I see a figure not far from where I stand lying on the grass. I take a tentative step closer and discover it's Maverick when he rolls his head to the side and his piercing hazel eyes land on me. For a few long seconds we both freeze, afraid to move. I don't know if he's feeling the same electrical charge that is pulsing through my limbs. Maverick blinks a few times before he pats the blanket-covered ground next to him.

With sluggish feet that feel way too big, I make my way to Maverick, kick my sandals off and sit beside him on the green and black plaid wool blanket. Stretching my legs out next to his, I lean back on my elbows and throw my head back, admiring the stars. Other than the crickets singing us a cadence, the only other sound is a slight whisper of wind.

Aware of his gaze on me, I feel my cheeks heat as I say, "It's a beautiful night."

"Yes, it is," Maverick replies in a low voice without taking his eyes off from me. The deep notes of his voice resonate through me. My body is painfully aware of how close we are to each other.

He rolls onto his side, putting a little more space between us, and I already miss how close he was to me. I take a chance and turn my head toward him, our eyes lock, and my breathing slows. I have to flex my fingers to stop myself from running my hands through his messy ebony hair. I wonder if it's as soft as it looks.

I make the mistake of looking down at those gorgeous full lips and involuntarily lick my own, causing his eyes to darken. He reaches a tentative hand out and places it on my flat stomach. Fireworks light up under his touch, and as I switch to my side, his hand trails to my waist. Placing my palm on the center of Maverick's chest, I'm rewarded with his heart beating a frantic rhythm through his t-shirt.

Time stands still as he dips his head and finally places his mouth on mine. Kissing him is like heaven, and I swear I can hear the angels above belting out a chorus. Everything else disappears from my mind besides the feel of Maverick's tongue mixing with mine and him pulling my body closer to his until there's no space left between us. He breaks the kiss, and I'm flooded with needing him more than my next breath.

"Emma," he begins breathlessly. "I can't promise you more than this one night." The unspoken threat that he may not be coming home tomorrow night lingers between us.

"Then we should make it one that neither of us will ever forget."

"It wouldn't be fair of me to put you through that." The concern in his eyes tell me he really doesn't think he'll survive.

"Well, it wouldn't be fair of me to hold back what I feel for you." I swallow. "You deserve to know how hard I've fallen for you, Maverick." I pull his chin back up to kiss him, but he holds back.

"Are you sure? But if I don't make it-" he starts.

The thought of him dying nearly rips a sob from my chest. I place my finger over his lips, cutting him off before he has a chance to say what I think he's about to say; if he doesn't make it back.

"It's only us that matter tonight. Everything else can wait until tomorrow."

I know once I cross this line, once I allow myself to fully fall in love with this man, there will be no escaping it. The hurt will tear me apart if he doesn't walk through those doors tomorrow night. But I can't live one more day in fear of what's to come, not when everything I want and need are right here in front of me. I've been punishing myself for making up for my parents' behavior. If this really could be our one and only night together, fear and pain have no place here. I'll give him everything that's good and pure in me, and maybe that alone will be enough for us both.

The crickets and stars no longer exist in our little bubble, just the love that we'll finally allow to transcend us to a place we've both never been before. True, no holds barred, love.

Chapter 12

DANTE

The night sky is dark and clouded over. You can only see the twinkle of a star here and there, making the perfect cover for us. The team is all in position on the coast of Murud, which is just a short distance from the island. With our enhanced night vision, we immortals can see the looming walls that tower nearly forty feet in the air, effectively keeping out any unwanted guests.

Portal jumping in different time zones really messes with your head especially when traveling from the mid-afternoon in the Caribbean to the early hours in India. It's about two o'clock in the morning. The team, consisting of a total of 58, and I chose this time to strike because the guards at the Murud-Janjira fort are the least active. Apparently, Excalibur thinks he's so badass that nobody would bring the fight to him, so he doesn't have a shield around his fort. Boy, do we have a surprise for him.

It's silent save for the waves breaking close to us, the calm before the storm, literally. Sierra, Konstantina, and Reid are all upfront against my better judgment. I should be going in first, not her. We were lucky when we raided the FBI to have just enough bulletproof vests for our whole tactical team. We left five trained immortals and a pair of warlocks behind to protect our compound and the humans we left behind. Humans are no match for what we're up against tonight. As much as some wanted to help, they would just be sheep sent to slaughter.

Eric gave us a good idea of how many dark ones to expect. I double checked with Michael, but he couldn't tell me much since he's still locked up in the dungeon below ground. I hate not being able to trust Eric, but I have no other option. He's supposed to be at the fort when we storm it. I just hope and pray that he really is on our side. If not, we could be walking into a blood bath.

We're all equipped with various weapons such as daggers, katanas, stakes, and a few crossbows. Some of the immortals have extra abilities that help, dreamwalking doesn't help here unfortunately. But the main gift that really matters is Sierra's. That's why Reid and Konstantina will be staying by her side. Earlier, they cast an energy spell that allows Sierra to draw energy from them.

Maverick and I will flank both of them, and the others will follow. I'm hoping not to lose any of my teammates today, but I know there's a slim chance of all of us making it out alive. I walk to the front of the group by Sierra and give her hand a tight squeeze.

"To all of my brothers and sisters, I want to thank you for all the hard work and dedication that you've shown. I want you to take a minute and look to the left and the right of you to your fellow teammates and know that there's a chance some of you may not make it through tonight." I pause, and Sierra tightens her hold on my hand. "But today we stand in solidarity against the wrongdoings of Excalibur and the shortcomings of the High Council. Tonight, your sacrifices will be known to the rest of the world that lives in the shadows. They will know that this team of exceptional beings did the unthinkable and brought justice to the man that was untouchable. We will tear down his reign. We will bring peace again to our people. Until we meet again, my friends, stay safe and kick some ass!"

Hushed battle cries sound out among the crowd as they embrace one another. Sierra looks up at me with a gleam in her beautiful hazel eyes.

"That was one hell of a call to action," she says, smiling at me.

"I practiced many different speeches, but none of them had me prepared for what I would actually say," I answer truthfully. "Looking out at all of them, I really am amazed at what we're about to do here."

"So am I. We'll get through this, handsome." She places a chaste kiss on my lips. Still somehow able to be sweet in the midst of the chaos.

"Are you ready, beautiful?" I crack my knuckles out of habit.

This will be the first time Sierra has ever gone up against anybody other than the Scylla. I've been itching to fight since we left Graystone. It was nothing for me to have several confrontations a week when I was an immortal guardian. I do miss the adrenaline rush of banishing demons and chasing down dark ones. After we bring in Excalibur, the High Council has to let us back in. I don't know what I'll do if they don't. I'm not meant for a sedentary lifestyle. I need to fight worthy opponents who I risk my life with.

"Let's do this," Sierra replies confidently with her chin held high.

Her actions say one thing, but the troubling look in her eyes tell me another. She's scared. Sierra takes a long deep breath, closes her eyes, and bows her head. She chants so low I can't make out the words. When she lifts her head back up, she brings her arms out to her sides.

The clouds above the fort start to darken into an angry dark gray with black in the center. I can barely make out the rain from this distance. The wind picks up and whips Sierra's brown hair into the air. The rumbling of thunder in the distance is a welcome noise. It'll help to block out any sounds that we make getting to the prisoners.

"South wall, lawn," Eric speaks quietly into the earpieces we're all wearing.

"Okay," Maverick acknowledges the place Eric is directing us to, where the best site to portal into is.

Lighting flashes and the low growl of the thunder are our signs to move now. Maverick pulls out his long blue benitoite portal stone and points it toward the rocky beach just ahead of us. Slowly the swirling cloud of a door shows a grassy landscape with a stone keep castle as a backdrop. With a nod and an I love you mouthed to me, Sierra steps through the portal with Konstantina and Reid on either side.

I step through next, followed by Joe and Lucas. Maverick stays behind to keep the portal open for the others to come through. The bright flash of light followed by the loud crack of thunder above us briefly illuminates the area. Luckily nobody is around. It's monsoon season, so it's not out of the ordinary to have a storm pop up.

Eric's off in the distance waving for us to follow him. He's mapped out the entire compound for us, but I still would rather lean on anybody else. Sierra is doing her job at keeping the storm at bay and conserving some of her energy for when Excalibur shows his face. Joe, Lucas and Thomas are each leading a group of six in three separate teams for the extraction of the prisoners.

As soon as we know the prisoners are off the island and safe, we will hunt down Excalibur. Our hope is to deliver him to the High Council and demand justice. I reach for my stainless-steel katana strapped to my back and pull it out of its scabbard, holding it out in front of me. The weight of it is comforting. Maverick is on the opposite side and holds out his matching daggers. We're both ready for anything. The battlefield creates a calm in me like nothing else. This is when I'm at my best.

SIERRA

Shouting and crashing noises come through the earpiece in my right ear. No one has reached the prisoners yet, and I suspect they've been made by the sounds that greet me. I watch the archway Uncle Joe led the groups through, waiting for anybody to return. The echo of the thunder's boom across the night sky causes a percussion in my chest each time it follows a flash of lightning.

Dante and Maverick move closer together in front of me, and I'm not surprised to see Roger among the immortals who chose to encircle me. I've come to rely on the silent strength that he offers. We've built a community back in the Caribbean, and I hate the thought of them risking their lives. Even if it's for the greater good. Reid and Konstantina have linked themselves with me so that I can sustain manipulating my element for extended periods of time.

I can't tell how long we've been here; time seems to stand still. I know at any moment the fighting will come to us. I'm supposed to stay and provide cover for the extraction teams unless Excalibur comes out, then he's my main focus. According to the prophecy, I'm the only one who can defeat him. No pressure at all there.

Out of all people who had to be the savior, why me? I'm barely an adult, still trying to find my place in this crazy world we live in. I've been trying to keep the rain off my comrades, but it's hard with so many obstacles I need to avoid. At least it's still hot out, so the rain shouldn't feel too bad.

An explosion off in the distance grabs my attention, and I wait impatiently to hear anybody on the wire. Nothing, just silence. Not even the sounds of fighting are carrying through now. The earpieces aren't working. They must be being blocked by something or someone.

A ball of angry red fire barrels through the night sky directly toward me. I throw my hands up, directing my energy into shoving the fireball away. The man of the hour has finally come out to play. I was hoping to get my mom and dad back first before dealing with Excalibur. I'm still at a loss for how I'm supposed to defeat him. Surely rain won't wash him away, and apparently his gift is fire so I can't fry him with lightning, or can I?

He's slowly making his way to me, he's about fifty feet from where I stand. I increase my focus and point in his direction, and a lightning bolt lands about five feet away from Excalibur, lighting up everything around him. The darkness can't hide the hatred he has plastered on his face. He's even more menacing than I remember, with his muscled frame like a bodybuilder on steroids. His shoulder length jet black hair is tied back behind his head. A jagged scar that runs the length of his left cheek resembles a bolt of lightning. He clearly wasn't expecting us to come at him in his own home. I'm glad we were able to get the element of surprise, even if just for a short while.

"Sierra, my dear, you've come a long way since I saw you last. My offer still stands. Join me, and we will rule the world together," he bellows above the thunder and the rain pattering down around us.

"I'll never join you. We both know how this ends. How the prophecy says you can't win against me. Give up the prisoners willingly, and we'll show mercy!" I shout back, feeling more empowered.

If there was ever an evil villain laugh that is what he just did. I thought the lunatics only did that in the movies, but here we are. He lifts his left hand, and a flame appears above it as if sitting in a torch. I challenge him by sending a rush of water to his hand and drenching the fire.

He laughs again.

What is wrong with him? How can he be amused at this? Another fireball comes flying toward us, this time at Maverick. Instinctively I jump in front of him, and I direct a wall of water in front of us with my hands, extinguishing the fire. Another one at Dante and I do the same. He's targeting those that stand with me.

"Get behind me!" I yell to those trying to protect me but are only providing targets for him to aim at.

"Oh, Sierra, when will you learn? You are just a child; you are no match for me." He rumbles his deep baritone as a mix of vampires, werewolves, and other immortals emerge behind him and flank his sides.

I send a water ball at him, but he manages to lunge to the side to avoid it. I see movement to my left, and it's my Uncle Joe ushering what looks to be some of the prisoners back into the doorway they came from. Too late, though, Excalibur sees them also and sends a large fireball in their direction. I throw an even bigger water bomb fast and knock it out of the air just in time for them to duck safely back in. I hate the silence coming from the earpiece. I need to know what's going on. Did the extraction teams get to my parents yet?

"Well, well. What do we have here?" Excalibur tilts his overly large head in the other direction, hiding the ugly scar.

Hordes of his followers leak out around him and start engaging in battle while my team surges toward them. Sword's clanging, fists hitting, and bodies thudding on the ground are sounds I don't think I will ever forget. And yet he's still laughing like a mad man and standing still in a sea of fighting.

I create an enormous amount of water above me and fling the torrent of liquid at Excalibur. The water knocks him off his feet, but he bounces back up with a scowl. Dante is muttering something behind me, but I don't understand what, and I don't want to take my eyes off of Excalibur to look back at Dante.

When my mother appears to the left of Excalibur wielding a large black-handled sword, fierce as can be and is fighting her way closer and closer, my mouth gapes open. She's magnificent. I've never seen anything like it before. She takes out opponent after opponent with my dad trailing behind. Standing back-to-back they were a force to be reckoned with, and I pry my eyes away from them to focus on what we're up against. Forty or so of our team are fighting what seems like hundreds of his army.

I start to doubt we'll be able to overtake Excalibur. Was Uncle Joe able to create a portal to get the prisoners free?

Among those on Excalibur's side were vampires, immortals, and werewolves in their wolf form. The canines, larger than any wolf, bare their teeth. Then, jaws snapping, they leap toward my friends. I tried to send shockwaves of water in the direction of our enemies, but it's hard to single them out amid my teammates. Out of the corner of my eye, I catch a glimpse of Uncle Joe emerging from behind the archway alone. I can only hope that means the prisoners who had been with him have been portaled to safety.

"Take out her circle but leave the girl for me," Excalibur orders his followers, locking his gaze with mine in a staring contest.

His followers charge, and my team tries to counter and move around me. I try to tell them to stay behind me again, but they won't listen. I still don't know how I'm supposed to be able to defeat him. The water from my bombs has left the lawn a slick and dangerous mess. I direct a lightning bolt toward him, but he holds his hand up at the last second, and a shimmering force field surrounds him, effectively ricocheting the energy off into the wall with a loud crack as the wall crumbles in on itself.

So, he not only can mind control other immortals but can wield fire and have a shield? How the hell is this a fair fight? He slowly walks in my direction, his gaze never leaving mine. A thought occurs to me then—there's other ways to use water. I stop the storm clouds from drenching everybody and instead focus on making a spear out of ice. I close my eyes and take a deep breath.

I imagine a long sharp icicle like what you would find hanging off a roof in a snowy northern winter. Slowly the ice starts to form in my hand, not as big as I want, but it'll do. I need to wait until the right time to throw it. My parents and Uncle edge closer and closer to him from behind. My dad lunges at him with his dagger out and manages to stab him in the side. Excalibur cries out and twists too fast for my dad to react. Excalibur grabs my dad by the throat, and I take my shot, praying that I don't hit my dad.

The ice lodges itself in Excalibur's shoulder blade, and he screams out in agony. My dad falls to the ground as Excalibur releases his grip on his neck. With a flick of Excalibur's wrist, a wall of flames bursts up from the ground surrounding him and forces my family to back away. My dad scrambles to his feet, thank God. Excalibur roars in fury. He glares at me as he marches in my direction, his wall of flames moving with him. He reaches behind him with his hulk sized arm and pulls out the ice that had already started to melt from the flames around him. I put up my own defensive waterfall around myself and those next to me.

My palms are sweaty, and my arms hurt from holding them upright for so long. Dante is standing to my right, Maverick and Roger to my left. They all have their katanas and knives out, ready to strike him when he gets closer. I quickly scan the lawn transformed into a battlefield and wish I hadn't. There are at least thirty or so lifeless bodies sprawled on the ground. It's hard to tell who they are, but I recognize a few as our own by the vests on them. I have to fight back the tears that threaten to spill out. I can't show him weakness. He has to pay for what he's done. There will be time to mourn them after. I make a huge effort to focus on my enemy.

Our guys with the crossbows have started assaulting him from all directions. He doesn't slow his approach; he just puts his shimmery forcefield up like a bubble between him and the ring of fire he's created around him. The arrows bounce off and fall to the ground. I try more ice and water bombs, but nothing will go through it. I can't reach him.

"Your water is more potent than his fire," Dante shouts to me over all the chaos.

"What does that even mean?" I shout back, frustrated at the impasse.

"Go under. He's not blocking you from there," Maverick suggests.

That's true. The forcefield looks like it disappears at the ground level. I pull all the water from the ground around Excalibur and force it up into the bubble that protects him. I use as much of my will as I can to force the water level higher. The water rapidly fills the fishbowl up to his chest, and he's forced to drop his shield to let the water out before it drowns him. The water exits and extinguishes the flames around him, which makes him vulnerable.

Arrows fly at him as I ready more ice spears. Another one of my spears pierces his thick leg, my mother thrusts her sword into his abdomen. Excalibur wails, the sound rivaling the thunder booming above us. Uncle Joe and my dad, unable to join my mother in attacking Excalibur, are forced to fight off a werewolf and a vampire.

Excalibur swipes a hand in a circular motion, and flames leap up around him again, this time, though, trapping my mom inside with him. Dad and Uncle Joe are too far away with too many opponents between them. I send as much water as I can pull from all around us to put out the flames, but it isn't enough. Excalibur lifts my mom's small body up by her throat and into the air. Her legs kick at him as she wraps her own small hands around his massive neck.

Nobody can get close enough to help her. I run toward her, my feet pounding into the grass. I send a river of water rushing ahead of me, putting out the flames that surround him, only momentarily. I throw several ice spears, but the partial shield that surrounds him blocks them, shattering them to the ground. His shield doesn't reach the ground this time, so I'm unable to drown him with his own sphere. A high-pitched scream of pure agony cuts through all the noise, and all the fighters from both sides freeze and stare in its direction.

"No!" I shout as I throw water bomb after water bomb and spear after spear forcing them to go through the small opening at the bottom, hitting both Excalibur and his shield. I douse my mother in water to try to stop the fire from burning around her again.

Her screaming continues as a bright light emanates from within her, and my water is helpless against the fireball he creates inside her body. She's burning to death from within. I bring on a torrential downpour as well as a river up and over them. But it's too late. The screaming stops. Excalibur drops her lifeless body to the ground as smoke billows from her mouth. My raging river of water pulls Excalibur away from her. My dad sobs as he drops to his knees beside her. Making a sound that's even more pained than the screams that came out of her just moments ago.

He killed my mom. That monster just murdered her. This has to end now before he takes the lives of anybody else.

CHAPTER 13

ERIC

The time has finally come to deceive my dad and his boss. As much as I despise the man and the things he's done and made me do, he's still my dad. I want to spare him and Charlotte, but I don't know how I can manage it. After I kept watch and told the team the best place to come in, I headed in the direction of the dorms. Because I'm invisible now, nobody will notice me walking around this late at night.

I come to a standstill in the dark hallway. Raymond and Charlotte's dorm is just about fifty feet from me. He's been staying here more and more lately. They hardly ever come back to our house in Colorado anymore. It's actually been kind of nice to have the house to myself. I'm debating on whether or not to wake them so they can leave before shit gets dangerous. Raymond may deserve it but not Charlotte. She's just a human entranced by Raymond.

I knock softly on the door and wait. I haven't heard anybody else. I drop my vanishing act just in time as muffled footsteps on the other side reach the worn wooden door. My hands are shaking with nerves as the door whips open, blasting me in the face with wind.

"Eric, what's going on?" Raymond wipes away the sleep from his eyes.

"We need to talk. Can I come in?"

"This better be good. Do you have any idea what time it is?"

Raymond opens the door enough for me to step inside, and after shutting us in, he takes a seat at the small round table. Charlotte stirs in the bed on the other side of the room but quiets quickly. Raymond's icy stare prompts me to start talking before I back out.

"Listen, Dad, there's something-"

A loud explosion rocks the floor beneath us.

"What have you done?" Raymond snarls at me as Charlotte jumps out of bed, frightened by the noise.

"About the prophecy, there's another way. Sierra can-"

"You know nothing about the prophecy!"

"Sierra can defeat him, and she will. I'm telling you; she's got her own team. They can free us from Excalibur."

"Why couldn't you just leave it alone?" Raymond shakes his head. "What the hell's going on out there?"

Charlotte comes up behind him and places a hand on Raymond's shoulder, reminding me why I'm here.

"You need to create a portal and get out of here, get her to safety." I nod toward my step-mom.

Raymond stands so quick that the wooden chair he's sitting in falls backward, clanging on the hard floor. He strides around the table and stops in front of me. He then pokes his index finger into my chest hard enough to bend his finger.

"You do not tell me what to do, you understand me, boy?"

"They're getting the prisoners out and arresting Excalibur. Which side do you want to be on?" I whisper harshly as I poke him back in his sternum.

"I don't think that's what this is about at all. Not you doing what's right. Your moral compass is jaded just like mine. I wondered why you weren't capable of bringing

Sierra in. It makes perfect sense now." His eyes narrow at me as if I were nothing but a bug to be stepped on.

"What does?"

"You're in love with Sierra, aren't you?" he barks out the words as if they disgust him.

"That's got nothing to do-"

"Answer the damn question, son," he says in a deep growl as he cuts me off.

"Fine, yes I am. Are you fucking happy now? It doesn't change anything. Get Charlotte the hell out of here. She doesn't deserve to pay for your sins," I bark back at him.

"Then you're a fool. Love makes you weak. I raised you better than that." His upper lip curls in a snarl.

"No, loving someone isn't a weakness. It gives you something worth fighting for, a reason to live. A reason to be a better man."

"No, power is something worth fighting for. Excalibur has more power than you'll ever know because he didn't let a piece of ass get in his way."

Another explosion sounds. Whatever, I tried. There's nothing else I can do to change his mind. I walk out the door giving one last sympathetic look at Charlotte and hoping she can get out of here. I cloak myself again before jogging back the way I came, stopping by the window that overlooks the lawn. I scan the entire area until I find Sierra. She's toward the back of the lawn, close to where they portaled into. She's balancing a ball of water that she throws at Excalibur. Her brown hair blows around her as if she's in front of a fan. She's fierce and queenly standing there holding her own.

I was hoping it wouldn't come to this. I thought they could sneak in and get the prisoners out without Excalibur knowing. He's standing at the front of his small army of followers, and the odds aren't in her team's favor. I have to get down there and help her. I sprint toward the dungeons to make sure they're all out. I come around a corner too quickly and ram into somebody's hard body, and they yelp.

"Shit, I'm sorry." I quickly reach a hand out to steady the short red-haired woman I almost took out.

She jumps away and yells, her brown eyes darting around. With sharp daggers in both hands, she's standing guard, with her feet planted shoulder-width apart and in front of four sickly-looking people who I can only imagine would be some of the prisoners. I quickly drop my invisibility before she can stab me.

"It's okay." I hold my hands up to show her I'm not a threat. "I'm Eric, Emma's brother. What are you guys doing over here?"

She relaxes her stance a bit. "Oh! I'm Ruby. We got turned around when that ass-hat bombed our way out of here. We're just trying to find the others. For some reason, I can't create a portal."

I take out my blue benitoite wand and point it at the wall in front of me, but nothing happens. Huh, that's a new one. It must be Kairos's doing. I saw that bony freak show standing to the right side of Excalibur. I've been too drunk to be able to create a portal before, but I'm stone-cold sober, unfortunately. I think the whiskey would help calm the mess in my head right about now.

"Follow me. I can get you out of here."

"Lead the way, Casper."

I grin at her. I think I'm going to like this girl.

I direct them through a doorway a little farther down the hall, which leads to some tunnels that run underneath the fort. We should be able to go through those to get to the other side. Hopefully, the bomb didn't cave these in as well. Once we reach the right door, I see that it's locked. I take out my own knife and jam it under the hinge on the wood. I hit it hard with the palm of my hand, causing the hinge holding the padlock to break free.

I slowly open the door and peek inside. No noises are stemming from the tunnels. It's dark, but it seems like we're alone. I walk down the creaky stairs first and gesture for them to follow me once I reach the bottom. There are no wall sconces or torches down here, just darkness. I let my eyes adjust to the lack of lighting before proceeding down the dirt walkway. The walls were constructed out of reddish clay, and the ceiling was reinforced with thick wooden poles, making the tunnel look like a mineshaft.

It's been a long time since I've been down here, but I'm confident I'll be able to remember the way. Being here brings up another not-so-good memory. I used to meet a pretty little fairy that worked for Excalibur now and then. Once Raymond found out I was sleeping with the help, I never saw her again. He said she works in another country, but I wonder what really happened to her. Bringing my mind back to the present, I glance behind me to see Ruby holding up the back of our train.

There's something about her that draws me in. I'm not sure if it's her shiny stainless steel horseshoe gauges in her earlobes that match the thinner one hanging from her septum. Or if it's her tattoos running the length of her slim arms that beg me to take a closer look. It's as if she feels me looking at her; her sultry brown eyes meet mine and hold my gaze. I break away from her gaze to keep our pace going in the right direction. I can't get distracted by yet another woman.

I have to slow down because the prisoners behind me are falling behind. I knew withholding food and water was a way for Excalibur to get what he wanted from them. You'd be surprised what desperate people will do when they're on the verge of starvation. My body involuntarily shudders at the atrocities I've witnessed here. Some of them wished death would come, but he kept them fed and hydrated just enough to keep the angel of death away. We have to win today; I can only imagine what his sick twisted mind would think up to torture us.

We reach the end of the underpass, and I push my finger against my lips, shushing them while I place my ear against the wooden door we've come to. Satisfied that there's nobody on the other side, I turn the handle, but the door won't budge.

"Get back," I tell the others.

I take a step back and kick my right foot hard into a spot just next to the handle. The wood splinters and groans but otherwise holds steady. I do the same thing again, but I put all of my weight into it this time. The door breaks free from the handle, and slowly swings open, revealing a grassy lawn. This tunnel dumps out to the side of the fort through a hill. I try to make a portal again but still fail. The sounds of battle greet our ears, but they'll be safe here until we can get a portal open.

"If you stay here behind the mound, you should be safe. I doubt anybody will come out this far." I put my knife back into the sheath at my waist.

"I can't stay here; I have to get back to join the others. My team needs me," Ruby pleads with me.

"Yeah, but so do they." I wave a hand to the four prisoners standing silently behind her.

"Even though I highly doubt anybody would come back here, they aren't in any shape to fight off anything."

"I know." She lets out a frustrated growl as she fists her tiny hands.

"I'll see you around, Black Widow." I wink at her before turning and walking away.

This wasn't part of the plan. Get the prisoners, make them a portal to safety, defeat Excalibur. Standing guard with the helpless wasn't on the list. It sucks to do, but I would rather she stayed back here safe and I go back into the shit show. As I stick to the relative safety of the hills in hopes to come out by the side of the castle so I don't give away their position, a blood-curdling scream breaks over the noise of the battling on the front lawn. As I race toward the building to learn what's going on and who made that awful noise my breath is raspy. My clammy skin makes me shiver. It can't be Sierra, it just can't.

SIERRA

Excalibur manifests his wall of flames as he pulls a few stray arrows out of himself, grunting at each one. I don't see how he is still standing after all the times he's been hit. My emotions are affecting the weather without my control. The wind is whipping around us, the thunder rolls loudly, and the lightning is lighting up the scarified earth he left in his wake.

It's just him and me. The others have been knocked aside by the battle raging between us. Excalibur's fire to my water. It's exhausting to use my gift relentlessly like I've had to do. Nobody else can get close enough without getting harmed. I tried to protect them, to shield them from his fireballs but I failed.

The rage building inside me is like nothing I've ever felt before. He killed my mom. I will never see her face again, hear her sweet voice or feel her loving arms around me ever again. I thought I would lose my composure if something happened to anybody I cared deeply about. But there's nothing but anger and deep, dark hatred.

Excalibur has his shield up again, and I don't think the fishbowl trick will work on him a second time. He keeps leaving a small gap at the bottom. There's another water source that calls out to me. It's within the monster who destroyed my life. It's calling me, baiting me, begging me to use it. I twist my wrist as if I'm pulling on a string. Excalibur tilts his head as if wondering what I'm doing. Don't worry, you'll find out soon enough.

There it is. His eyes grow wide as he reaches for his throat. I pull on the water harder. The storm around us calms as I focus only on his water source. He's digging at his neck with both hands now. It's clear he can't breathe. The water I'm stealing from his body is stopping his lungs from expanding. He drops to his knees ten feet in front of me, shock written across his face. He knows he's lost. I finally found out how my gift is stronger than his. Our own bodies can be made up of sixty percent water. Excalibur is gasping for breath as his body crumples inward on itself.

Excalibur reaches out a hand and is able to create a small fireball, but I put that out easily. He's too weak to be able to manifest his shield again that dropped when he fell. I can feel him trying to invade my mind. My thoughts are starting to get fuzzy. I stare down at him into his blood-red eyes. I'm no longer afraid of him. I hold the power now. I push him out of my head with my own thoughts.

"Please, stop! We won't fight you anymore. Just please let him go!" an unknown voice yells out to me.

I look toward the voice and am taken aback by the face I see. A pretty brunette with shoulder-length hair and eyes that match mine. She holds a helmet in her hand by her thighs.

"Rosalee?" Uncle Joe asks, unsure of himself.

"Hello, brother," the woman he calls Rosalee answers him with a slight smile.

Brother? Is this Rosa, their sister who went missing?

"We thought you were dead, Rosa. Have you been helping him all this time?" His forehead wrinkles.

I watch the exchange between them, still keeping my hold on Excalibur.

"Please, he's my anima gemella," she pleads with me, her own eyes begging for me to show mercy. A mercy he doesn't deserve.

"And she was my mother!" I shout back.

As Rosalee's hazel eyes stare back into mine, the irises start altering until they turn into an almost pure gold color. A strange sensation comes over me, and I start to feel true terror. My throat closes up, my heart beats rapidly and my palms start to sweat. I take several shallow breaths. I blink a few times to clear the unshed tears in my eyes, and I place that strange feeling. That bitch was in my head. I snap out of the fear and twist my hand in her direction. I start draining water from her as well.

Her eyes widen and her mouth falls open. Rosalee drops to the ground beside Excalibur. Her gaze begs me to stop.

"Sierra! Stop! This is not who you are!" Dante shouts to me from a distance, an echo in the mayhem.

Even though the flames have been extinguished, both sides of the fight stay back and watch the drama unfolding. I ignore Dante and keep taking what belongs to me, all the fluid in Excalibur's and Rosalee's bodies. Excalibur's large soot-covered hand reaches out to me as if that would get me to stop.

"Don't become the monster that he is," my dad pleads in a strangled cry.

"He deserves to die," I say coldly as I continue to take his life little by little. The callousness in my voice surprises even me.

"He does, but not by your hand. He's down and not a threat. If you kill him now, that would be cold-blooded murder. You don't want that on your conscience." Dante's voice wavers.

"You don't know what I want." I narrow my eyes at Excalibur as he falls to his side, hitting the ground with a thud.

I keep Rosalee immobile with my powers as she struggles to breathe. I won't kill her, though; she didn't kill my mom. But he did. He needs to pay.

"But I do, Sierra. I'm your anima gemella. I'm the other half of you. We were born from the same flame. You're kind and caring. Show him mercy. Be the woman that your mom knew you were. The woman I know you to be. Don't let him dull your light." The last part was almost a whisper, a prayer for me to do what he thinks is right.

The prophecy. *Only her light can keep the darkness away, for without it, there is no hope.*

The tears welling up in my eyes are making my eyesight blurry. Dante's right. My mom wouldn't want this. She wouldn't recognize me if I did this. But he doesn't deserve to live either. I'm frozen, stuck between my choices. I don't know what I should do.

I release my hold on Rosalee first, allowing her to scramble over to Excalibur's body. I drop my hand in defeat, allowing Excalibur to start gasping for air. My teammates immediately surround Excalibur and Rosalee.

My dad's sobbing cuts me like a knife, and I slowly walk over to where he's sitting on the ground. He had pulled my mom into his lap, and he's rocking her lifeless body back and forth and kissing her forehead.

"I'm sorry, Sophia. I'm so sorry I couldn't save you. I love you." He repeats that mantra over and over again.

I kneel, place my arms tightly around him, and let a few tears begin to fall. My mom's expressionless face nearly makes me drop to my knees and beg her for forgiveness. The guilt of not being enough to save her is too much to bear. On shaky legs, I get up and walk back to where Dante and a small group of our team have assembled around Excalibur and my aunt Rosalee if you can even call her that. She's not deserving of that title.

The fighting ceased from both sides once my mother was killed. I think they all knew the war was over at that point. Or at least, it was only between him and I.

"Can you make the portal to the guard in Graystone?" I ask Dante, not trusting my own ability to create one. We took our sapphire allegiance stones out of Shanghai for this reason.

"Hey, beautiful, take some time. We can take care of them in a little while. I'll make sure they get where they need to be. Go be with your dad; he needs you now." Dante wraps his arms around me.

I hug him back, but I'm not going to rest until he's in jail. "My dad needs that murderer to be locked away, so that's what I'm going to do," I tell him in a stern voice.

"Okay, if that's what you want."

He takes out his wand-shaped portal stone and points it to the ground in front of us. The scene swirls around and around until it creates a portal to Graystone. There's a large stone building with huge iron doors on the other side. I've never been there before, but I recognize it from the descriptions Dante has given me.

"Let's go," I snap at both Rosalee and Excalibur.

Excalibur's deep red eyes narrow as he lifts his chin up in defiance. I twist my wrist and start to pull water from his evil body again as a reminder that I'm in charge here, not him. His lips grow into a tight line.

"Ah!" I yelp as my stomach starts to get hot.

It's as if a hot poker was stabbing me in the abdomen. I clutch at my belly and hunch over. It dawns on me then what's happening. This is what Excalibur did to my mom. I'm going to die too. I struggle as I continue drawing water from him and direct the liquid into myself to try to put out the fire burning within my body. Our eyes are locked together. A battle of wills.

Maverick drives his blade into Excalibur's side which only seems to make my pain worse. He doesn't pull his gaze away until another scream lets out beside me.

"Excalibur, let her go or I'll do it!" Dante shouts.

Rosalee is kneeling in front of Dante while facing Excalibur. Dante has a fistful of her brown hair in his hand pulling her head back and baring her neck. Tears stream down her face. The sharp tip of his dagger breaking the skin. Blood beads up and makes a trail down the pale column of her throat.

Excalibur's nostrils flair and he closes his eyes tight.

"Now, or I'll kill her," Dante growls.

The pain eases in my stomach and I yank hard on my grasp of his liquid, until he can barely breathe. Dante shoves Rosalee to the ground as he rushes to me.

"Are you okay?" his voice trembles as he runs his hands all over my body looking for injuries.

"Thanks to you, I am." I lean against Dante's side.

Maverick and Thomas drag Excalibur up to his feet while Tony and Roger man handle Rosalee into Graystone. Excalibur shuffles his feet as Maverick hauls him through the portal. I immediately trail behind. I'm not going to let them get away this time.

Some of my team stays back on the other side of the portal to make sure all of the traitorous bastards come through. I take a deep breath and try to clear my head. I can't fall apart yet. I owe this to my mom. Just as I thought, the familiar welcoming party of the blue-uniformed immortal enforcers arrive right after us.

At first, they look a little confused at the number of immortals, werewolves, and vampires coming through the portal, then they notice me.

Asher, the lead enforcer says to me, "You?"

"We need to see Ryker immediately," I command him in what I believe is an I-don't-take-no-shit voice.

"We don't answer to you," he scoffs.

"Well, maybe you and every other enforcer should, seeing as how our team was able to capture Excalibur and his Revolution while everyone here sat on their asses in their well-protected cushy little buildings." Wow, I need to think before I speak. Or maybe not. I really don't care at this point. What do I have to lose?

Asher looks around our bruised and beaten crew as more and more come through the portal from India. He grabs the radio off his belt.

"This is Asher, I need all available enforcers as well as the High Council at the guard."

"On our way." The radio crackles.

I still have a hold on Excalibur in case he tries anything again. One look from Rosalee, and I'll do the same to her. She doesn't need to be messing around in my head either.

Chapter 14

DANTE

I thought the way Sierra wielded her gift in the beginning was magnificent, but after her mom's death something changed in her. There was a darkness inside her that I'd never seen before. When she almost killed Excalibur, she seemed cold and calculating. I'm not saying he didn't deserve to die because he definitely does not deserve to live. I know what it's like to take a life, and that really messes with you. Unfortunately, that's a part of being an immortal guardian. But Sierra has yet to go through all the training that prepares her for what she'll need to do. Killing Excalibur the way she was going to was wrong.

I wasn't quite sure what was going on with some of the Revolutionaries that we captured at first. Quite a few of them were crying or straight up wailing. In the beginning, I thought they were just showing remorse for their actions or trying to get out of being sent to the guard, but as I listened, the reason became more and more evident. Before we attacked, Reid and Konstantina weren't able to find a way to break the hold on those being mind-controlled by Excalibur. But somehow the link broke. All of these immortals and dark ones are coming to terms with all they have done against their will. I can only imagine the brutalities that Excalibur had made them commit.

"Hello Dante, I'm Nilo. I'm acting Master Council while Ryker and two others are taking a leave of absence." The burly built councilmen with the brown wide-set eyes gives my hand a firm shake.

"Hello Nilo. What happens now?" I ask.

"I'm dispatching enforcers to take statements from each and every person involved from both sides. Everybody who fought alongside Excalibur in the battle will be held in a cell until my enforcers can clear them of any wrong doing. Some chose to be by his side of their own free will."

"What about Excalibur?" I've barely taken my eyes off that vile man since he was able to put a fireball in Sierra. My fists clench.

"I have a special place for him. Excalibur happens to be my half-brother and I've been trying to break his hold on the High Council and everybody else for centuries. There was no way to fade away the glamour he held on them." Nilo pauses. "Excalibur had to die in order for him to release them, or in this case, Excalibur was brought to the brink of death and chose to let go of them to use what little energy he had left to fight for his life. Excalibur knew his end was near. Nobody was powerful enough to kill Excalibur before now. Before Sierra."

My beautiful, courageous Sierra.

"How did he have multiple gifts? I've never heard of that before." I glance at Sierra beside me to make sure she's okay. The fire that burned inside of her didn't do lasting damage.

"He found a way to alter his own genes by transfusing his blood with others' in a ritual much like the transition ceremony. Unfortunately he took the shielding ability from my blood. But that's how he wasn't able to control me, because of my gift." Nilo shakes his head as he turns his gaze to Excalibur.

"Is that why he was drawing blood from the prisoners?"

"I'm afraid so. All these years working alongside Ryker and watching his every move, knowing that Ryker was being manipulated, as were many others, has finally paid off. My team has created a prison that is off the books specifically to hold Excalibur. I was aware of the prophecy and knew this day would come eventually. The prison is located at the top of Mount Olympus in Greece, where Excalibur will be held prisoner for the rest of his life."

The remaining three black-robed councilmen and women who were left command the scene with such grace that it demands respect. Nilo turns his attention to Sierra whose been silently watching Excalibur and Rosalee this whole time.

"Ms. Walker, I'm truly sorry for your loss, and I know this is a bad time to ask anything of you, but I do need your help." Nilo's kind eyes look down on Sierra with warmth.

"Where were you when we needed help?" Sierra lifts her chin and glares at him in defiance.

"Fair question." He pauses. "I'm afraid I had to wait for the right time. If I had helped you before now, Excalibur would've known, and we wouldn't have been able to imprison him."

"What do you need from me?" Sierra looks in the direction of Excalibur, and her eyes narrow.

I know she still has a hold on him. Sierra won't let him get away this time. There are three other enforcers with Asher, the lead enforcer surrounding him. Excalibur's hands are bound behind his back with iron handcuffs. I'm sure he's been taking the pills to block the iron's ability to block his gifts, unless iron doesn't affect him either. Who knows how many tricks he has up his sleeves? An immortal has never had more than one gift before, and he had three that we're aware of.

"I'll need you to keep Excalibur compliant while we transfer him to his permanent location and help us with the spell that will bind him there." Nilo rubs his arm under his robe sleeve, revealing leathery-looking pale skin.

"I don't know how much more she can withstand, sir. She's been using her gift constantly for the past few hours. Even being linked to Reid and Konstantina, she'll run out of energy soon." I cross my arms over my chest. Who the hell does he think he is? Hasn't she done enough already?

My thoughts think back to about two weeks ago in Mongolia when she passed out because she overused her gift. I reach an arm out to Sierra and hug her close, fearing that may happen again.

"It's fine. I can do it." Sierra's exhales a deep breath and her lips form a tight line.

"We'll depart in ten minutes." Nilo walks away from us and toward another group of enforcers that I don't recognize.

I watch as Nilo converses with the group, they're wearing the same dark blue uniform as the rest of the immortal enforcers, but the shoulder sleeve insignia doesn't resemble the typical immortal enforcer shield with the swords behind it. These have a mountain with the sun just above the ridges. The badge is familiar, but I can't place it. Then I notice the handgun in a black holster at each one of their hips and wonder if these were the men that shot our people. My eyes find Reid's, and it's clear he came to the same conclusion when he gives me a curt nod. We can't let our guard down yet.

Sierra's getting more and more tired by the minute. She has dark circles growing under her eyes, and her breathing is growing labored. The energy she's siphoning from Reid and Konstantina is ending. This is what I was afraid was going to happen. Luckily, they had anticipated the possibility of them not being enough to sustain Sierra on their own. Reid and Konstantina had done another linking spell tying themselves to Levi and Maggie. The spell had already been cast. They just had to finalize it by sliding the gemstone bracelets on one of each of the four warlock's arms. Nilo is true to his word. Ten minutes later, we were ready to transfer Excalibur to his prison. They had six immortal enforcers chained at the waist to Excalibur encircling him in a mass of iron and brute strength. They weren't taking any chances of him breaking free, I hope.

The brawny enforcer with the buzz cut is barking orders at his men as he paces back and forth in front of those who are chained to the enemy. The flint-eyed immortal gives off major drill sergeant vibes as I watch him with wary eyes. I really hope these are the good guys, I can't handle another horrible twist of fate. He stops his measured steps and faces Nilo.

"We're ready when you are, sir."

"Are you ready?" Nilo asks our group but looks to Sierra for confirmation.

"I'm ready," Sierra replies in a powerful voice resembling somebody who hasn't been through the wringer.

Nilo takes out a blue benitoite portal stone and points it down. Slowly a doorway to a rough-mountainess looking landscape forms on the other side. Nilo steps through first, then the drill sergeant, followed by the group of 7. Sierra and I trail behind Excalibur so she can keep him in her sights, the four warlocks behind us lending Sierra their strength. The chill of the breeze coming through the trees makes me shiver involuntarily. Once we're all on the other side and greeted by a land full of trees and rock ledges, Nilo closes the portal and addresses us again.

"We have to walk the rest of the way to the top of the peak. There's a barrier that nobody can portal through."

That would have been nice to know beforehand, seeing as how my team is in t-shirts and the others have robes or full sleeves. I tuck Sierra into my side, trying to shield her from the bite of the wind as she instantly wraps her arms around herself. We follow along quietly as Nilo leads us farther and farther into the mountainside. We portaled about three-quarters of the way to the top. The higher we go, the thinner the trees and air become, making it cold enough to see our breath. Just when I think we need to find a way to warm ourselves, a cave appears around a bend in the trail.

The entrance is guarded by four more enforcers wearing the same insignia on their shoulders. They step aside silently to allow us to pass through, and I can't help but feel even more outnumbered. I wish I would've brought more of my own team with me. Excalibur has been eerily silent this whole time, making me even more nervous. We stop a short way into the cavern, a wall of bars blocking our way. A frail-looking old man with long gray hair slowly gets up from a stool by the opening to the blockade. As he gets closer, I notice his eyes are clouded over. The knobby wooden cane he's leaning heavily on seems to also aid his blindness.

"Don't be fooled by appearances. I may be blind, but I see more than you'll ever know." His deep raspy voice fills the walls of the cave.

It's as if he's reading my mind, which is unsettling.

"Ms. Walker, my name is Teiresias." The old man holds a hand out for Sierra to put hers in.

Sierra looks at me, and I shrug as she reaches her small hand out to his. As soon as he clasps it inside his own, she lets out a gasp. I lunge toward him, thinking he must be hurting her. "It's okay." Sierra holds her other hand out, keeping me back.

I'm left there hanging in the balance as her eyes close. I look at Reid and the others, and they look as uncomfortable as I feel. Konstantina seems to be the only one at ease with this situation as she looks admiringly at the elderly person. I scrunch my eyebrows together at her, hoping to gain her attention, but it's useless. She's just as raptured as Sierra is with her eyes shut.

Sierra slowly pulls her hand out of his as she nods to him like he'd see her with his sightless eyes. What am I missing here? What the hell is going on? I hate being left out. Her eyes finally find mine in the dimly lit cave, and she mouths the words, "trust me?" I nod for an answer even though I have no clue what's going on.

"Ms. Konstantina and Mr. Reid, will you follow us, please?"

"Yes, of course, sir," Konstantina replies without hesitation.

Reid raises his eyebrows at me, clearly just as confused as I am but answers the man with a yes.

"Unchain him," Nilo orders the sergeant, making me question his loyalties. Every muscle in my body tenses, ready for an attack.

Sierra holds her hand up, her beautiful eyes begging me to wait this out. So instead of following them into the dark unknown of the cave, the rest of us are forced to wait at the entrance. Only Teiresias, Konstantina, Reid, Sierra, Nilo, and Excalibur walk past the barriers protruding from the walls. Every instinct I have is yelling at me to follow them; we don't know these people. I told Sierra that I trust her, and although I don't understand what passed between Teiresias and her when he took her hand, the way she looked at him tells me that she trusts him. I shove my hands in my pockets and start pacing the small space in the cave, hating that there's nothing for me to do.

SIERRA

When Teiresias took my hand in his, it was like one of those old analog projectors flashing through my eyes. So many pictures flashed in front of me it was dizzying. I saw what appeared to be a much younger Teiresias writing the prophecy that has plagued me down on parchment. Fast forward a little, and there's a young boy who looks like he could be Excalibur being held down and tortured by doctors. Later on, it shows him getting revenge on his tormenters as a young man. He's identical to Excalibur, just without a face full of years of hatred and the scars that mar his features. The last image that burned into my eyes was my mother, her stomach swollen with late pregnancy as she kneeled at the feet of Teiresias. She was looking up to him with a radiant smile on her face and tears glittering her eyes.

Seeing my mother's beaming face makes my heart hurt even more. I long to see that beautiful smile of hers. I don't know how she knew Teiresias, but she trusted him. I know I can too, then. Does that mean she knew of the prophecy? That thought lingers in my brain as I follow the others farther and farther into the mountain. It's surprisingly warmer in the cave than I thought it would be.

Torches lit aflame on the walls light a path forward and cast the hall in a flickering orange glow. I'm not letting go of my hold on Excalibur. I increased the amount of water I drew from him as soon as Nilo ordered his men to unchain him. We've come so far; he will pay for what he's done if it's the last thing I do. I can feel my energy waning a little the farther we get from Maggie and Levi.

I narrow my eyes just thinking about her. That blonde bimbo better not even think about making a move on my man, witch or not, I'll wreck her. Even though she's helping me at the moment there's something about her that sets off the alarm bells in my head. I can't put my finger on it, but I know it's more than just her flirting with Dante. She's hiding something, and I plan on finding out exactly what she's planning.

Scuffling feet draw my attention back up to the men walking in front of me. Excalibur grabs the cane from Teiresias, causing the elderly man to stumble. Nilo reaches out to catch Teiresias, freeing Excalibur from his grip in the process. I curl my fingers in tighter to my wrist as I point my hand in Excalibur's direction, and I jerk my hand toward my body.

Excalibur falls to his knees on the stone floor, grasping his throat and glaring at me. If pure unadulterated hatred had a look, that would be what he shows me now.

"Enough, we're almost there," Teiresias's raspy voice cuts through my thoughts of just ending this bastard. "Trust me, this will be worse for him."

I know he's right, so I let up just enough to allow him to stand and follow Teiresias. Finally, after about a mile hike through the tunnels, we round a sharp bend that opens into a large cavern. Torches line the walls and a large iron-barred cell with a bed, a toilet, and a sink rests in the center of the space. The only other furniture in the room is a teak wood table.

"This won't hold me, brother," Excalibur huffs out.

"I wouldn't be so sure, *brother*," Nilo replies, gesturing for him to walk into the open cell door. When Excalibur doesn't move, Nilo shoves at his back and thrusts him forward.

Once Excalibur is in the prison cage and Nilo locks it shut, a woman steps from the shadows. She resembles Konstantina's features but not her fashion sense.

"Hello my friends, my name is Willow."

The hem of a long black dress with cap sleeves, trails along the floor as she draws a large circle around the cell block with a line of salt. A candle and box of matches sits on the ground along six points of the circle of salt around Excalibur's new home.

"Sierra, if you can come stand here, please," Willow says is a sweet comforting voice.

I go to the spot she indicates. Then Willow goes clockwise to the next candle.

"Konstantina, I'll have you stand here."

Konstantina takes her place.

"Here, I will have you, Nilo."

"Yes, ma'am."

"Reid, you will stand here."

He comes to stand stiffly across from me.

"And lastly, Teiresias-"

"I know where to go, Willow," he says teasingly.

Willow picks up the empty table save for a small white selenite plate and carries it just past the salt line into the circle. We follow her lead of picking up our white candle and matches. As we light them, a faint vanilla smell envelopes the room. The sweet scent instantly calms some of my nerves. This is almost over. Just a little longer, then I don't have to worry about Excalibur ever again. I can do this.

Willow starts chanting in another language as she moves clockwise from person to person with a large gold chalice embedded with gemstones around the center ring. Starting with me, she reaches out for my hand, and I can already tell I'm not going to like what's going to happen next. Sure enough, from her black dress's pocket, she pulls out a dagger with a black handle embedded with purple taaffeite stones and a shiny silver blade, similar to my transition back in Graystone. Why do these things always have to be sealed in blood?

I swallow hard and grind my teeth together as she slices the razor-sharp blade through the meaty part of my palm, creating a gash about an inch and a half long. My dark red blood wells up and drips into the cup below. After just a few seconds, my blood is already starting to slow its trickle, I squeeze my hand into a fist to make the blood drip faster. The sun-kissed witch walks to Konstantina and does the same and repeats the process with the remaining three. After she takes Teiresias' blood, she walks over to the small table and sets the chalice on the round selenite plate and cuts herself.

She pulls a large black leather pouch from around her neck and slowly puts the contents into the chalice. The way her body is angled, I can't see what's in the bag. She steps back to her spot at the circle and chants again. This time Konstantina and Reid join her spell that was written and placed with their candles.

Each verse is louder than the previous. A gust of wind rushes through the cave and lifts my hair as the candles flicker. A coolness settles over me like when I call to my element. Next, I'm warmed as if I'm next to a campfire or fireplace as the small cavern is filled with the earthy scent of composting leaves from the forest.

"The ancestors have heard us, and they agree that Excalibur should not be allowed freedom to cause more harm to others. They will bind us and these stones to the spell that entraps him here for the rest of time."

She grabs the chalice of our blood sacrifice and walks up to me, taking another smaller leather medicine pouch from around her neck. Handing the bag to me, she says, "For you Sierra, Immortal Savior, I give you black obsidian to aid in the protection of our spell."

She reaches into to chalice and pulls out a quarter-sized black stone stained with our mixed blood and places it into the open black leather satchel. She walks to Konstantina next, "For you, Konstantina, daughter mine, I give you red jasper to give us all the courage we need to do our duty." She places a tumbled red stone with brown streaks into Konstantina's black leather pouch.

Konstantina's her daughter? That's why they look so similar.

"For you Nilo, protector of the prophesied ones, I give you celestite to aid in the divine's help." A pretty pale blue tumbled stone goes in his.

Willow reaches back into the cup and pulls out a small amber-colored stone with dark brown stripes. "For you, Reid, master enchanter, I give you tigers eye to protect our binding from curses of evil. And for you, Teiresias, soul seer of the deities, I give you lapis lazuli to protect us all from psychic attacks." A smooth striking cobalt stone goes into his small bag. "For myself, enchantress of the ancestors, I will take onyx to protect this tomb from negative energies." She places the last of the stones, a small black stone closely resembling my obsidian from the cup and into her own pouch that's around her neck.

"Sierra, you can let go of your hold of him now. He's not going anywhere." She places a firm hand on my shoulder, her warm motherly eyes telling me it's okay.

As I slowly release the water I have been pulling from Excalibur's eerily silent body, exhaustion creeps into me. Half way out of the cave, Teiresias stops and turns to us.

"Unfortunately, the spell's strength will wane in time and will need to be maintained every month during the full moon for the best protection. The only way to break this spell and free Excalibur is for somebody to be able to get all the stones from us and cast a reversal spell." Teiresias clasps his pouch in his hands. "Each of us must protect our stone at all costs, and if any ill will comes to you, your child or closest family member will inherit the responsibility of being one of the six keys."

The reality of what he's saying is setting in. I will never be free from Excalibur and the pain he's caused my family. I have to come here every month until I die? It seems I'm being punished right along with Excalibur. I can't help but think if I just killed him back in India, he wouldn't have a hold on my life anymore.

"It is with profound gratitude that I thank each of you for your ongoing sacrifice. I know this isn't the outcome you thought we would come to." He glances at me. Crap, I need to remember this guy always seems to know what I'm thinking. "We all have a destiny we follow that's been laid out before our time. We are but instruments of the divine."

The rest of the walk back to the cave entrance is quiet. Each of my steps feeling heavier than the previous. I can't wait to go to sleep I'm so tired. The increase in sunlight trickling into the cave alerts us that we're close to the exit.

CHAPTER 15

ERIC

I was one of the last to go through the portal to Graystone. I wanted to ensure every single person willingly helping Excalibur, would be charged with whatever the boys in blue decided they deserved. Just as I suspected, Raymond didn't heed my advice. He and Charlotte were forced into Graystone by an immortal from Dante's team. He's made an impression on me, but for the life of me, I can't remember his name. The poor guy has a face only a mother can love.

Ruby and the four prisoners she's escorting are making their way over to where I'm standing. An immortal enforcer put cuffs on Raymond, and once they bring him into the prison, it felt as if a weight is lifted off from my chest. His hold over me is over. I can be who I want now, not his little pawn. Charlotte is cuffed too and imprisoned. I feel bad for her, though. She's just a simple human caught up in immortal affairs.

"Was that your dad?" A soft voice breaks my gaze from the building.

I turn to find Ruby standing beside me, rocking back and forth on her combat boots, a knowing look on her face. "That obvious?"

"Well, besides the resemblance, I figured nobody else can make you look that way." Ruby shrugs.

"Are you okay?" I look at her from head to toe, searching for any signs of injury.

"I'm good. I wasn't hurt. How about you?"

"Nah, I'm fine." I run my hand through my short black hair. Suddenly I feel exhausted. "Are there any hotels here where I can crash?"

"Right, you've never been to Graystone, have you?"

"First time." I shove my hands into my pockets.

I don't see Sierra and Dante anywhere, there are so many immortals, witches, and warlocks in the grassy area around me. I don't spot anybody else that I know besides Maverick, and he's busy with the enforcers.

An immortal enforcer comes over to us and takes each of our statements and determines that we're free to go, for now anyway. A medic tends to the four sickly thin followers Ruby had led from their cells. Leaving the enforcers to take care of the prisoners, Ruby starts to walk toward more tall buildings.

"Are you coming, Casper?" Ruby asks, looking back at me over her shoulder, a grin on her face.

"Right behind you, Widow." I jog to catch up to her.

Ruby and I walk side by side through the narrow alleys leading to the town square. The heart of Graystone is a large open space with shops encircling the perimeter, doors held open to the public. A large round water fountain sits in the center, with a few people sitting on the concrete sides. She points out several places to eat and shop and other places to avoid. I can't believe my dad kept me away from here. This place looks astonishing.

Raymond doesn't have the immortal tattoo that I've seen on most of the others. Maybe he's never been here himself, and I wonder how long Excalibur had Raymond under his wing. Ruby continues walking past the center and underneath a stone archway. We follow along the cobblestones until she stops in front of a towering brick building with large glass doors.

Opening the glass door for her, I let Ruby go in first, her clunky boots echoing off the tile and bouncing off the high ceilings. The tall blonde girl standing behind a dark wood podium offers Ruby and I a friendly smile.

"Checking in?" The woman with a gold name tag that reads Natalie asks.

"Yes."

"Would you like the honeymoon suite?"

"Um, uh, no," Ruby stammers.

"Two separate rooms, please," I tell her while grinning at Ruby. She can be ready for the battlefield without a sweat, but the thought of sharing a room with a man makes her clam up? This is going to be fun.

We finish checking in and grab our key cards. Ruby and I take a right past the lobby and wait at the elevator in awkward silence. I've held my laugh in, but I can't fight the grin. She rolls her eyes. Once inside, we travel up to the fifth floor. My card says 518, and hers is 520. Moving down the corridor, we reach my room first. She walks a few more feet and stops. Our rooms are side by side. Perfect.

"You sure you don't want to come in?" I wiggle my eyebrows at her.

"I, uh. I have some things I have to take care of, but I'll see you later?"

"Sure." I didn't think she would anyways, but why not try. "How about you show me around some more tomorrow?"

"Yeah, I can do that." She nods as she slides her key card into the slot on the door. "Later."

"Goodnight."

She quickly enters the room. I slip into my room and flick the light switch. Damn, if this is a regular room, I can only imagine what an upgraded room would look like. Every piece of furniture screams high class with its gleaming dark gray wood and black accents. The bathroom has a large white Jacuzzi tub surrounded by light gray walls. The counter is the same shade as the tub, with trial-sized toiletries set on the counter.

I walk across the plush carpet to the large queen bed with light gray bedding and fall backward onto it. The squishy mattress envelopes me in comfort, the memory foam forming to what my body needs for support. I could get used to this; my bed back home is a flat unforgiving board in comparison.

Sitting back up, I pull my phone out of my pocket. I should call Emma and let her know what happened. She answers the call on the first ring, and I tell her everything that I know. I wish I could've seen Sierra, but the enforcer said she left with the guards holding Excalibur. She must be a wreck. We had some get-togethers over the years with both of our families, and I really liked Sophia. You could tell she really loved Sierra, the way a parent should, not like my dad. I don't even know who my real mom is. Raymond told me she died giving birth to me, but I don't believe him. I just have this feeling that she's out there somewhere.

I talk to my sister for a while until I know she's okay. Emma spent a lot of time over at Sierra's; it's no wonder that she would be this upset over Sophia's death. I wish I could comfort Sierra too. She must be hurting so bad, and again there's nothing I can do. I have no idea where she is. I pinch the bridge of my nose, feeling so many conflicting emotions at once. I blurted out to Raymond that I was in love with Sierra. Why would I do that? Nobody knew besides me -Dante and Emma both suspect it, but I didn't voice it- and it should've stayed buried. That's just another piece of ammo for dear old dad to use against me. He's right, he did raise me better than that. The bad guy never gets the girl.

I grab the remote on the nightstand and flick through the channels on the big screen T.V. hanging on the wall. I stop at an action movie I don't recognize and walk over to the mini bar in the corner of the room. The glass front door reveals a few bottles in there that catch my eye.

After selecting a cold bottle of Bacardi rum and a ginger ale, I pour some into a disposable cup from the coffee caddy and mix them together with a plastic coffee stirrer. I sit back on the pillow-top mattress and watch the movie without really paying attention.

What am I going to do? Now that I'm the captain of my own life, with endless possibilities at my fingertips, I just don't know what to do. I know one thing for sure, I'm reaching out to Sierra tomorrow. I can put my own stuff aside. She lost her mother and I won't abandon her yet. As painful as it'll be for me, I want to be there for her.

RUBY

After I shut the heavy hotel room door and lean my back against it, I slide down until I sit on the thick rug. I don't know what it is about Eric that makes me so flustered. I've always been known to flirt with the guys, but it doesn't come easily to me with him. His tantalizing eyes roaming over my body does things to me that I haven't felt in a long time. I've heard little snippets of rumors about him trying to get in between Dante and Sierra. I can't fathom anybody being able to do that, but I don't want to encourage a relationship with Eric if he's pining over Sierra.

I agreed to show him around Graystone tomorrow without really thinking. I feel for the guy, I do, but I get attached to people far too easily. I don't want to set myself up for heartbreak, but God, those striking dark blue eyes show years of pain hidden in them, which makes me want to help him more. Maybe I can be for him what Alex has been for me all these years. If not for Alex, I really don't know where I'd be, possibly in a shallow grave for my uncanny addiction to getting into trouble.

I have a place in town. I don't even know why I booked a room, to begin with. He's muddling my thoughts and jumbling my brain like a washing machine. Maybe I didn't want to go home to an empty apartment, or maybe I knew deep down that he needed me. That's what I'm going with. I pace the room long enough to think that I can call Alex without sounding like a babbling lunatic spouting off random crap.

He answers on the first ring. "Are you okay?"

"Yes, you're not going to believe this, but we pulled it off. Not without casualties, unfortunately." My heart aches for those that we lost.

"I'm so sorry, Ruby. I wish I could've helped," he sighs.

"I know, Alex. I'm just glad you're safe from this mess." I sit in the chair overlooking the hotel's courtyard. It's super late at night, so it's completely barren. The little bistro tables look inviting, though.

With Alex being the beta werewolf, he stood to lose everything he's worked so hard at if he gave us an assist. He would be exiled from his pack, and other werewolves in the area wouldn't accept an exiled wolf into their pack. He would literally turn into a lone wolf. I don't want that for him. This world is cruel enough already to the dark ones. But that, I'm afraid, is a battle for another day.

Excalibur caused such a ruckus with the dark ones by having them come out of the shadows of the humans. They won't disappear from the world again, and I don't blame them for that. I wish humans weren't so arrogantly greedy and having to be at the top of the food chain. They're the reason we can't live out in the open. I've only voiced these opinions to Alex, just saying the words out loud can get me in a shit ton of trouble.

I know it makes me sound as mad as Excalibur is, but I think in the beginning maybe he too had good intentions. He just got so twisted with greed and vengeance that it darkened his soul for good. Speaking of dark souls, Sierra, so filled with light and goodness, even has a dark spot. That was made apparent after Sophia was killed. That was a plot twist if I ever saw one. I never thought her capable of something like that. Grief can do some awful things to people.

The sounds of pure agony coming from Michael, though, is something that's going to stick with me. I shiver. I haven't personally met somebody whose soul mate has passed, but I've heard of them; they're called the wanderers. They spend the rest of their living life searching for their bonded one. Most are never the same again, just an apparition of the person before their loss. Then there are those who completely turn off their feelings and turn into killing machines for the High Council. They take the jobs even we SIAs won't take. Most are straight-up suicide missions. But I guess when faced with the opportunity to be united with your soulmate again, death by someone else's hand will get you there.

I vent to Alex, careful not to talk about certain topics over the phone. You never really can trust any government's overreach. Hopefully, tomorrow I'll find out what's in store for me after leaving Graystone. Eventually my mind shuts down and allows me to fall into a deep sleep.

The following morning a knock at the door wakes me. I clamor out of bed and throw the soft plushy pink robe on and check the peep hole. Sure as the sun comes up, it's Eric. Ahh. I throw my head back and roll my eyes. I'm not ready for this yet. It's only—I squint my eyes trying to read the green digital display of the alarm clock—noon! I feel like I just barely fell asleep.

"Just a minute," I call to him as I dart into the bathroom to see how much of a train wreck I am.

Damn, I'm a bit rough. Maybe it'll be enough to get him to back off a little, but is that what I want? Well, there's no time to fret over it. I take the safety chain off and open the door to see him standing there holding two trays of food and barely able to stop himself from dropping them. The cups look precariously close to their tipping point.

"I thought I'd score us some breakfast before they closed. Can I come in?" He flashes me a grin.

I push the door open wider to allow him to pass through. "I'm sorry, I just woke up when you knocked. I haven't had time to shower and dress yet." I pat down my pixie hair that no doubt looks like I stuck a finger in a light socket, suddenly feeling too conspicuous.

"I noticed." He winks, actually winks at me. "I don't mind. I think it's a good look on you."

Feeling too exposed, I grab my clothes that I threw on the floor last night in my haste to get to bed, paling when I realize my bright red bra and panties are on the top of the pile. Just what he needs to see, not! I wrap them inside my pants and head to the loo, hoping against all odds he didn't notice them.

"I'll be right out," I say while shutting the bathroom door. I dress quickly and splash cold water on my face. I gently press the soft terry hand towel to my face trying to smooth out the lines made from my pillowcase before walking back out.

"Thank you for bringing me breakfast." He's already set plates and two hot cups on the small round table when I come out, as well as an unmistakable black bottle of Bailey's Irish Cream. Well, hello, how did he know I liked me some Bailey's in the morning?

"I figured it was the least I could do if you're going to put up with me all day." Eric shrugs like it's not a big deal to bring a chick you barely know breakfast.

The morning light peeking through the barely-there lace curtains highlights the dark circles under his eyes. This man in front of me has some demons hidden away in his closet, but who am I to judge? I have plenty of my own. People don't usually do things like this for me without a catch. My mistrust of men stems from my childhood but doesn't end there, unfortunately I seem to attract the bad ones. There really is no shortage of assholes in the world. I'm really hoping he doesn't fall into that category.

"I'm putting up with you all day?" I ask as a joke, and a smile comes easily to me as I think about spending time with him.

"If you'll have me." Eric smiles but it doesn't reach his eyes. It's more for show. I have a feeling he and I are more alike than I realized.

"Have you heard anything about what's going to happen to everybody that deflected?" I ask to change the subject.

"I heard that Nilo arrived back in Graystone in the late morning hours. Obviously, they're overwhelmed with the amount of people to deal with, so I think it's a safe bet that we have a few days before they get to everybody." He forcefully stabs a chunk of bacon with his fork, and I watch as it disappears between his pearly whites.

He licks his lips after swallowing the greasy goodness. Forcing myself to look away as I start to pick at my own food, I'm taken aback at how good it tastes. My stomach growls as I begin to eat my eggs, bacon, and hash browns

"I didn't know if you like Bailey's or not, but I can't have my coffee without it, so don't mind me," Eric says as he pours a hefty amount into his white paper cup.

"It's actually my favorite, so don't mind if I do." I reach for the bottle and our fingers just barely touch, but it's enough to send heat coursing through my body. I gasp. Our eyes meet and my cheeks heat under his intense gaze.

I decide a large amount of alcohol may be a good idea and douse my own cup with it. Once we finish with our breakfast, I hold up my end of the deal. It's surprisingly nice to be able to spend the day with him. We walk around the heart of Graystone for hours. I'm not usually the type of person to bring somebody on a tour, but I make an exception for him.

CHAPTER 16

DANTE

The relief that floods out of me when Sierra steps into view is unsurmountable. I don't know what I expected when she disappeared with the others. They were only gone for about an hour, but it was hell on me. I'm sure someone will have to even out the ground from the new trail I left from my pent-up pacing.

"Hey, beautiful." I kiss her gently on the forehead before I wrap my arms around her as she comes to stand beside me.

"Hey, handsome." She smiles, but it doesn't reach her eyes.

"We rented out a bed and breakfast in a nearby town for all who want to rest before returning back to Graystone. I know many of you are exhausted after the day's events."

Even if one of them made us a portal to get back to Graystone, we would still have to summon enough energy to make our own for home. I'm sure I can do it if Sierra wants to go back to our place. I look to her and shrug; she nods in reply. It looks like we're staying in Greece for the night. But there's a question that's been burning to get out of me. I have to know if Nilo's behind the bullets that shot my teammates and me.

"Nilo, can I have a moment privately with you?" I ask as all eyes land on me.

"Yes, of course," Nilo replies, gesturing for the others to go ahead of us.

Once we're alone, I rub at my stubble. "There's no way to dance around it. I need to know if your team's responsible for the altered bullets that shot my teammates and myself?"

"In a way, they are. This side project of mine was completely off the books, I had my own separate team at a facility outside Graystone, and the scientists there were the ones who created the bullets. The information somehow got leaked to Ryker, so I had to come up with a cover story that ammunition could be used for dangerous rogue immortals who we weren't able to capture. He couldn't know I was testing them to take down Excalibur."

"Who shot us?" I ask, gauging his reactions for a lie. Everybody has a tell.

"That would be the High Council's hunters. Ryker was so thrilled with the invention that he armed them with the specialized bullets, and since he's master council, I couldn't stop him." He sighs. "I'm sorry that they were used in that manner and stripping the hunters of their pistols will be one of the first things I take care of when I get back to Graystone."

"And you truly believe Excalibur won't get out of there?" I dare to ask as I jab my thumb in the direction behind me.

"I can't say that it's impossible because nothing is ever truly impossible if one puts their mind to it. We've been working on this spell and perfecting all its gears for centuries. I'm confident in all of our abilities to keep him imprisoned."

"Okay then, thanks for everything that you did."

"It's my sworn duty to protect the people of Graystone and the rest of the world."

I catch up to Sierra a little farther up the trail and am happy to find there will be a bus waiting at the trailhead to take us all to Old Panteleimon Village. We can't create a portal to a place like that. All these outsiders literally popping out of thin air would cause too much attention. Sierra leans heavily on me the rest of the walk. She's exhausted and has been through so much in such a short time.

I offer her one of the peanut butter granola bars I had stashed in my pants pocket. She takes it and eats it quietly as we walk along the narrow trail to where the bus is. Once we reach the end and climb into the bus, she rests her head on my shoulder and nods off within a few minutes. The town is just a short ride. The bus stops just outside of town, since vehicles aren't allowed in, just foot traffic. Normally I would prefer that type of village, but my girl is already drained. I'd offer to carry her, but I'm sure she'd reject it. From that determined look in her eyes, she doesn't want to seem weak in front of the others. I can respect that.

The sun is setting off in the distance and is throwing rays of oranges and pinks into the clear night sky. We walk side by side along the cobblestone walkway following closely behind the others. It seems like a cute little town with its little shops and taverns. Hopefully, Sierra will be up for exploring it in the morning before we return home. I think it'll do her some good to get her mind off everything that's transpired recently and what's waiting back home for us.

The group stops in front of a large stone mansion and files in, slowly getting checked in for our rooms. We all had the same idea about staying the night. Only Nilo and his team decided to head back to Graystone since he's acting master council in Ryker's absence. After checking ourselves in, we walk to our room. This place is huge, with large exposed beams framing the inside of the building and radiating a welcome feel.

We reach our door and are greeted by the sweet scent of the pink flowers in a vase on the entryway table. There's a queen-sized bed in the center of the room with a colorful handmade quilt covering the top of the mattress. To the left of the door is the bathroom with a small shower I may be too tall to fit comfortably in.

Sierra silently makes a beeline for the bed, she strips down to her tank top and underwear, tosses her clothing to the floor, and slides under the covers. I think she's asleep before I'm even able to climb in. I can only imagine how much her gift took a toll on her today.

I settle in beside her and wrap my arms around her body as she sighs in her sleep. What a day this has been for all of us. With my face buried in her soft wavy hair, I close my eyes, inhaling the scent of cherry blossoms she always embodies. The feel of her chest rising and falling against me steadies my own breathing. I wonder what tomorrow will bring? I can only imagine the commotion in Graystone right now. I know the guard has quite a few cells but I'm not sure there's enough for all of Excalibur's minions. I hope in the confusion of that aftermath none of them were able to slip away.

SIERRA

The sound of mumbled voices awakens me. I open my eyes and am momentarily confused about where I am. The light seeping around the pale blue curtains reveals a white stucco room that I don't recognize. I blink a few times and rub the sleep out of my eyes. Looking around the small space, I find my mind flooded with memories. The storm I made to cover us, getting into the fort and rescuing the prisoners, then the fighting.

Mom. Oh God, my mom is dead.

The tears stinging my eyes trail down my cheeks and soak into the soft blue pillowcase my head's on. I remember everything now, even though I wish I didn't. Why couldn't I be one of those people who after a traumatic event gets amnesia? I want that. I don't want this tremendous sadness that's setting into me, weighing me down and pushing me harder into this plush-top mattress. The small soft leather pouch that holds my black obsidian stone is sitting on the nightstand beside the bed taunting me. One of the six keys that could grant that monster his freedom. As much as I hate the situation I've been backed into, I'll never give mine up. He won't see the light of day ever again. I will fight til my last breath and survive just to make sure he rots in his custom-made prison.

Dante stirs behind me, so I still. I don't want him to see me cry. I can be strong; I need to be. I can't fall apart yet. There's still too much I need to take care of. I have to get back to my dad and make arrangements for my mother's funeral. I'm sure Dad is in no condition to do any of that. I owe him that and so much more.

"Good morning, beautiful," Dante says in his husky voice, raspy from sleep.

I could've lost him too.

"Good morning, handsome," I reply automatically, cringing inwardly when my voice cracks. I hope he didn't hear it.

He gently pulls on my shoulder and rolls me onto my back to face him and searches my face. Sure enough, he saw the tears, and his face softens. "Hey, come here, baby. I'm so sorry."

His sympathetic eyes make it hard to hold back the sob clawing its way out of my lungs. He doesn't have to say what he's sorry for; it's the unspoken elephant in the room. I don't answer him but just snuggle in closer and let him hold me. And when he wraps his arms around me, I sob quietly into his chest. He gently rubs my back in a soothing motion.

Once my sobs have stilled for a few minutes, he asks me, "Why don't we get up and get showered. There were some clean clothes dropped off for us last night. We could go grab a bite in the cafe down the hall. You must be hungry. I know I'm famished."

"I'm not that hungry." Food doesn't interest me right now. My stomach is twisting and turning like a runaway hamster ball.

"After all the energy you used last night, you need to refuel your body, though. If not for you, then will you eat for me, please?" He sits up on the edge of the bed.

I don't answer him. How can I say no to him after everything he's done for me?

Dante ducks his head into the hall and grabs the clothing left in a white canvas bag outside our door. I groan, scrambling out of the bed, and it feels like I got ran over by a mac truck. I grab my pouch off the nightstand and carry it with me. Every muscle in my body is screaming in pain as I walk cautiously to the open bathroom door.

I catch a glimpse of myself in the mirror, and I look like a zombie out of a horror movie. My pale face stands out in contrast to the dark puffy circles under my eyes. Even my lips are chapped and peeling. I set my key down on the counter, my gaze lingering on it. Wishing there was another way this could've ended.

"Are you okay?" Dante asks as he comes into the tiny bathroom with me. His presence makes the room feel even smaller than it is.

"I'm just really sore, my whole-body aches, and I'm still really tired." I stifle a yawn. I haven't told him yet that I will have to go through this once a month for the rest of time. Maybe if I don't say the words, it won't be real.

"That's understandable." He gently tucks a stray lock of hair behind my ear. "How about after the shower, I go get us something to eat and we just stay in here for the day?"

"That sounds wonderful to me, but I should be getting back to my dad soon." My gaze falls to the floor. I feel guilty not going back home last night to see him. I was just so exhausted, though. Even if I did make it home, I wouldn't have been any use to him.

"Okay." He gives me a reassuring smile.

If I thought the bathroom was cramped that has nothing on the shower. Not only is it made for short people but also very thin ones. I'm average, but Dante's built like a UFC fighter. I just barely fit under the shower head; Dante has to maneuver in a weird way in order to be able to wash his hair. It's actually kind of comical to watch him struggle. I think he's being overdramatic to lighten the mood, which he did a little.

"I have to tell you something..." I begin.

"You can tell me anything."

"The ritual I had to perform last night." I sigh. "I have to repeat it every month to keep the spell from waning."

He pauses mid shampoo, his hands frozen on his head. "Are you up for that?"

"I have to be. Each one of us that were part of the original spell are one of the six keys. That's what's in that black pouch. My obsidian stone." I reach up and place my hand on his bare chest. His heart beat is a steady rhythm that's calming me.

"Whatever you need baby, I'm here." He wraps his soapy fingers over mine. "We'll get through this, I promise."

The hot water cascading down my sore muscles feels soothing. The shower does make me feel a little better just from getting clean again. The fairy godmother that delivered our clothes while we slept also brought my hair brush and our toothbrushes from home. I suspect Maverick probably had a hand in that because the others that came here to Greece with me were just as tired. I know I drained Konstantina and Reid, and Maggie and Levi expelled quite a bit of energy too.

Dante was true to his word; he said he'd go find food and let me relax for a bit. I drank one of the strawberry banana flavored elixirs that were with our stuff, and I can feel it lessoning the deep ache in my muscles. What I wouldn't give to soak in a hot tub right about now with a book, just to get lost in the pages and make everything else disappear. To be able to live in a fantasy world even if for just a little while. Or let the side effects of a stiff drink take the edge of the pain away. The fogginess in my head is saying I really need coffee, though. I haven't had much alcohol since Excalibur took my parents hostage. I was too focused on getting them both back. Which I failed. I wish I could go back to the careless teenager who was only guilty of partying.

I open the curtains to the bedroom and glance outside. I feel like I've been transported back in time. The roadway is paved with cobble stones and there are no vehicles in sight. Just humans, or so I suspect they are, walking down the streets and perusing through the little pop-up shops that line the narrow drive.

Wooden balconies flank some of the buildings, and on one of them across the street from the hotel we're staying in, there's an older woman, and the slight breeze is blowing through her long silver hair. She's wearing a shirt that matches the colorfulness of the blanket on our bed. She stands out against the gray rock wall of her house as she watches the people below through her wire-rimmed glasses. A bakery down the street is wafting what can only be described as heaven my way, and my stomach growls at the sweet scent of baked goods. I guess I am hungry after all. Where is Dante? I lean out the window, hoping to spot him, but I don't.

This brings me back to when Emma and I used to people watch at the mall. I wonder how our little community we built in the Caribbean is holding up. I haven't asked yet how many we lost. I'm afraid of the answer. I know there are more who died than my mom. I just want to put off that guilt for a little longer. I could have been better. I could have been stronger. That will never happen again. I'm making a vow to myself from here on out, that I will be my strongest self. I won't fail the next time I'm faced with a challenge.

Almost as if he heard my thoughts, Dante walks up the cobblestone road toward the bed and breakfast I'm in. Wearing his black tactical pants and a dark grey t-shirt, Dante looks so cute toting two small boxes, a bag, and thank the heavens he has what looks like coffee cups. He looks almost domesticated even. I huff a laugh at that thought; he's far from. I see some women giggling as he walks by them, no doubt thinking he makes a good-looking tourist. Ha! If they only knew what he did for a living. Or does he anymore? I'm hoping us capturing Excalibur for the High Council will force them to allow Dante to be a guardian again. I know that's what he wants. He took a huge risk with my family, and I feel guilty for that too. The list of things I feel responsible for keeps growing longer and longer. I couldn't have done it without him, though. He's been my rock through it all.

He disappears from view as I continue to watch with envy the people out and about without a care in the world. They can all continue their lives freely without ever knowing what it takes to keep them safe. A soft knock at the door breaks my trance at watching the world outside continuing on without my mom. It's Dante with something that smells amazing in his hands. My mouth waters as he sets it down on the small round table.

"I don't know why you're hovering by the table. You said you didn't want any. These are all for me, but I did get you a coffee," he says with a straight face handing me the paper cup with a little brown cardboard sleeve.

As he starts opening the boxes, the smell gets stronger, and my stomach growls in protest. Dante lifts the box high enough so I can't see what's inside.

"Oh really?" I cross my arms.

"Yeah, your words. I'm not that hungry." He cracks a smile as I swat at his shoulder. I take a step closer to get a peak, but he pulls the lid down too quickly with a playful grin.

"So, what did you get?" I have to know what that smell is. The anticipation is killing me.

"Well, there's these loukoumades and tiganites as well as some frouto. But you can only have some if you're able to guess what they are." He snickers at the pouty face I made.

"I'm guessing their food and they're edible. There I guessed, so can I have them now?" I put my hands on my hips to drive the point home. I take a sip of my too-hot coffee before setting it on the table by the little white bakery boxes.

"Close your eyes and open your mouth."

Not what I expected. "Why?" My eyebrows raise in suspicion.

"Don't you trust me?" Voice low, Dante pulls two chairs out for the both of us.

"Always." I sit and do as I'm told. Well mostly, I try sneak a peek through a partially closed eyelid.

"No peeking," he commands in a stern voice.

I close both eyes and try to sit back into the chair, and I open my mouth, feeling awkward as heck. The moment the fluffy dough touches my tongue, I know I'm hooked. I chew the small round ball, and hints of cinnamon and honey explode in my mouth.

"Mmm, that's really good. What is it?" I open my eyes and meet his dreamy deep emerald green ones.

"Those little beauties are the Greek version of a donut. They're called loukoumades. Close them again."

The sound of boxes sliding around on the table is begging me to look, but I control myself this time. Patience is not one of my best qualities. I lick my lips in anticipation for the next treat.

The next item Dante offers me is warm and flat like a pancake but almost the same consistency as the donut I just ate. Flavored with honey and walnuts and topped with the unmistakable tangy, salty mixture of feta cheese.

"What do you think of that one?"

"That one's good too." I like this game. I've always loved food. There's no secret there, and he knows me more than anybody. Well played, Dante.

"That was tiganites, and as I'm sure you guessed, it's their pancakes." Dante clears his throat. "Okay, last one."

A sweet and juicy strawberry is what comes next. There's nothing fancy about it, but you can easily tell farm-grown berries from commercially grown berries. The flavor is much sweeter and rich.

I sit up straighter and grab a bottle of cold water Dante had in the bag. My coffee is still piping hot. He insists on feeding me the rest of the food, alternating bites between him and me. It was such a sweet way for him to take care of me.

"Oh, I almost forgot. I thought you could use this." Dante reaches into the bag on the table and pulls out a small tube of beeswax lip balm and hands it to me.

The thoughtfulness he shows others never ceases to amaze me. My eyes water with unshed tears. He'll never know how much this means to me. "Thank you, handsome."

"Anything for you, beautiful." He flashes me a smile that makes my knees grow weak.

Once we're done cleaning up, we start packing up the few toiletries and clothing we have. Once checked out, we stroll through a few shops on our way out of the village, vowing to come back and spend more time here next month when I have to return to maintain the spell. I did unfortunately tell him. I made it real. Looking behind me as we pass the last of the buildings, I have to smile at the simplicity of the lives of those that live here. It's like seeing a live page ripped out of history. We continue down the dirt road until we're a safe distance away from anybody and hidden in between the roaming green grassy hills. Dante pulls out his blue benitoite portal stone and creates a doorway back to our compound. I hesitantly step through first, and he follows and closes the portal before tucking the wand-shaped stone safely into his pants pocket. I breathe a sigh of relief to be back in the safety of our own home. It seems like it's been longer than twenty-four hours since I was last here.

Too bad the relief won't last. I have to go find my dad. Then I have to figure out how I'm going to be able to live in a world that my mom no longer exists in.

CHAPTER 17

Dante

"**N**o! Please stop. Please don't kill her. Take me! No!"

Sierra's screaming wakes me from a sound sleep. I bolt out of bed and swipe my daggers off my night stand. I hold them both out in front of me as I whip around surveying our bedroom for what threat was hurting her.

Nothing, again. Just her night terrors. Placing my weapons back where they were I climb back in bed. Sierra's eyes are open now and she's sobbing quietly.

"Come here. It was just a dream. You're safe at home. I got you, I won't let anything happen to you, sweetheart." I rub circles on her back and kiss her forehead.

I always hold her until it passes. She never tells me what happened in her nightmares, and I don't try to pry it out of her. By what she shouts I can use my imagination to fill in the blanks. I had traumatizing reminders for a while after that mess in Attica. I still see that replay from time to time.

"I'm here whenever you're ready to talk," I murmur against the top of her head.

Her only reply was a nod.

Her nightmares have been happening almost every night since we attacked Excalibur's fort in India six days ago. She doesn't sleep much, and when she does manage, she's awoken like this. I feel useless, I have no way to protect her from what her own mind conjures up. I tried to dreamwalk with her several times, but that only works when I'm awake. Once I fall asleep, her demons are free to unleash their own personal hell on her.

I don't know how to help Sierra through this. It seems no matter what I do, it doesn't do much. I know she's grieving and trying to process all that has gone on in the past several days. To be honest, I'm surprised she's held up this well. I think she's blocking out most of what happened to protect herself. I know from experience that won't work; it'll just make it harder when the wall crumbles down. And it will crumble; they always do.

Sierra falls asleep tucked in close to me, her face buried in my chest. I continue to run my hand over her in a soothing motion hoping she'll stay sleeping for a while. Sierra hasn't been eating hardly anything, I even offered to go to Greece and get her some of the food I brought her before that she loved so much. That was the most she's eaten since the battle in India.

Michael has been staying here in the cabin with us as well as Joe and Grace. Michael's in rough shape, and I worry for him and Sierra. I don't think he would take his own life and leave Sierra behind, but he's not exactly in the right frame of mind. I can't imagine losing Sierra, and I haven't been with her nowhere near the amount of time Michael and Sophia were together. After the last honors are held tomorrow, I think it would be a good idea to look into the rehab facilities they have for those grieving the loss of an anima gemella. I think they could help Michael, and I don't want to chance Sierra losing her dad as well.

Sierra stirs in my arms and stretches her legs out.

"It's okay, baby. I'm still right here," I say as the sun starts to wink through the gaps in the curtains.

Talking has almost been futile with Sierra. Emma isn't getting anywhere with her either. I'm man enough to admit when I need help, and I'm going to call Eric today to take her someplace to see if that will get her some closure. Maybe getting away from all of us would help. I'm not sure if she'll go with him willingly, but I'm at a loss for what to do.

It's going to be hard as hell to be stuck here at my home trying to be a good man and support the love of my life while she's out with him. But I owe her that. For her, I will do anything. I know she wouldn't cheat on me, and sex is the last thing on her mind anyway right now. Her lips have barely brushed mine since the attack.

I know Eric loves her even though he won't come out and admit it. I can only hope he loves her enough to help her and do the right thing. I imagine asking him to see her with me is equivalent to stomping on his aching heart. As much as I don't like Eric for what he's done in his past, he is a good man. I know he'll sacrifice his pride to make sure Sierra will be okay. For that, I will always be grateful to him.

I lie awake for a few more hours watching the rise and fall of Sierra's breathing. I wasn't able to fall back asleep myself. My stomach keeps twisting just thinking about calling Eric. What if he doesn't answer? Something's got to give here. There has to be a way to help Sierra be more than just a shadow of herself.

ERIC

The shrill ringing of my cell phone jolts me awake. I don't look at the name on the screen before swiping my finger to the side to answer.

"Yeah?"

"Eric, it's Dante."

The mention of his name is like a bucket of ice water over my head. I sit upright.

"Is everything okay?" Worry seizes my breath.

"No. Not really." He pauses. "I need your help with Sierra."

Anxiety bubbles up. "What kind of help?"

"She's not herself and I've tried everything. So has Emma. I know she's going through a lot but I don't know how to help her."

I rub my face and don't answer.

At my silence he continues, "I hate to ask but can you come pick her up and, I don't know take her someplace to get her mind off everything."

"Send me your address and I'll be there as soon as I shower."

"Thank you, Eric."

"You're welcome."

I hang up and toss my phone on the bed beside me. What did I just agree to? I talked to Sierra briefly over the phone the day after the battle, but I haven't heard from her since. I haven't seen her close up in weeks, not since I walked away from her. I told her I wanted to do right by her even if it killed me. It almost has already, and today will prove to be one of the hardest trials.

I don't even know what I can do to help her anyway. If Emma isn't able to break through, why would I? I can't stand the thought of Sierra hurting, and I would help regardless if Dante wanted me to or not. I just signed the lease to my apartment yesterday. I don't have much but living above a furniture store has its perks. I did score some sick deals on some less than perfect furnishings. A scratch here or a dent there won't matter to me anyhow.

I've thought about her so often and have almost gone to her multiple times. My morals are the only thing that stopped me. I really do want to be a man who is deserving of a woman like her. Every morning I wake up to an empty bed is like a kidney shot. Bottles of Jack are the only thing that numbs some of the ache I feel.

I scrape my rough hands over my face. I suppose cleaning myself up should be the first thing I do. I don't want to show up there smelling like a bar. I shower quickly and throw my only clean set of clothes on; I haven't gone to the laundromat yet. I look longingly at the black glass bottle sitting on my nightstand before walking out my front door and down the steps.

I pull up my navigation in the truck and type in the address Dante texted me. It's about an hour's ride from here. Perfect, just what I need, more time to be by myself and get lost in the circus pulling out all the stops in my brain. At least the sun is out and there's barely any clouds in the sky. The temperature is already climbing, and it's only ten in the morning. It's going to be a scorcher today.

I top off my tank and grab a bag of ice and some drinks. I always keep a cooler in the backseat on the floor of my truck for backup. Unfortunately, I passed on the alcohol in favor of a few bottles of soda and water. As much as I need the liquid courage, Sierra needs me sober today. Dante really does live out in the middle of nowheresville. I finally make it up to his gravel drive, and I'm blown away by the house that sits in the center of the meadow. It resembles something from a Thomas Kincaid painting, all-inviting log home surrounded by lush gardens. All he's missing is a lake with a fishing dock and some ducks playing in the water.

I grip the black leather steering wheel until my knuckles turn white. Every muscle in my body tenses at the thought of being so close to Sierra again. I pocket my keys and slowly make my way up the flagstone path as the birds sing a cheerful melody around me. I exhale slowly, but as my hand reaches up to knock on the door, I hesitate. What if I only make it worse for her? Does she even know I'm coming to pick her up? I don't get a chance to knock before the door opens.

"Hey Eric, thank you for doing this." Dante gestures for me to come in.

"Anytime." I hope this doesn't become the norm; I won't survive punishing myself like this every day.

"She'll be out in a minute; she's just changing." The hard set to his jaw lets me know he isn't comfortable with the situation any more than I am.

I still haven't figured out just what the hell to do with her today. We've never really spent much time alone before; we were always with Emma and our friends or family.

We stand in awkward silence until the muffled footsteps draw our attention to the hallway. Sierra appears in the opening wearing a light blue pair of blue jeans and a teal-colored t-shirt that really brings out the green flecks in her hazel eyes. Taking in her appearance, I feel like the floor drops out from beneath me. She's always been thin, but her cheeks have hollowed, and the dark purplish circles that surround her normally bright eyes make her look like she's aged ten years in a span of just a few weeks.

This isn't the Sierra I know and love. She gives me a weak smile; one I know is for my benefit. My anger quickly ratchets up at Dante. How could he let her get this bad?

"What do you say, we gonna blow this joint and paint the town red?"

Sierra only shrugs in response. I meet Dante's worried gaze, concern etched in every wrinkle at the corner of his eyes and his own exhaustion-ridden face. I have to turn away as she reaches her arms around Dante to hug him before leaving with me. It's one thing to know he has her, it's another animal altogether to be a witness to it.

Once she climbs up into the truck, I just pick a direction and drive. My anxiety is palpable as I tap on the wheel with my thumbs to the beat of the rock music pouring out of my speakers.

"What would you like to do?" I ask.

"I don't know." She stares out the window.

Okay rephrase. "Where do you wanna go?"

"I don't care," she says quietly. Her voice so timid it's as if someone else is possessing her.

After driving for about a half-hour with no success of getting anything else out of her, I pull the truck over to the side of the road and slam on the brakes. Sierra smacks her palms against the dash to catch herself as I throw the Tundra in park.

Her eyes widen. "What the hell, Eric?"

"There she is, at least the Sierra I know is still in there." I pivot to face her.

"You're wasting your time, Eric. That Sierra is long gone," she mumbles as she looks out at the thick pine trees lining the road.

"No, she's not. She's still in there." I have to squeeze my hands into fists to stop myself from pulling her into my arms. "You forget I had to do the same thing long ago, lock a part of myself away so nobody could hurt me anymore."

"That was different." She swallows, still staring off into the landscape, then finally whispers, "People you love didn't die because you weren't strong enough to save them."

Screw the consequences. I unbuckle and slide over to her tugging her close to my aching chest. Resting my chin on the top of her head, I inhale her sweet-smelling shampoo. "Sierra, it's not your fault. None of this is because you weren't strong enough."

She sniffs into my shirt but rests her head against my chest. I tighten my grip on her. I should have known she would blame herself. Desperate for a way to help her without touching her any more than I have to, I ask, "What can I do?"

"I just want to forget everything, even just for a day." Her voice is hoarse from unshed tears. And damn it if that sound coming out of her doesn't make them well in my own eyes. I'd do anything to take the pain away from her. Even jeopardize my own sanity in the process.

Against my better judgment, I make a pit stop at the local liquor store down the road from my apartment before bringing Sierra back to my place. I don't have much here, but I do have one thing that I know will be able to take her mind off the misplaced guilt she feels. I may not be able to offer her much but making her forget about the shitty cards she's been dealt for a day is something I can manage. One of the few things I did grab from my home in Colorado is our video game collection. Sierra has a history of whooping me at guitar hero. Video games and drinks I can do. Anything deeper than that and I may forget my reasons I should stay away.

Several hours later and my living room looks like we had a frat party with the number of empty bottles floating around. The more we drank the lighter her mood became. I'm afraid we may have over done it, neither of us are able to walk in a straight line. She's laughing though and that's all that matters. Plus, I should get a medal for being a good little boy. I've been able to control my urge to touch her and kiss her all night.

It has not been easy. Every time I thought I'd lose control I'd pinch myself until the wave passed. It's getting late and I should probably call Dante to come get her. I can't make a portal when I'm drunk and I sure as hell will not be getting behind the wheel like this with her in my truck.

He's going to be mad. A laugh springs free. Oh well, he'll get over it. He should just be happy she's going back home with him. I pull my phone out of my pocket and stare at the screen.

"Eric, it's your turn," Sierra calls out from the living room.

"It's okay, you go another song. I have something I have to take care of."

I sit at one of only two kitchen chairs I have at the small table and wait until I hear the music start before I dial Dante's number.

"Eric, is everything okay?" he clips out.

"Yeah, she's okay. You're going to have to come get her, though. I can't drive her home because we've been drinking."

"You got her drunk?" His tone is accusing.

Are you kidding me?

"Listen man, she wanted to forget everything for a day. So, we drank and played video games. She's more herself now than the zombie I picked up this morning. Don't think this was any easier on me than it was for you. She gets to go home with you, doesn't she?" My teeth grind together as I try to keep my voice down.

I don't want Sierra to overhear and feel worse than she already does. That poor girl has enough guilt she's carrying around.

"I know, I'm sorry. Thank you for helping. I'll be right over."

I hang the phone up without saying good bye. Going back to the living room and longingly watching her hit all the notes of the song, I have to admit even though it was torture, I enjoyed my time with her. Within minutes there's a knock at the door. I reluctantly get off the futon and let lover boy in.

"She's right in there." I point to the room as I stay in the kitchen.

Dante peeks his head around and watches her finish the song. A smile forms on his face as mine falls.

He turns his gaze back to me. "I really do owe you. Thank you, Eric. I'm sorry I got short with you on the phone."

"It's fine," I say as Sierra comes out to the kitchen shuffling her feet so she doesn't trip and I have to grin at her.

She wraps her arms around my neck and for a few seconds I can't breathe before putting my arms around her slender waist.

"Thanks Eric. I needed this." She smiles as she takes a step back.

"Anytime, Sierra. Just call me, okay?"

"K," she says before walking out the door with Dante and taking my heart with her.

SIERRA

I was surprised to hear that they're giving my mom a traditional immortal guardian burial, considering the High Council thought of her as a traitor for many years. I still can't believe she's really gone. I mean, I was there, I saw what happened, but I keep thinking she'll be walking through that door at any time. Every once in a while, I'll hear her sweet laugh carried by the wind, and I turn to see she's not there. She'll never be there again.

I struggle to be around my dad. The pain is just too much. It's my fault she's gone. Not only was I the one in the stupid prophecy but if I had thought to steal Excalibur's water before it got too far, she'd still be alive. I'm no Immortal Savior. I failed her because I wasn't good enough. I'll never hear her voice again, never feel her loving arms wrapped around me, never see her beautiful smile again. I just can't believe that in this magical world that was hidden from me for so long, her coming back to life is so out of the question.

She wasn't the only one I failed that day. We lost five others as well, and all six of them will be laid to rest today. I'm in the master bathroom of our cabin looking at myself in the mirror. Unlike human funerals, where everybody wears black, at an immortal gathering everybody is required to wear white to help the fallen pass on to the afterlife. In Graystone, they call the service the last honors, which is a fitting title for those who live their lives in honor of their duty to protect the world from those that wish to destroy it.

I dab some concealer on my face to hide the contrasting colors that seem to always show now. The puffy black circles under my eyes are made even worse by the paler of my face. Sleeping and eating have been really hard to accomplish since that day. Sighing, knowing that no amount of makeup will be able to hide how I feel, I resolve to put my mother's pearl earrings in that my dad insisted I wear today. They were my mom's favorite jewelry. I'm afraid that after today I won't ever be able to put on a set of pearls again without thinking of this terrible moment in my life.

I smooth out the slight wrinkle in the creamy white shift dress before taking one last look at myself. I switch the light off and walk back out to the kitchen to where Dante, Dad, Uncle Joe, Aunt Grace, Maverick, Emma and Eric are waiting. It's strange to have them all in the house at once. We're taking two vehicles to the chapel. I'm thankful for the support they all try to give me, but I don't deserve it.

The ride into the center of Graystone was the most somber I've ever endured. There's already a swarm of people gathered outside the large white chapel. The sharp tip of the steeple points directly to the clouds above. I follow Dante's lead since I have no idea what to do.

All the guests who arrive make a road of standing silence leading up and into the large black doors with ornate crosses carved into them. The bodies of hundreds will line the street like an honor guard when a first responder dies in the line of duty. We all stand and bow our heads as even the Holy Ones who traditionally wear only cobalt blue robing are also dressed in white as they pass us. The Holy Ones are leading the way for the caskets to be carried through.

I take a deep breath and blink several times, trying to clear the tears that threaten to fall. Once the deceased start coming, I won't be able to stop them. The first caskets are hauled out of the back of the first black hearse at the end the street. Several men and women dressed in white suits are tasked with bringing the fallen to their final resting place. The men are all wearing crisp suits and the ladies have ankle-length gowns with scoop necks. White gloves line all the hands that will be lifting the caskets.

Dante intertwines his fingers with mine, and I reach for my dad's hand on my right. My father's grasp is firm as I watch him slowly breathe in through his nose and out his mouth. He's only hanging on by a thread too. He's told me it's not my fault, and he doesn't blame me. He's only showed love and support since then, but I carry enough blame for the both of us. Several long and steady breaths pass before I'm able to pull my gaze from his tortured expression. The wrinkles in his forehead show he's trying to fight back tears.

When there is a last honors ceremony for more than one person, they do it in alphabetical order. My mom will be the last one to be carried past us. Each light oak casket is draped with a white pall with the immortal guardian's mark in the center. Other than the sounds of the dress shoes clapping on the pavement, sniffing and crying mingle. I swallow and continue to bow my head, glancing at each wooden box that floats by.

Amelia's casket comes by us first. I didn't know her well, but she seemed like she would be a great friend. Ari is next. He never got the chance to find out that his father Josiah had been abducted and later rescued by our team. Julian, I believe was the eldest who was among our team, but his years of experience were no match for Excalibur's onslaught.

Lucas, on the other hand, I knew rather well. He was my friend, and I let him down too. He was always part of Dante's inner team when they did special missions. Dante was close to him. I sneak a glance at Dante and notice the wetness that coats his eyes. I have to look away. So much pain and sadness bears down on him. Miguel's arrival follows Lucas. He was one of the newest members of our team. He joined about a week before we attacked. I was so focused on the mission by the end that I didn't allow myself time to get to know him. I regret that decision now. He deserved to be known by us all.

The sharp intake of breath from my dad alerts me that it's my mother's turn to be hefted on through the sea of people. My dad's hand nearly crushes my own with how hard he's squeezing it. I swallow down the acid that rises in my throat.

After all the deceased have been brought into the church, the honor guard follows behind. The pews fill up fast, and the people continue to flow in until we're packed in like sardines in a tin can. Everyone here wants to pay their final respects to those who sacrificed their lives so that they may continue to live. The Holy Ones take the stage, and we all sit as they begin an emotional sermon and chanting, I'm not sure which. My eyes won't stray from my mother's casket, while my ears are ringing so loud, I'm not aware of what's being said. The body heat stemming from the crowd of people in the house of mourning is making me sweat.

I'm still holding the hands of the two most important men in my life and trying to be strong for my dad because I owe him that much. I fight the images of her final moments before she died. I hope she knew how much I loved her and wish I could have saved her.

I blink in surprise when Dante and Dad stand and pull me up with them. People start filing to the caskets and placing flowers on them that the Holy Ones hand out. When it's our turn, Dante whispers to her before kissing his fingers and places a firm hand on top of the wood. He leaves the white rose he was handed on the top of her casket, and I do the same.

"I love you Mom, please watch over Dad. Rest in peace." Choking on my own hot tears in my throat, I blow her a kiss.

With gut-wrenching sobs, my dad falls to his knees behind me ."Sophia please don't leave me. I can't do it; I won't live without you," he cries and mumbles incoherently. I stand there frozen, not able to move.

My Uncle Joe kneels beside him and consoles him in a way I'm not capable of doing. Because at that moment, it's as if the grim reaper reached into my chest with his skeletal hand and grasped my beating heart, yanking it free from my body and squishing the organ in his unforgiving hands until it crumpled into dust and falls to the floor. I've got to get out of here. The walls are closing in around me, and I can't breathe no matter how much my lungs expand. Nothing goes in.

Dante tries to reach for me, but I just shake my head at him. I can't do this. I take off at a run, maneuvering around all the other guests and bolt out the front doors held wide open. I portal to the only place I can think of to go. The only place it's safe for me to fall apart.

CHAPTER 18

SIERRA

I flee the ceremony and run to the side of the building, where I create a portal to the only place I feel close to my mother. Colorado Springs. The house I grew up in. I step through the portal and look to the home that has more secrets the closer I get. But this place is better than where I was....

I couldn't do it anymore. I had to get away from everyone. They're sympathetic gestures are too much to begin with but watching my dad fall apart like that? That's what broke me. My guilt over the death of my mom keeps eating away at me. I can't eat, I can't sleep, I can't even breathe without inhaling her sweet flowery scent.

The house looks the same as before, but the white building that I grew up in seems to hold more secrets the closer I get. My beat-up blue Dakota sits parked in our drive. The little blue shutters accenting the windows show some fading from this past summer's sunshine. This is the first time I've been back home since we left for Ireland two months ago. It feels like another lifetime ago since I last walked out that front door and into my parent's SUV.

I walk up the stone sidewalk lined with white daisies, purple asters, and pink mums, bringing about happy memories of my mom. My dad and I always bought her flowers for Mother's Day. The pink mums were the new addition this past year. She had a love of flowers that rivaled my love for coffee. I bend down to inhale their sweet earthy scent, and I wonder if I'll ever be able to look at flowers again without this dark cloud of misery. Dante's cabin in Graystone is surrounded by flowers too, and I don't know if I can go back to his place anytime soon. I hope he can forgive me. I have to close my eyes or stare at my shoes every time I walk past the multitude of flowers his private oasis offers.

I take my keys out of the small hidden pocket in my white dress. My house keys were one of the few things I didn't lose in the plane crash that ruined my life. I've kept them on me most of the time, even knowing I might not get another chance to come home but not willing to lose them. I guess I could have just portaled inside if I did misplace the small keychain of a sea turtle with a few jingling keys. There are still so many questions I want answered, so much about this life I still don't know. I'm supposed to enroll at the Guardian Academy for the next semester, which starts in a few weeks. I don't know if I want to go now. I'm not sure I want that life. My mom protected me from it for a reason. Although I don't agree with her hiding who I truly was from me, she was my mom, and at the end of the day, she was just trying to protect her only child. I can't fault her for that.

I reach the wooden steps and amble up them while running my hand up the white railing until I reach the covered porch. I smile as I run my finger over the scratches etched into the wood. Every year on my birthday since I was one, my parents would have me stand next to it and carve a line into the wood and mark my age next to it. The last time had been my 18th birthday when I stopped by with Emma to eat Chinese food and have cake. I thought it was silly of them at the time and almost refused that one small thing. If I had known it would be my last birthday with my mom, I never would have left that day.

So much has been taken from me, from my dad, and from the world. My mom was an amazing woman and I'm only now finding out I didn't even really know all of who she was. I push my key into the multiple locks one at a time in the blue painted door and take a deep breath before turning the handle to go inside. The beeping of our security system reminds me to enter my code to stop the incessant noise. Now all the locks are starting to make sense because of who they were hiding me from. And yet Excalibur still managed to ruin me and take her away from us. Her screams as she was killed still haunt my dreams. That's why I can't sleep. When I do allow myself to fall asleep, I see her murdered again, as clear as the day it happened. Her agonizing wails that ring in my ears linger long after I've woken up.

After stepping across the threshold, I walk around my house as if I'm on a tour. Each room was another memory, her laughter drowning out the painful screaming in my head. I can smell the sugar cookies as we frosted them this last Christmas Eve while listening to holiday music. Then my dad stole my mom away from frosting them to dance barefoot in the kitchen to their favorite song, "All I want for Christmas is you." I can picture it as if I was still there. They looked silly dancing with their green aprons covered in flour dust and speckled with dropped frosting. We'll never have that again, though.

I should have killed him when I had the chance. I wish they hadn't stopped me. If I could've let out all my rage like I wanted to do, I'd feel better. At least then, I would've avenged her death. After all the lives Excalibur ruined, how can he live with himself? Does he not have any morals or conscience? How is he able to keep living his life? And why did Rosalee help him to destroy her own blooded family? I get he's her anima gemella, but there have to be some limits to that bond. Surely it can't just be blind love, right? I don't think I could be with Dante if he did such evil things. I'm thankful I have an honorable man waiting back in Graystone for me. I know it pains him that I didn't want his comfort, but he's so understanding.

There's an emptiness to the house that I've never felt before, almost as if even our home misses her. I know I do. Hot tears stream down my face and splash on the black granite countertops of our kitchen as I recall our last few weeks together. I was mad at them for hiding things from me, but I didn't realize the reason. I spent more and more time away from them the closer we came to leaving for Ireland. I wish I could go back. My whole existence was a lie. I can't help but wonder if things would have turned out differently if I had known who and what I was before. What if I grew up in Graystone like they did and went through training? Would I have been strong enough to help them take down Excalibur before that deadly fight last week? All of the what if's keep replaying in my mind. All the things I could have done another way and perhaps had a better outcome.

I wipe my tears off my face and make my way up the carpeted stairs to my bedroom. Flicking the light switch on, I find the light purple room exactly as I left it. I sigh and walk over to the large window and slide open the deep plum black-out panels to let the sunlight in. It's odd how so much has changed since the last time I was here, yet this place is like a time capsule, perfectly preserved to a time when I was happier. When I wasn't broken beyond repair. I take it all in, the posters of bands I liked hanging on the wall, the stack of unread books on my desk, and the lavender paisley printed comforter. My problems back then looked so small and insignificant compared to the issues that plague me now. If only I could go back a few months and just stay there. Let time stand still. I think I could manage being happy knowing she'd still be here with us.

I climb into my bed, pull the blanket up around my waist, and let the tears come. I let down the dam that's been holding them back. I've tried to be strong for everyone else, especially my dad. God, my dad. He's a hollow shell of the man he was before, my mom taking his life with her as she left this world. He's more of a zombie than a human or immortal. The first few days were awful, and as if there was no emotion behind those hazel eyes, just emptiness. At least until he saw the oak box that carried her lifeless body at the last honors ceremony.

I'm not that strong, though. I can't keep hiding the pain. The more I hold it in the harder it is to keep the lid on it. I took my amulet off that Dante gave me on my birthday. I left my necklace in my nightstand back at his log cabin. I know if my emotions are strong enough, he can feel them, and I can't bear the thought of hurting him too. I feel like there's been a large cavern torn open in my heart and I'm flooded with sadness and hatred. I want to spare him from the broken pieces of me. I love him, and I know he's been trying to help me. I just need to let it all out on my own. I don't want him to see me this shattered.

I cry for so long I can feel the puffiness of my eyes clouding the edges of my vision, slowly swallowing away my sight. Thoughts and memories continue flowing through me like a river of images I can't hold back any longer. So much has happened in such a short time. I didn't have enough time with her. I'm only 18. There's still so much I need her for. I curl up in a ball and keep crying until there's nothing left of me. The sleep I've managed to stave off finally overtakes my exhausted body.

DANTE

After the ceremony celebrating the lives of the six casualties, including Sierra's mom, I wasn't surprised when she left. I thought she would've at least told me where she was going, but she just ran out and disappeared. I know she needs time. If she needs me, she knows where to find me. Her shaking her head at me when I went to follow her hurt more than I care to admit. She wanted to be alone, though, and I respected that at first.

Several hours have passed since she ghosted me, and I'm getting worried. I checked in with anybody she could possibly be with, including Eric. Now that was an awkward conversation asking if my girlfriend was seeking comfort from the only man on the planet who has the ability to make my relationship with Sierra feel threatened. The relief I felt that she didn't go to him makes me disgusted. If she felt like she needed to go to Eric to help her with her grief, then she has every right to. I trust her, and I love her more than anything. Whatever Sierra needs to get her through this, I'll support it. However, I wasn't too happy to discover her amulet back in our bedroom. If something terrible was to happen to her, the necklace would allow me to find her faster.

I don't know why I hadn't thought to check her parents' house before, but once the thought came to mind, I knew that was where I'd find her. I portaled into the kitchen. The worn blue cushions of the breakfast nook were just as I had remembered. The home is silent, but I catch sight of Sierra's white shoes by the front door. Knowing her room is on the second floor, I search for the staircase that leads to the upstairs.

I climb the steps quickly, taking them two at a time. She has to be here; I looked everywhere else for her. As I reach the top landing, I hear sobs coming from the right. I immediately pick up my pace and startle her when I come in fast. She's curled up in the fetal position holding a pillow to her stomach. Her hazel eyes are red and puffy as she looks up at me. She's been crying for a while by how swollen her eyelids are. I gently climb into bed with her, pull her in close and hold her tightly.

"I'm here, baby. I'm so sorry." I rub her back.

Each sob from her creates another crack in my heart. My sweet Sierra is in so much pain, and I'm helpless. All I can do is hold her as she cries into my chest, trying hard not to cry myself. She's lost so much, and she was carrying too much responsibility. This world hasn't been fair to her. We stay wrapped around each other for close to an hour before she says anything.

"I'm sorry I left," she croaks.

"Hey, shh. It's okay. You have nothing to be sorry for." I kiss her forehead as I brush her tear-soaked hair from her face. "I'm here now."

"I wasn't enough to save her, Dante," she whimpers.

"It's not on you to save everybody, Sierra. That's not your fault."

"I could've done more. If I had thought to take his water before, my mom would still be here."

"You don't know if that would've made any difference." When she opens her mouth to argue, I place a finger gently on her lips to. "Listen, we all did everything we could've done, but sometimes things happen that are out of our control. If you want to blame somebody, blame Excalibur. He was the one who did this."

"I know he did, and I want him dead." She sniffs and wipes the tears from her cheeks as a steely glint lights her eyes. "I want to watch as he dies a slow, painful death. The first chance I get, I'm killing him."

I take a deep breath, trying to collect my thoughts. "I know the feeling all too well. I want him dead for hurting you. But that won't change what happened. It won't bring any of them back."

"Am I broken?" Her question catches me off guard. The pain in her voice tears at my soul.

"No, why would you be? It's normal to grieve, and everybody does it in a different way." I rub circles on her back.

"The thoughts I've had in my head are so dark sometimes they scare me," she whispers.

I lift her chin so I can look into her eyes. "Don't let him take more from you. You are stronger than you think. Even the ancestors knew. That's why you're the Immortal Savior. Your light will drown out the dark. You just have to give it time. We'll get through this, baby."

"I don't think I can." Her hand fists my white t-shirt like a lifeline, and there goes my heart down on the floor getting stomped on.

"To be honest, we're all a little broken and damaged. That's the only way we can survive this world." I sigh as I rest my chin on the top of her head, wishing I could take all the pain and suffering from her.

"Not you, though. Nothing rattles you. Well, besides Eric. You're like Superman."

"Even Superman has his Kryptonite." I smirk at her reference. "Some of us become good at wearing the mask that everybody expects. I have dark parts of me I keep hidden. I've done things that I regret and wish I could've done differently." I don't want to burden her with things that trouble me, but she needs to know I'm not a man made of steel either, as much as I wish I were.

"Why haven't you told me?" She furrows her brows.

"I wasn't ready to tell you, but I will in time. I've had more than my fair share of dark days too, but do you want to know the good part about the darkness?" I ask, cupping her jaw in my palm and caressing her soft tear-stained cheek with my calloused thumb, wishing I could rub the sadness away.

"How is there a good part in this?" Her bottom lip quivers.

"It makes the light that much brighter when it does come out of hiding. It makes you revere that which gives you a reason to look for the stars among the darkness of despair. And you, my beautiful Sierra, are my north star." I give her an achingly tender kiss, hoping she feels all the love I'm trying to pour into her broken heart to mend the cracks.

When her eyes close and her breathing slows, I grab my phone from my pocket and send a quick text to our friends and family to let them know she's safe. Hours before, I'd had my doubts.

CHAPTER 19

SIERRA

Today I have to head to the Guardian Academy to get my room all set. When I agreed to go there, they left out the part where I would have to stay in the dorms from Sunday night til Friday afternoon. Even though it feels like I'm going away to college, I'm actually enrolling as a high school student. I graduated from a human high school in the beginning of the summer, but their teachings don't apply to this place. Go figure.

Dante and I split our time between his cabin in the woods and our castle in the Caribbean. I'm not ready to leave him. I've grown accustomed to waking up beside him every day and spending almost all of my time with him. I can't imagine what it's going to be like to go days without seeing that handsome face. After everything that I've been through and the stuff that I've done, high school just seems so trivial. Why can't they just stick me in a different training program?

The only silver lining to redoing those years is that Emma is also enrolling with me, and we're supposed to be sharing a dorm room. Although she is a half-breed, they agreed to let her in to study medicine. There are far too few doctors or nurses that are immortals, but I think they were more worried about sending her back into the human world with so much knowledge of our existence. This was their way of keeping tabs on her.

I never had to transfer schools growing up, and I always felt bad for any kids that did. I'm glad Emma will be there, though, so I won't be totally alone. Emma and I took a day trip last week and surprised our friends back home in Colorado. Kayla, Amanda, and Cynthia never knew what happened to us. We both just up and disappeared. I went "missing" after the plane crash, and many back home thought I'd died along with hundreds of others. That was a hard pill to swallow to not be able to tell them I was alive.

We told them that we were abducted into a human trafficking ring, not too far from the truth. And that we were now working abroad to help others in that situation. It's a stretch, but it lets them know Emma and I are safe, and we can still have them in our lives, even at a distance.

Dante and I load up my few small bags into the backseat of his black Silverado. It's mid Sunday afternoon, and the sun is shining, promising to be another beautiful day outside. Too bad I have to head to the academy; my classes start early tomorrow morning. Emma's meeting us there; she was staying at a hotel in the meantime. There's really no point in her getting a place of her own when she'll only be there two nights a week.

Dante is unusually quiet this morning. He starts working again tomorrow as well. He told the High Council he wasn't going back to work until I left for the academy. I know he's still worried about me, but I'm doing better. I'm taking things day by day. That's all I can do. I'm so thankful the High Council decided to reinstate any of the guardians who deflected. I'm going to really miss seeing Dante on a daily basis, though.

The hour-long ride seems to fly by. Next thing I know, the large building made of huge gray bricks enters my vision. The black wrought iron fence surrounding the campus is more for show than anything else. A four-foot fence won't keep anybody out. Dante pulls the truck up behind a long line of other vehicles dropping students off and puts it in park.

"Do I really have to go?" I whine and lean back into the suede seat.

"Unfortunately, yes, you do." Dante laughs easily.

I look out across the green front lawn and see clumps of students gathered and chatting. I thought I was done with high school; Emma and I will probably be the oldest ones here, and yet we'll know the least about what this school teaches. These kids must be better than human teenagers, right? I hope that's the case. Teenagers can be so cruel, especially girls.

I reach for the door handle and reluctantly hop down onto the blacktop and grab one of my bags from the back. Dante does the same on his side grabbing the two he placed in there earlier. After we shut the doors and walk up the concrete sidewalk leading to the massive building, I can feel everyone's gaze on us. Great, not so much different than humans, after all. I fight my chin from wanting to dip to the ground.

The short walk up the stairs and into the large open door feels as if I'm walking into a lion's den, and I'm the gazelle. Here for the taking. I swallow down my anxiety. I've faced far worse than a school of all things, how bad can the place be? Dante registers me at the little desk we checked into when I came here for my qualification evaluation around two months ago. The young man working the desk hands me over some paperwork that lists my dorm number.

Of course, since Dante went here, he offers to show me around and help me get settled. I haven't seen Emma yet, so hopefully she'll be here soon. We walk down the long narrow corridors of the main building, and I try to ignore the stares and hushed conversations that are obviously about me. We exit out a side door to the left of the building and enter into another fairly large structure that looks almost identical. This is one of the two co-ed dorms they have. The dorm for the younger kids is on the other side of the academy. For obvious reasons keeping teens and elementary students apart is a good idea, no matter immortals or not.

My dorm number is 307, which is two flights of stairs or a long line at the elevators. Dante opens the large metal door to the stairwell, and chaos erupts on the other side. Students spill out of their dorms into the hallway, music blasting from many of them, and of course, a good number of students gawk at me like I belong on center stage of a circus.

Luckily my door isn't far from the stair entrance, and I slide my large brass key into the lock, avoiding looking at all the students watching me warily. The dorm is about what I expected to find, each half of the room has a bed, a bureau, a writing desk, and a book case. I put my bags on the bed to the right. I don't think it'll matter to Emma which side she has. Luckily, we have our own bathroom attached.

"I know this is a lot right now, but I think you're doing the right thing." Dante places his arm around my side, pulling me closer to him.

"It just sucks that I can't stay with you. I just don't get why I have to stay here." I shake my head.

"It's how they've always run it; I'll still be able to see you on the weekends if I'm not out on a mission."

That's what I'm afraid of, that he'll be working while I'm free. That would be my luck lately.

"At least Emma will be here with you."

I've been trying hard to find the light in the darkness like he said to do. Some days are just really hard to get through. I have a feeling being stuck here may do more harm than good. Dante is my bright spot, but when he's not around?

I hope to God Emma can fill in.

EMMA

I see the way everybody looks at me. I know I don't belong here, but I don't care. I owe it to myself and others to become the doctor my father should have been. I knew it was going to be tough. I can't wait to see Maverick this Friday; he's taking me out to dinner at this fancy restaurant in town. I just have to keep thinking that the both of us can get through this. We've been seeing each other these past few weeks, but we're not official, yet anyways. Since we had that one night under the stars, he's been taking things painfully slow with me.

Sierra is already in our dorm upstairs. She texted me a little while ago. Eric dropped me off and didn't want to come in with me. I didn't want to come in either. He said he has a "thing"—whatever that means. He's been acting off for a few weeks, and I worry about his mental health. Sierra told me about their talk, and it was so out of character for him to act that way. I think he's in love with her and doesn't want to admit it to her. Of course, I didn't tell her that. I don't want her to feel guilty about being happy with Dante. Eric should have made his move sooner. He had plenty of chances. He's always been more of a suffer-in-silence type.

I reach the little registration desk and wait my turn. There's a cute red-headed guy giving out the packets to the students. His blue eyes light up when I reach the desk.

"Welcome, what's your name?"

"Emma. Emma Jones." I bite my lip.

"Jones?" His face loses all expression.

Thanks, Dad of the year.

"Yes," I say politely forcing a smile.

He hands over the packet. "Room 307. Your key's inside as well as a map." He nods to the next person in line.

I fight the tears that threaten to come. Is this what my life will always be like now? Maybe I should change my name. I quickly make my way to the dorm house by following the map from the folder. This place is so huge it rivals many large universities back in the states. I know most half-breeds like me are left completely unaware of immortals, but many do live here and go through the academy. It's my right to be here too, so all these prissy girls sliding me nasty faces can take their snooty looks and shove it.

I toss my long straight blonde hair behind me and square my shoulders. I was popular in high school, but I don't care if I get invited to all the parties and such here. I just want to be left alone and do what I can to pay for my family's sins. I finally reach dorm room 307 and give a gentle knock on the door before putting my key in. I don't want to catch them in a compromising situation. Not like she never walked in on Carl and me. Sigh, oh Carl. I thought I would miss him more than I do, don't get me wrong, some days really suck. But most of my time has been filled with much bigger things than tossing a football.

As soon as I step into the room, Sierra wraps me in a hug. She's been spending most of her time with Dante these last few days. We haven't seen each other much. I don't blame her I'd want to spend as much time with him as I could too.

"Hey, roomy!" Sierra says into my hair.

"Hey, yourself. Hi, Dante."

"How are you doing?" He gives me a quick hug as well.

"Not exactly thrilled to be back in high school," I say with a face that makes Sierra laugh.

"Me neither," Sierra agrees.

I toss my bags on the bed to the left. It's obvious Sierra has already claimed the other side by some of her stuff on the bed and in the white bookcase against the far wall. I start unpacking my texts that I already picked up from the book store down the road and begin placing them neatly on my own shelves. I don't really have much else besides clothes and toiletries. I haven't been back to my home in Colorado since I first went to the compound in the Caribbean. I just wanted to distance myself from anything to do with my parents.

I figure if I need anything, I can just buy it here. I guess inheriting my parents' money wasn't exactly a bad thing. It's not like they can use it anyways. The High Council hasn't formally sentenced all of Excalibur's followers yet. They're still working through the numerous trials. At least they're jailed until then. I was surprised they didn't charge Eric with anything, even though he was blackmailed. Eric played a huge part in making the job successful. I think that's why they spared him. They wouldn't have Excalibur in custody if it wasn't for him.

I couldn't imagine losing him as well. Speaking of loss, Sierra looks a little better. Her skin isn't as pale, and she looks rested. I worry that she hasn't spoken much about what happened with her mom. We usually talk about everything together. I don't want to bring it up on the off chance she's not thinking about it. I don't want to cause her any more pain than what's already been done to her.

I'm always a bundle of nerves right before the new school year starts, but this time seems worse than usual. There's so much for me to learn with the new world I face-planted into and the anatomies of all the beings that belong to it. I studied and read almost all the texts the library offered back in the Caribbean and Ralph taught me a lot. I'm hoping that'll give me a jump-start here, and I won't be stuck here til I'm thirty.

Dante and Sierra are cuddling close on her bed and talking in hushed tones. I continue unpacking my clothing and bathroom stuff to give them some privacy. A loud rap on the door breaks them apart.

Sierra clamors out of bed and opens the door. A dirty-blonde guy with an athletic build stands on the other side. He flashes her a too-white to be real smile.

"Hello ladies, I heard there were some new girls on campus. I wanted to introduce myself. My name's Jack."

"Hi Jack, I'm Sierra and that's Emma." She opens the door wider so he can see me.

I have to smother a laugh when I see Dante rolling his eyes off to the side. Jack can't see him.

"Hey, Jack." I wave.

"There's going to be a party late tonight. You girls interested? We can get pretty much anything, booze, pills, I've got the right hook ups." He shrugs and tilts his head.

And that's when Dante decided to step into view. All hulking six and half feet of muscle makes that boy look like a child.

"If I recall young man, parties are frowned upon. Drugs are forbidden."

"I. Um. I was just making conversation. I didn't mean anything by it." He slowly backs away from the door like he worries if he turns around Dante will pounce. "See you around, girls."

Sierra shuts the door and turns to Dante and slaps her forehead. "Did you really have to do that? He was just being nice."

"I was that kid at one point. Trust me, when I say he wasn't just being nice." He air quotes the last three words.

"We'll be fine, Dante. I can handle teenage boys." She raises her eyebrows at him.

"I know. I just worry about you two being new and alone here. Promise me you'll find some other friends as well." He looks to both of us.

I save Sierra from having to answer. "We will, Dante."

He nods. "I should let you get settled in. Call me if you need anything at all, anytime."

"I plan on it, handsome." Sierra stands on her tiptoes and kisses him goodbye.

When Dante turns to leave, he says over his shoulder, "See you later, Emma."

"Bye, Dante."

"Don't forget to pee on the door on your way out." Sierra bursts out laughing.

Dante grins. "Would it make you feel better if I marked my territory?"

Oh boy, I know that heated look. I turn back around and fumble around in my bag for nothing in particular.

"Don't you dare," she warns before screeching.

The sounds of gross wet kissing and bodies being pressed roughly against the wall is all I can hear. There's nothing to block them out. I groan.

Thankfully it's over, and Dante leaves without a word. I hesitate before I turn around to face her.

"Don't look at me like that, you've put me in more awkward situations." She smirks, a red mark resembling a hickey stands out on her neck.

"I didn't say anything at all." I pretend to zip my lips and toss the key.

I go back to arranging my stuff as she puts her own belongings away. I can't wait to check out the library here. I want to covertly research half-breeds who transition into a full immortal. Nobody even asked me if I was interested in it and assumed I wouldn't want to. The risks are greater for somebody like me, but I still want the option. I don't know what I would choose if given the opportunity. The draw to transitioning is that I get to live longer. I could help more people and be with my friends and family for possibly centuries. But then again, I could die and help nobody. And there I go again, spinning around and around in this head of mine.

I'm so glad Sierra is here with me; I couldn't imagine being alone in a scary place like this. We take our own tour of the campus with our little maps; we look like tourists on vacation. A couple students talk to us, but most of them just watch from a distance. Which is totally fine by me. As we compare our schedules, we notice we're in a few of the same classes.

They have so many different programs here, even though it's called the Guardian Academy. They know not all will either want to or will be able to become a guardian. I shouldn't be surprised by Sierra's choice of wanting to protect the humans. She's always had a big heart and wanted to do something that makes a difference in the world. I still remember when she finally told me everything in that mall cafeteria over our greasy cheeseburgers. The tale she wove was so unbelievable, but it made perfect sense. All but the part that my parents were the bad guys. I never saw that one coming. I was hoping she was wrong. I still wish there was an explanation for why they would become so cruel. They are the only ones who can answer that, but I'll be damned if I visit them anytime soon.

ERIC

After I drop Emma off at school, I convince Ruby to go out to lunch with me, not at my work obviously. There's a place called the Stone Diner that she says is one of her favorites. I figured if I offer to take her there, she won't be able to say no. After doing the right thing and walking away from Sierra, I thought I would never be able to do anything without thinking of her. For so long, thoughts of Sierra were at the forefront of my brain. Always taunting me to go steal her away from Dante. I still have them frequently, but they're not as ruthless as before. Ruby isn't Sierra by a long shot, but the more time I spend with that snarky beauty, the pain from losing Sierra eases little by little.

Ruby makes me want to be worthy of love again. I think I can grow to love this woman. Ruby tries to act like I don't affect her that way, but I'm not blind. I see how she looks at me when she thinks I'm not paying attention. The little hitch in her breath she gets when we touch and the way she tries to pretend spending time with me is a chore. Some ladies love to play hard to get. It's okay. I like the chase.

Pulling my silver Tundra to the side of the road, I check the address on my phone again. I was able to find a flower shop just on the outskirts of town that carries black roses. She told me they were her favorite a few weeks ago when she showed me around town. Another way I know that I'm getting to her is how Ms. Badass is easily flustered around me and will start chattering about random stuff when she's nervous. Give her a weapon and a target, and she's as calm as a glassy lake.

I'm still learning the ins and outs of Graystone. I'm glad I decided to stay here instead of back in Colorado. I'm blown away by how good it feels to not have to hide who I am. That's kind of a double-edged sword at the moment, though, with the wonderful legacy my father left for Emma and me. I can feel their burning eyes on me everywhere I go, always watching and waiting for me to slip. Knowing that the High Council is keeping me under a microscope makes me want to prove everybody wrong even more. I may have inherited my cocky attitude and my good looks from him, but that's where the similarities end. I am nothing like my father.

There's the road I was looking for. I finally come to the little blue house with the greenhouses and barn off to the side. I slow down as I pull into the gravel driveway. Dirt and a mixture of flowery scents slap me in the face as soon as I step into the building. I spot the roses out of the corner of my eye and head toward that cooler. I grab the bouquet that looks the darkest. I bring the deep burgundy-black petals to my nose and inhale their heady, intensely sweet scent.

I have the florist cut and arrange them into a crystal vase etched with swirl designs. The baby's breath stands in stark contrast to the deep red in the center of the flower, which changes to a near black hue on the edges. I think Ruby will love them, and I'm excited to see her face when I get there.

Once I pull up to the front of her white apartment building, I shake my shoulders out and twist my neck to both sides. The cracking at the base of my head releases some of my built-up tension. I knock on the door and try to wait patiently. Waiting patiently is not one of my talents. Footsteps come closer, and the unmistakable sound of a brass peephole cover lifting and closing.

"Hey, Eric. Come right in, I'm almost-" Her gaze finds the flowers I hold in front of me, and her glossy red lips turn up in a smile as she brings her eyes back up to meet mine.

Taking her in from head to toe, I find her a sight to behold. Ruby is wearing a high-waisted black and red plaid skirt that falls just above her knee caps, and wow. Those black fishnet stockings don't hide that this girl has legs for days. Her tight-fitting black long sleeve top hides all of her ink that I know sits right below the fabric. There's a large black tattoo that peeks just below the hem of her skirt that's begging me to get a closer look. She's a bit shorter without her heeled combat boots.

Other than dark eye shadow, eyeliner, and mascara, the rest of her face is make-up free, just the way I like it. Her skin doesn't need anything added to it to look beautiful. She doesn't need to fix up her eyes either. The cocoa-colored irises are tempting enough.

"Hey, Ruby." I flash her a smile that comes easily around her.

I feel a little underdressed in my nicest pair of blue jeans, paired with a white long sleeve Henley. She reaches for the roses and brings them up to her face. Closing her eyes, she breathes the aroma in and sighs.

"They're beautiful, thank you." She leans in for a one-armed hug, her own flowery scented perfume like heaven on my senses.

"You're welcome," I reply, following her into a small kitchen with off-white walls.

She sets the flowers down on the marbled white countertop and proceeds to sprinkle some fish food into the small aquarium. The rectangular glass houses an unnaturally large goldfish hiding amid the pale green silk ferns that decorate the space.

"What do you feed that thing?"

"You mean Goldy? Just goldfish flakes." She shakes her head as she puts the orange cap back on the container.

"You named it Goldy? Isn't that a little cliche? Don't all kids name their goldfish that?" I start to laugh at her when her eyes widen.

"Hey! I didn't get to have a pet when I was a kid, so this is my first, and the name is fitting. Are you jealous you don't have a goldfish too?" Ruby laughs and puts a hand on her hip.

"Are you ready for lunch or what, woman?"

"Only if you buy." She lifts her nose up to the sky.

"I already plan on it."

"You know I'm just joking right? I can pay for my own food." Her face grows serious.

I step closer to her until mere inches separate us.

"Where I'm from the man always pays on the first date."

"Oh, you think this is a date?" she asks coyly.

"Yes, I do. Do you have a problem with that?"

Ruby clams up before she says, "No. I don't."

I don't think she was expecting me to call it a date. After all, it's lunch not dinner. But I figured if I asked her out for dinner it would be a no right off. She's quiet on the short drive there. Once we arrive and climb out of the truck there's a line of about twenty or so people. At least with the lunch rush we know the food will be fresh.

We get to the vestibule and there's hardly any elbow room in there. Instead of standing too close to a man who reeks of stale cigarettes I inch closer to Ruby. When my arm naturally rests on her low back the muscles below tense.

"I'm sorry," I say before removing my hand quickly.

The way she warily holds back from my advances tells me she's been hurt pretty bad by a guy before. I would love to put my own hurting on any man who toys with women's hearts. I may have been a player before all of this but I was upfront about it, there were no expectations from the beginning. I may not believe I'm as good a man as Sierra says I am, but that's one thing I will never be guilty of.

The waitress with the bleach blonde hair seats us in the back of the restaurant. I wonder if it's because she knows who I am and she doesn't want to frighten the other diners. Just as well. That means this little corner is mostly private save for a passerby here and there heading to the restroom around the corner. I pick up the laminated menu and start to look over my options. There are so many that sound good.

Feeling my indecisiveness Ruby pipes up, "The fried chicken and mashed potatoes are amazing, that's what I'm ordering."

I decide to go with that and it did not disappoint at all. The retro diner has an appealing atmosphere, made even better by her sarcastic personality. I find myself laughing with her more than I have with any other woman. Every time I try to make a move on her, though, she shies away from me. It's just going to make my job of winning Ruby over even harder.

It's a good thing I like a challenge.

CHAPTER 20

SIERRA

Smack! Another student flops onto the mat, the wind knocked out of them. Dragging my focus back to the instructor, Audrey, in the front of the class, her black hair wound tightly in a braid that swings just above her butt. She's taken a liking to pulling those not paying attention to the front and making an example out of them. I underestimated Audrey during my prequalification evaluation, and I won't do that again. Her body is about the same size as mine but she's far more dangerous. Lethal even.

I know she didn't give me her full force that day. I didn't know that at the time, though. When she lets go on these kids, I cringe. She doesn't hold back. She kicks their ass and then tells them what they did wrong and how to fix it. She's been a guardian out in the field before. Her reputation has said that much. I don't know what forced her to come back and teach. As much as Dante said he was fine not being an immortal guardian while we were away, he was chomping at the bit to get back to it.

Audrey is a shining example of what I want to be known as. I don't want to be remembered just for my gift. Or even for my continued role in the prophecy. I want to be able to take all those who misjudged and underestimated me and lay them flat on their backs as easily as she does. That's my new goal in this life, to not be the girl that needs saving, but instead to be the one that does the saving.

"How many times have I told you this?" Audrey snaps at Jack.

"I know! I'm sorry, I tried!" he shouts back at her.

"Not hard enough. If I was a vamp, you'd be dead."

"But you're not!"

"And your damn lucky of that."

Her eyes meet mine briefly and my whole-body tenses. Please don't call me down there. I don't want to make a fool of myself in front of them. I've only been here about a week so far. The other students have years on me. Audrey has been giving me private lessons after school to try to get me caught up. I've made a lot of gains so far, but I still have a lot to go to make up for lost time.

"Adeline, you're up."

Adeline stands gracefully from her chair and struts to the front. She's one of the more advanced in our class, and she sure likes to flaunt it. She has her platinum blonde hair pulled up high in a pony tail. Where her muscles are more pronounced mine are still developing. She likes to take cheap shots at me when Audrey isn't looking.

The two women square off with each other. Audrey perfecting the student's form where needed. Adeline holds her own for a while with Audrey, even getting a few hits in. But I know Audrey isn't giving her all yet. Sure enough, Adeline misplaces a step and the instructor finds the weakness. Audrey grabs a hold of Adeline's arm and twists her fast before pinning her to the wall.

I don't care what it takes, I want that guardian star added to my immortal mark. I deserve it after everything I've already done, yet I still have to go through all the training and tests. Each day is getting a little better. I'm stronger and making more gains than before. I check in with my dad every other day now. He's still torn to pieces over the loss of my mom, but the rehab facility we sent him to is helping him cope.

I don't think he'll ever be the man I remember, though. I know I'll never be the girl I used to be either. Grief has a way of ripping you apart until you don't even recognize the pieces left behind in a crumpled heap.

I still have a darkness that surrounds me when it comes to Excalibur and I still think he doesn't deserve to live after what he's done. I keep having flashbacks of that night. Just a scent or a noise is enough to send me back there. I know I still have a long road ahead of me to heal myself from the trauma I've faced.

I know I'll never have answers for most of the questions and whether my mom knew about the prophecy or not. When I went to Greece last month to help lock Excalibur away, Teiresias touched my hand, he gave me the vision of my pregnant mother kneeling in front of him. The way she looked up to Teiresias was as if she adored him. She had to of known then, right?

If she knew about the prophecy, why didn't she prepare me? Did she know she would die fulfilling it? Did my dad know too? He's too fragile right now to ask, but I'm pretty sure he didn't know. Thinking back to when our family was still together, I remember seeing him look sick. Maybe my mom's death was in one of his visions?

I have to go back to Greece during the full moon this weekend. It's classified where they're holding Excalibur. Only about thirty or so people know his true location. Everyone else knows he's locked away and can't escape. Rosalee is held in Graystone with most of the other traitors. But that doesn't mean there aren't twisted individuals willing to try to break him out.

The longer class drones on and on I have a hard time focusing. My nightmares recently have evolved from not only the horrors I witnessed but of a looming threat. The deep bellow that awakes me from a deep sleep all but promises me that he will indeed break free. The dreams almost feel like a Dante dreamwalking dream and I wonder if that's another of his endless abilities. To continue to reach out with his mind while is body is still caged within those walls. The dream this morning was the most unsettling yet. He told me he'll be seeing me on the outside real soon. And something about the way he said it made me believe him.

I haven't spoken a word about the night terrors to anyone yet. I've woken Emma up from screaming in them but she doesn't pressure me to talk about them. I'm scared if I say something to any of them, I'll be the next one getting shipped off to a treatment center. But if I've learned anything it's to trust my gut and it's telling me something isn't right here.

"Sierra, since you think it's in your best interest to daydream while in my class, it's your turn to show me what you got," Audrey barks out.

Crap. And here I thought she was taking it easy on me.

As I walk past Adeline, she sneers at me from her seat and mumbles quietly, "Good luck, water girl."

The class erupts in laughter. Just peachy. I walk proudly down to the front to where Audrey stands.

"Did you have something to add, Adeline?" Audrey narrows her eyes and silences the class.

"No, ma'am," she says sweetly.

"I don't take kindly to name calling Ms. Simmons. Make your way to the front as well."

Double crap. If she thinks pairing me with Adeline will help matters, she's dead wrong.

"Both of you go to the fencing wall and suit up, we're trying something new today."

I've been short tempered since the battle with Excalibur, and dealing with the crap here at the academy from the other students is tiring. For the most part, they leave me alone unless we're in combat training. Then they like to outshine me, because as much as I improve, they still have more experience in that field than I do. They grew up doing this. There are no classes to work your magic with or I think I would blow them all away with my gift. They like to keep our extra abilities under wraps, so we each meet with a professor in private.

Zuri is the professor who's assigned to me. To be honest, she's not really much help. Nobody has experience with an elemental gift, so we've been learning together as I go. It's no secret to anybody on campus who I am and what I'm capable of regarding hydrokinesis. They've all heard the rumors about the battle in India and what I had to do to stop Excalibur.

Adeline and I both suit up in the armor and head gear that still smells of sweat. I select a sabre from the rack that looks promising and stand in the center of the arena. She's not far behind me.

"But we haven't practiced much with these yet," she whines.

"Well then, I hope you paid attention during practice. Water girl here might teach you a thing or two." Audrey grins.

Ha! Take that! I snicker behind my mask as I plant my feet and wait.

The whistle blows and I charge at Adeline. I advance on her so fast she didn't have time to block the first few strikes. Once she realizes what's going on she starts blocking my swings. Muscle memory takes over from here. I fenced with my mom frequently growing up and I was good. Within a span of a few minutes, I have her on her back with the rubber safety tip of my sword at her throat. Her breaths are coming in hard and her eyes narrow into slits.

"Well done, Sierra. Now if we learned anything at all from today's lesson it's this, don't get cocky in the field. You never know what the other being is capable of. You'd all be wise to remember that. Class is dismissed."

I take my gear off and go back to my desk to grab my backpack when Audrey calls for me to stay a minute. I walk up to her desk while the rest of the class exits the room.

"I don't know what's going on with you the past few days but I've noticed you're having a hard time staying focused." Her kind eyes read me like a book.

"I've had a lot going on lately, I'm sorry. I'll get better. I promise." I nod.

"I hope so. I don't have favorites but, I've taken a liking to you. I see the potential in you. I know you haven't had it easy lately but, I can't be seen showing leniency to you, or it will just make it worse. You're lucky she chose then to call you that."

I smirk. "It was good timing."

"Indeed, it was. I don't offer this to many of my students but, I'm here if you need me. Even if it's just for a sounding board. I've been here a while; you'd be surprised what I've seen."

She reminds me so much of my mom, I wrap my arms around her before I even know what I'm doing. She hugs me back tightly.

"Thank you, for everything Audrey." My eyes are wet, I need to get out of here before I really embarrass myself.

"Anytime, Sierra."

I'm actually kind of looking forward to going back to Old Panteleimon. My mouth has been watering for the food I ate the last time I was there. Leave it to me to think of food first, but hey, a girl's gotta eat. If that's one of the only bright spots from the worse few days of my life, I'll choose to hold onto that. I have to hold on to that one sweet memory mixed in the sea of despair.

The ritual will be held Saturday night, but Dante and I will be arriving Friday after I get out of school and when he's done his shift. Nobody knows about the ceremony that is required to keep Excalibur imprisoned, and they definitely don't know the part I play in that. Nilo is the new Master Council and has already made the school aware that he has me working on a special project for him and will require me to be available when he needs me. I guess there's some perks to knowing the Master Council personally.

I can't wait to explore all the cute little shops in the area. If I'm stuck doing this for the rest of my life I might as well enjoy a tiny sliver of it. Not to mention being alone with Dante for a few days each month. That was another exception Nilo made. Dante will never have to work during the day of or the day after the full moon. Each person with a key is assigned our own personal guardian for those days to ensure our safety, and of course, mine is Dante. There's no question about that.

EMMA

I don't know how other half-breeds have made it out alive after attending the Guardian Academy. The immortals are cruel. Every day is a test of my ability to outsmart the guardians in training. They all seem to have it out for me, though they hide it better when Sierra is around. The whispers of "blonde spawn" follow me wherever I go. It's obvious they're referring to who my father is. I haven't gone to see him once since he's been locked up. I want to see my mom, but she stood by and allowed Raymond to commit vile, unspeakable acts. I would rather separate myself from them so people know I'm not like them. I want to be better than the reputation they left for my brother and I.

Eric didn't want to attend the academy. Instead, he chose to work at one of the restaurants in town. I'm glad he decided to stay. We've always been close, but now that I know how much he's had to endure while keeping me safe, it made us even closer. Eric faces some of the same backlash as I do for our namesake. Other than Sierra and Ainsley, one of the very few half-breeds here, I don't really have any friends here at school. I haven't told Sierra the extent of the bullying I've been dealing with. She has far too much on her plate right now to deal with my crap too.

At least during class, I can submerse myself in the learning and tone everybody out. The teachers don't say much to the other students if they do hear what's going on. I think the professors think the same about me. That it's only a matter of time before I snap and proceed with Excalibur's evil plan. Whatever, they can believe what they want. I know who I am and what I stand for. The dreaded bell rings, signaling the end of the third period. Now it's time for me to try to make a mad dash to my calculus class on the other side of the building.

Switching classes is usually when they target me. The students are all walking this way and that, so if the teachers even care what happens to me they're less likely to see it in all the movement. I keep my head down, but I catch a smirk from one of the girls who's been mean to me. She jumps out and body slams me into the white lockers that run along the hall. Pain lances through my arm and hip as my bones crash into the cold metal. My books scatter across the floor with loud slaps. I look up to see the normal group of bitches surrounding me.

"Please just leave me alone. I don't want any trouble," I manage to say without my voice trembling.

"Then I guess you should drop out, blonde spawn. You're not welcome here." The prettier of the four sneers at me. Her name is Adeline, and she's the queen of the popular girls who attend the school.

I cover my face. One pulls at my hair while another slaps me against the back of my head. I kick out and use a shoulder to shove another away, but there are too many of them and I'm outmatched. They will always be stronger, so the four-on-one crap they pull is made even worse.

"Someone help me!"

The others in the hallway circle around us to watch the show. Like I'm the new toy everybody wants to try out.

A ball of water smacks one of the girls in the back, ruining her perfectly straight hair before splashing down to the floor. Adeline's face turns an angry red as she spins around on her heels to face Sierra. "You can't use your magic on us. It's forbidden!" she shouts above all the chatter in the hall.

"So is bullying, and yet here you are." Sierra shoves each of them aside. She then helps me pick up my now wet books from the floor.

Sierra mouths an apology for the ruined texts before putting herself between me and the four girls. I don't care about the books. This is exactly what I didn't want happening, Sierra getting involved. I knew she would... She's always stood up for others who couldn't advocate for themselves. This is why I didn't tell her how bad it was.

"Who the fuck do you think you are? Do you know who my father is?" Adeline spits the words with as much venom as a cornered pit viper while she pushes Sierra's shoulders, trying to slam her into the lockers.

"Does it look like I care?" Sierra bats Adeline's hands away with a complicated-looking flourish.

The snotty bitch snaps her fingers, and two of the girls lunge at Sierra and grab her arms, pinning her to the lockers. The third girl grabs her legs to keep her from kicking as Adeline wraps her hands around Sierra's throat. I shoulder my way closer to help as Sierra cracks a smile, letting me know she's fine. A lot of good I would be to her anyway.

"Stop it!" I yell as Adeline squeezes her hands even tighter around Sierra's throat, causing her knuckles to whiten and match the color of the lockers behind us.

"You will learn your place at this academy, or you will be forced to leave. Do you understand, Savior?" Adeline snarls with disgust.

Bad move, blondie. Sierra doesn't take that role lightly.

Sierra's eyes darken with a hatred I've only seen when she talks about Excalibur. Then Sierra smiles, and I mean like, a full-on Cheshire cat kind of smile. I don't know how she can even manage that when this twit is cutting off her oxygen. Maybe that's why—the lack of oxygen is messing with her brain, causing her to do odd things.

They all release their hold on Sierra simultaneously as they start to gasp for breath and reach for their throats. Their fear-filled faces look at Sierra in confusion before they drop to their knees in front of her, struggling for every breath they take. As they scratch at their throats, they leave angry welts across their skin. It's as if something is stopping them from breathing.

Sierra tucks her long waves back behind her ears before squatting down until she's an inch from Adeline's face. Sierra's voice rumbles with menace, her breath stirring Adeline's blonde locks across her forehead. "Maybe you should learn your place, hmm? Don't you ever touch Emma again. Do you understand me?"

When all four of them nod feverishly, Sierra stands back up and wraps an arm around my shoulders and walks calmly away, urging me to do the same. Like what she did didn't just happen. The sea of students part as we move down the hall. Probably the smartest thing they can do.

"What's your next class?" She's back to her normal voice.

"It's calculus. Sierra, about what happened-"

"Why didn't you tell me you were being bullied?" She cuts me off as she stops in the middle of the walkway.

"I know you have a lot going on right now, and I didn't want to put more on you." I look into her eyes and see she's back to the caring, compassionate Sierra again.

"Emma, no matter what, I'm your best friend, and I will always be here for you. You have a lot against you right now too. We need to stick together." She continues to escort me to my next class.

"I hope you don't get in trouble for that." She doesn't need that too.

"All I did was throw a ball of water on them. They're the ones that physically assaulted us." Sierra glances behind her, revealing purple bruises forming on the delicate skin on her neck.

"We both know that's not true," I say, lowering my voice.

"They have to prove it first." She snickers as her whole face lights up with a mischievous grin. Maybe that was her plan all along. There really was no proof of what she did, is there? "You stay in the classroom until I come get you, okay?"

I nod, hating the fact that I put her in this position. I know they won't touch me again around her for a while, if ever. I can't help but feel both pride and fear at what Sierra is capable of. I've never seen this side of her before. It's scary as hell. I'm sure the bullies are pissing their pants and shaking in their designer shoes. Good, serves them well. Remember, Karma's always the winner in the end. I just hope Sierra doesn't take it too far.

Chapter 21

SIERRA

As soon as the bell rings, signaling the end of the school day, I bolt out of my seat and run down the hall to get to Emma before she walks the halls without me. I knew some of the students here were saying nasty things to her, but I never knew they were putting their grubby hands on her. The thought that she didn't think she could come to me with it pisses me off.

After everything we've been through together, especially in the last year, I didn't think she would keep things from me. I see the blonde halo of hair bobbing in my direction, and I'm grateful to see she's not being pestered. The bullies have backed off harassing her since I pulled the same trick I used on Excalibur and Rosalee. So far, the professors haven't breathed a word about it to me. And they don't want to either. I've been told they've turned their heads when the students started harassing Emma. They deserve the same fate those girls got. These teachers are supposed to make sure this is a safe environment for all students.

Emma frowns at me. "You know you don't have to babysit me."

"I'm not babysitting you; I'm babysitting them." I make a gesture to the students around us.

"Same thing." She raises her eyebrows, just a few shades darker than her golden hair.

As we walk closer and closer to the front entrance, my footsteps get lighter. Even though tomorrow night I have to see and deal with Excalibur, I've been excited to get out of Graystone for a bit. I still get sympathetic glances from some students, while the others stay away from me like they should fear me. Emma was planning on being able to stay on campus over the weekends, but I talked her into crashing on Eric's couch. There's no telling what those bullies will do to her knowing I'm not around to have her back. I might not be able to stop hurting them next time. That should scare me. But it doesn't.

We walk back to Eric's little one-bedroom apartment that's above a furniture store in town without incident. Of course, Eric isn't home but working. Not like he would want to see me anyway. He's still avoiding me like the plague, other than that one time he picked me up. That's really the only time I've seen him since that strange incident behind the barn. He really helped me that day we just drank and played video games. It was so freeing to not have the world against me for a change. And I really have missed him, though I did notice it was hard for him to be around me. I hope he gets over his feelings for me soon. I need him in my corner again.

Once I'm happy that Emma's home safe and nobody will bother her here, we say our goodbyes. I take my blue benitoite stone out of my jeans pocket to create a portal to Dante's log cabin. He says it's ours, but he had it before me, so I feel like it's his. Pointing the beautiful blue rock at the cobblestone archway in the alley, the bricks start to swirl together as if I'm creating a piece of spin art. Once I see the kitchen on the other side, I step into the doorway and past the threshold. Then I bring my palms together, shrinking the opening until it disappears.

I put the portal stone back in my pocket and head to the bedroom to start packing. Dante is done his shift in about an hour so he should be home soon. I don't plan on bringing a lot with me to Greece. After all, it's just the weekend, so I just only grab what I need.

I hear footsteps coming up behind me and turn to see my gorgeous guardian in the doorway. His handsome face morphs from happy to concerned in an instant. Dante rushes over and lifts my chin to get a good look. "What the hell happened to your neck? This isn't from practice, is it?"

Oh crap, I'd forgotten about the bruises, and I haven't spoken to him since it happened other than through texts. That's not exactly something I wanted to tell him through messages.

"I'm okay, really, just some girls giving Emma a hard time. But I dealt with it." I try to sound convincing. Now that I see him, I know what I did was wrong, and I don't want to tell him and have him think any less of me.

"Do I want to know what 'dealt with it' consists of?" Dante groans throwing his head back in exasperation.

"That's classified, sir." I smirk at him. That's the same line he used on me not too long ago. "I missed you, handsome." I stand up on my tiptoes and stretch my arms around his neck.

"I missed you too, beautiful." He wraps those big strong arms around me, and all the troubles plaguing me these last few days drift away. His lips finally find mine after five very, very long days away from him.

He lets go of me as he walks to the closet to start gathering his belongings. I can't help but devour him with my eyes when he's not looking. This whole staying away from him really sucks. He packs his stuff quickly, and before I know it, we're on our way to get the heck out of Graystone.

We portal into the hillside just outside of the little village we stayed at last time. Dusk is barely setting in, creating a beautiful mixture of hues in the cloudless sky. Walking on the worn cobblestone walkway, I feel like we never left. The whole place looks the same as I remember. Even my grief didn't darken this place.

We arrive at the large bed and breakfast and check in with the elderly woman at the counter. Her smile crinkles her eyes as she hands over a small white key card. This time our room is on the opposite side of the building.

As soon as we unpack our belongings into the rustic-looking bureau, my cell phone rings. "Hi, Uncle Joe."

"Where are you right now?" His tone doesn't sound like he's in a good mood.

"I'm doing my monthly extra credit." I snicker.

"I just received an interesting phone call from the headmaster." Well, so much for them leaving me alone.

"And?" I pry. I hope they didn't say what I think is coming next.

"He said you're looking at suspension or possible expulsion from the Guardian Academy. You want to fill me in on what's going on?"

"What? How can they do that?" My voice rises along with my rage. Dante comes to stand next to me, his heightened hearing already knowing what Uncle Joe is saying.

"He's saying you used your gift to harm other students. Tell me that isn't true, Sierra?"

I grind my teeth together. There's no point in lying to him. "A couple of students were bullying Emma; I threw water at them to get them to back off." That they can prove.

"That's not all they're saying you did." His tone is condescending.

"I'm 18. Why are they even calling you?" I bite out.

"You should've known better."

"I gotta go. I'll talk to you when I get back to Graystone." I hang up before he can say anything, my finger pressing the end call button so hard my now chipped fingernail bends. I don't want to look at Dante. I'm sure he'll have the same disappointment.

"Is that what you meant when you said you handled it?" Dante asks quietly.

"I don't want to talk about it right now." If I get kicked out of the academy, what will happen to my future? Worse, what will happen to Emma with those girls not being held accountable? They can't do this to me, not after everything I've done for all of them.

The following night I meet up with Konstantina, Reid, and Nilo about a quarter of the way from the top of the mountain. Each of them has an immortal guardian accompanying them as well. I don't recall the guardians' names, but I recognize them as part of Nilo's special team. We all came prepared this time with coats, hiking boots, and winter hats. Nilo leads the way through the thick brush that slowly thins until we reach the entrance to the cave.

The four guards at the front wave us on through. Teiresias and Willow are waiting for us inside. I thought I was prepared to see Excalibur again, but I'm dead wrong. The moment my sights land on that monster, I'm once again back in India watching him murder my mom. My fists clench as I lock my jaw shut, trying to remind myself why he has to rot away in a cage instead of me ending his life. The thought of killing him is far too tempting.

"Vengeance is not the answer," Teiresias speaks low, but the others hear and look at me with a sympathy I don't want.

"Hello, Sierra." Excalibur's deep bellow echoes against the cavern's walls. The same voice that's been haunting my dreams.

"Until the day somebody takes the stone out of my cold dead hands, I will live just to make sure you suffer," I mumble.

"What was that?" Excalibur's crimson eyes lock on mine.

I narrow my gaze at him, biting my tongue. I don't give him the satisfaction of repeating it. I didn't even mean to say the words out loud. I wring my hands out and take my place in the circle. The spell is identical to the last, right down to mixing our stones and crystals and having to slice our palms open. The ritual seems to go faster this time, which is good. I'm itching to get out of this mountain, with my unease growing by the second.

Once our parts are completed and we're back at the entrance, I finally work up the nerve to ask Teiresias, "Can I ask you something that's been bothering me?" I say quieter than I intend, sensing Dante's worried gaze sweeping over me, burning into me like a wildfire.

His clouded eyes look at me, and I'm again reminded Teiresias always knows more than he lets on. "Are you sure you want the answers to those questions, my child?" A heavy sadness takes over his wrinkled appearance.

"I have to know the truth." I swallow my anxiety. "Did my mom know all along about the prophecy?" I ask, surprised by the amount of conviction I show.

I squeeze my fingers tightly together as I await his response.

"Yes, Sophia was aware of the prophecy," he says kindly.

Okay, that's what I figured he'd say.

"Did she know she was going to die?" My voice wavered on the last word as my eyes fill with unshed tears.

"If you want to know, I will show you. Once you see the past, however, it cannot be unseen." Teiresias holds his bony hand out to me palm up, and I hesitate a moment before taking it.

My mouth goes dry. This could finally be the moment I know my mom's part. I choke down my resolve and reach for the soul seer's warm hand.

A jolt courses through my entire body until I'm transported back in time through Teiresias's memories. I'm blown away by the smile on my mom's face. She looks so real; I reach out to her, but my hand passes through her as if she's a hologram. This isn't like the last time Teiresias showed me the past. Those we're just images, this is like virtual reality.

The frail-looking old man places his hand on the swell of my mother's stomach. "She's a strong one, Sophia."

"I know. Sierra will have to be if she's going to be the Immortal Savior." She smiles as she caresses her belly. "I wish I didn't have to leave her and Michael so soon." Her smile falters. "Is there really no way to change the prophecy?"

"I'm afraid not, my dear. We all have a destiny planned for us from the ancient ones. Your destiny is bringing the Immortal Savior into the world and shielding her innocence from others until the time is right. Your duty is protecting this child until the last beat of your heart." Teiresias places a comforting hand on her shoulder.

"When will I know the time is right?" She crosses her hands over her lap.

"That is a question for us all, I'm afraid." He leans against the same walls that surround me now.

"How will I die?" Mom asks, her eyes watering.

"Sophia, you really don't want to know that." Teiresias shakes his head, making his long gray beard sway.

"Will it be painful?" Her lower lip quivers.

"I have seen your death as well as many others. Telling you how you perish will not help you in this lifetime." The old man looks away. My mom gasps and covers her mouth, obviously reading what he wouldn't say.

"When?" Tears freely flow from her light green eyes, wetting her pale-yellow shirt. "Please give me that."

"Your death will come when it is the only way for Sierra to succeed in her destiny. When her innocent soul, so full of light, is darkened by her grief, only then will she be able to come into her true power. You see, we all can't be pure and harness that kind of magic. This world thrives on balance, the light and the dark. She needs a touch of darkness at just the right time."

My mom wipes away the tears trailing down her pink cheeks. "Will they be, okay?"

I have a hard time not reaching for her again. I know it wouldn't help her.

"In time, yes. She will be met with devastation, but happiness will come when Sierra has a family of her own. Would you like to see them?"

"You can do that?"

"Sophia, my powers of sight are limitless. That's how I know everything will work out in the end. I have even seen you in the afterlife watching over them from above." He smiles at her, his beard pulling up on the edges of his lips.

He reaches a hand out to her the same way he did to me. I'm able to see what she sees while also watching her. I travel with her to a home I know all too well. A log cabin sits back in the woods, surrounded by flowers. The sounds of giggling draws our attention to the side of the home where a little boy with near-black hair is running around the yard with a much larger man with identical features chasing after him.

Dante swoops the boy up into his arms and tickles his belly, making him laugh so hard he screams in excitement, "Mama, Mama help!"

Watching my mom, witnessing Dante and my future unfold, I see her gently swipe away a tear by the corner of her eye.

I see myself then off to the side rubbing my own large stomach as I place a kiss on the toddler's head. Hazel eyes that mirror my own look up at me with an unconditional love that could only come from a child.

Just then, my dad comes out of the house carrying a picnic basket and a blanket draped over his arm. Dante puts the squirming tot down so the boy can run up to him.

"Papa, Papa!" he squeals as he wraps his tiny little arms around my dad's leg.

Dad reaches down with his free hand and picks him up, beaming at his grandson in a way that I thought I would never see in him again.

I'm sent back to this same room where my mom dries her tears as her radiant smile returns. "Thank you for showing me. Knowing that they can be happy again in this life makes it worth the sacrifice. I'm honored to fulfill my duty."

And that was the smile I saw the first time Teiresias showed me the past. That gloriously radiant smile shining with a mother's love.

I come back into my own body in the present time and wipe my own tears that are trailing down from my eyes. I wrap Teiresias in a hug. What he gave me today will help me to move forward with my life.

"Thank you so much for that gift." I don't think he could ever know how much that meant to me. "You can see her in the afterlife?" My voice is hopeful. That must mean she's okay and she made it there.

"I can, and in time I will show you. For now, I must rest. Like you, my gift takes a heavy toll on me." He leans heavily on the knobby little cane he uses until Dante places a chair behind him, allowing him to sit.

Looking at the father of my unborn children, my anima gemella, my aching heart torn to shreds from heartbreak begins to mend some. I know we'll be okay, as painful as it is right now. We'll get through this together, and we will be able to find happiness again.

DANTE

"Go ahead, my dear. I'd like a word in private with Dante," Teiresias says fondly to Sierra.

He reminds me of the loving uncle in everybody's family. The one they all look up to and love unconditionally. I know Sierra loves him in that way, he's also a connection to her mother. Sophia adored him as well.

Once Sierra's footsteps fade along with the rest of the small group, Teiresias' face takes on a grave appearance. I brace myself for what's to come.

"Dante, you need to listen very carefully to what I'm about to say."

"I will, sir." Instantly my unease grows with the seriousness of his tone.

"There's a darkness inside of her, and if nurtured can be more devastating than anything Excalibur could've accomplished." He pauses and takes a deep breath, letting that sink in. "I've shown her the best version of her future, the one where she allows the light to blossom. The other future I've seen, well, let's just say it's the darkest I've ever witnessed in my time."

"What can I do?" It feels as if somebody is choking the life out of me.

"Give her a reason to live, to love and above all, she needs to continue to be able to see the goodness in people. Once she loses the ability to see the light, that's when darkness will reign."

Only her light can keep the darkness away, for without it, there is no hope.

"I've noticed a change in her since Sophia died, but I didn't realize it was this bad. I should have." I scrub my face with my hands.

"We all see what we want to see, my boy. For if we all saw everything for what it was, the light in us all would dim." He rests a firm hand on my shoulder. "The future I showed her is possible and when she's ready she may share that with you. But until then, know that there is a consequence for every action. And whether the weight tips on the side of good or bad depends on the choices she makes. She will need your guidance, your support and most importantly your love. After all, love is what can conquer the darkness."

I clutch at my amulet that rests around my neck wondering how I didn't see her turning this dark. How I didn't see her pain. Am I really that blinded by love, I didn't see her struggling? Why didn't she come to me for help?

"I'll do whatever it takes. I vow to love her without condition for the rest of my life. I will spend eternity making sure she doesn't succumb to the darkness."

"I know you will. You're an honorable man, Dante. I'm delighted she has you to stand beside her to weather the storm together." He leans back in the chair and closes his eyes.

"I appreciate you helping us, Teiresias," I say before jogging to catch up to Sierra.

My footsteps are clunky and uncoordinated. I just can't get over that she's been hurting this bad and couldn't find comfort from me. I reach the front of the cave where Sierra is sitting cross-legged on the floor tugging her parka tightly around her, trying to stay warm.

"Hey, beautiful."

"Hey, handsome."

"Are you ready to turn in for the night?"

"Absolutely." She stifles a yawn.

I reach a hand down to help help her up. Once she's standing I wrap my arms around her and hold everything that's dear to me in my embrace. Thoughts racing through my mind of how I can help Sierra through this. I've found my own destiny, being the light in the darkness for the Immortal Savior.

The wind howling through the trees dotted along the mountainside is blowing snow wildly around us. Whipping it this way and that, pretty soon the snowsquall swallows the landscape into and endless sea of white. It seems, "weather the storm," is more fitting than I realize.

You can find out what happens to Sierra and her friends in the next novel in the Destiny Of Graystone Series, Thorn Of Darkness.

Katie lives in Vermont with her husband and their children. When she's not working or spending time with her family, she enjoys getting lost in a good book. Her favorite hobby is gardening, whether it is edible or decorative. In her opinion one can never have too many flowers! She may have a slight addiction to creating things in Canva and Procreate. Visit https://www.katierichard.com for more information and to sign up for her newsletter.

9 781737 145349